I0582734

THREE

HELEN JULIET

Three

Copyright © 2022 by Helen Juliet

This book is a work of fiction. Names, places, and incidents are either products of the author's imagination or are used fictitiously. Any resemblance to actual events, locales, or persons, living or dead, is entirely coincidental.

All rights reserved. No part of this book may be used or reproduced in any manner whatsoever without written permission, except in the case of brief quotations embodied in critical articles and reviews.

Trigger Warning

One of the kinks featured in this book is humiliation. Daddy says some pretty derogatory things, but his boy loves it. It is consensual and there is aftercare provided. It features in two chapters.

There is mention of physical abuse (beatings) at the hands of a parent. The description does not go into detail, and it is not featured on page.

1

SAM

It's the crying that wakes me.

I can tell Luke is trying to be quiet, but the walls in this flat are paper thin. Besides, his room is technically the living room, so there's only my door between us.

I debate for a few seconds if I should let him have some privacy, but my heart can't bear it. I have to help him.

I sleep in just my underwear, so once I've rolled out of bed, I pull on some joggers and a T-shirt, then creep across my small bedroom to ease open the door. The whole place is dark, but from the glaring street lights outside I can make the huddled form of one of my best friends under the duvet of his double bed.

I bite my lip before making my way over.

"Luke?" I whisper as I touch his shoulder.

He gasps in surprise and snaps his head around to look at me. "Oh no, did I wake you up?" he whispers back with a sniffle.

I shake my head, lying. "I wasn't asleep. Are you okay? How was your date?"

I don't really want to ask, but it doesn't take a genius to

1

work out that Luke went on a date with some guy he met briefly at a bar and now he's sobbing under his bedsheets, so something must be off.

Sure enough, his face crumples, and my heart cracks a little more.

"Oh, Sammi," he says, his lip wobbling. "He tried to get me drunk and made f-f-f-fun of my…"

He screws his eyes shut and takes a shaky breath.

It's not hard to imagine what that arsehole made fun of.

I swallow thickly, my love for my best friend throbbing in my chest. Without needing to ask, I scoot down the bed and open my arms. Luke throws himself eagerly into them.

"What a twat," I say emphatically, earning a sweet, wet giggle from Luke. "I hope you left him with the bill and blocked him already."

He sighs. "Yes, and yes," he says sadly.

I kiss the top of his head. "Good boy."

I feel the way he melts into me at those words. We all want to hear them. It's not the same when I try and say it, but I'm probably the most toppy out of all of us when I try hard enough.

I love making my bestie feel a bit better, but I don't get a rush out of it. Not like I would if I heard someone say that to *me*.

No. Not someone. A Daddy.

I sigh, the same worries rattling around my head as usual. The three of us are trying our best, but when are we going to catch a break? It's not just Luke whose love life has never got off the ground. And we're stuck in this small, damp flat, working all hours at low-paying jobs we hate…

I take a breath and grit my teeth. I have to be strong. Wishing for someone else to take care of me won't make it happen. Nor will wishing for Daddies for my best friends, either. Until something changes, I have to be strong and do my best to keep carrying this load.

Speaking of the three of us, Callum's door opens a crack, and he peeks his head out. There's a soft glow coming from his bedside lamp that illuminates his square jaw and angel-like strawberry-blond curls.

Below him pokes out a familiar stuffed piggy wearing a rainbow bow tie and tutu that he shakes.

"Are you guys cuddling and didn't invite me?" he asks in a squeaky voice, waggling his eyebrows. That gets another laugh out of Luke, and I feel a pang of warmth towards my other best friend.

"Get over here, you weirdo," I say fondly. "Bring Snazzy Pants and get Mr Bacon whilst you're at it."

Callum grins and dashes into my room before bounding back to us with a second stuffed piggy in his other hand. Mr Bacon has a smart suit on in contrast to Snazzy Pants' glittering attire. Callum tosses him to me before fetching a third piggy who's sitting on the bedside cabinet and passes him to Luke. Squish wears a pink jumper and has a felt wand sewn to his hand. We all got them made at one of those workshop places not long after we moved in together.

"There we go," Callum announces, jumping onto the other side of the bed and spooning Luke tightly from behind. "All present and correct. Now, what's up?" When Luke whimpers, Callam growls and scowls before kissing the side of Luke's neck. "Who do I have to pummel?"

I adore Callum's loyalty. He's like a big old puppy with boundless energy and enthusiasm. I sigh at his question, answering for Luke when it's clear Luke's clammed up again, his lip wobbling.

"Bad date," I whisper.

Callum huffs and rolls his eyes. "Why are all the men out

there so *shit?"* he demands. "There have got to be decent Daddies out there! Where are they all hiding?"

I have to agree. Rather than answer him right away, I bite my lip and stroke his arm, cuddling closer to Luke.

This is all my fault.

When we met in sixth form five years ago, we bonded over being gay and awkward, and later discovered we all leaned towards submission and the idea of being boys to Daddies. My protective instincts got a little out of hand, however. After seeing how many douchebags there were out there, the three of us promised we wouldn't give up our virginity to anyone less than amazing. We've fooled around with guys but never gone all the way.

It's getting out of control, though. I wish we hadn't put so much pressure on ourselves. I convinced the two people I love most in this world that they were worth being treated like princes, but perhaps we should have been having bad sex this entire time so we were ready when we met someone who might be a great Daddy.

If I could magic up three perfect men for all of us, I would. But…then I'd also lose what we have now. I love our snuggle times and easy kisses. More than once, the three of us have ended up in bed, laughing and wanking. I love it when we all come together. It's kind of magical how intimate we are.

But we all know what we *really* crave, and I'm being selfish not doing more to help my besties find that.

Even if it means breaking up the three of us.

It would just be different. A new chapter. We'd still be close, I'm sure. Hearing Luke try and hold back another sniffle makes up my mind.

"I think it's time for a new pact," I say before I can talk myself out of it.

Luke and Callum both look at me in the artificial light from the street.

"You want us to go out and shag any old bloke?" Callum asks, immediately guessing what I'm talking about, and sounding sceptical. I don't blame him.

"No," I say, shaking my head. "I think we should still have standards, but maybe we should focus our efforts. There's a new app out called Collr. It's a specifically kinky app, and you can filter not only for a Daddy, but also for what *kind* of Daddy. I think we should at least take a look."

Luke lifts his head, blinking spiky wet lashes at me. "Yes," he says firmly. "I've had enough of this waiting. This pressure. I kind of want to get it over with."

I try not to feel guilty, but on some level, I knew that was what was going on when he agreed to go on that date tonight even though the guy seemed sketchy. *Fuck.* This is my fault, and I really do need to help my besties fix it.

"I think it's *very* important we each find someone amazing still," I reiterate. "But maybe this app might help us be more proactive. The right Daddies aren't going to fall into our laps. We need to go on a Daddy hunt."

That gets another giggle from Luke, and I'm relieved. But then his expression turns serious. "By the end of the year," he says with conviction.

"To what?" Callum asks.

"To lose our virginity," Luke replies, completely serious.

"Wait, I'm not sure we should—" I begin to protest, but Callum wags a finger at me, that excitable puppy dog look in his eyes again.

"Yes," he says, nodding at Luke, who smiles warmly at him. "My ADHD arse loves a deadline. Otherwise, I never do anything. I agree with both of you. Let's all sign up to Collr and try really hard to meet someone great and just go for it before the year is out."

I look between the two people I care most about in this world. I guess it's only May, so that's loads of time. But… maybe Luke's right. Perhaps I scared them into waiting for the right Daddy to come to each of us, when life doesn't work like that. A deadline could help us focus, even if it's not imminent.

"Okay," I say with an exhale, then smile. "New pact. We each meet someone brilliant by New Year's Eve and stop living our lives with these self-imposed chastity belts."

I hold my fist out and can't help but grin when Luke and Callum enthusiastically clap their own hands over mine and squeeze tight. "We can do it," Callum says emphatically. "Because we're all amazing and gorgeous, and we just need to meet some men who can see that as well!"

Luke nuzzles closer to me and sighs. "Yeah," he says, not sounding completely convinced.

Now that I won't stand for. I let Callum's eagerness infect me. "Yes, we *are* amazing. And there are Daddies out there who are going to see that and love us and bring out the very best in us! We just need to try a bit harder to help them find us."

Luke smiles at me. "Okay, Sammi."

He's one of the only people who uses my full name, and only when he's feeling particularly vulnerable. So I kiss his lips, then kiss Callum's, too. "I promise we'll be okay," I assure them.

Callum nods and kisses Luke as well, stroking the side of his face. "We'll be okay," he repeats.

For a second, I imagine we could all meet Daddies who will be okay with us still being this close. It's a crazy dream, but I cling to it in that moment, hoping it will ease me into accepting this new chapter for us tomorrow.

I love my best friends.

So I have to let them be free.

2

JACOB

"Why am I so fucking *bored*, Harris?"

My executive assistant peers up at me from over her horn-rimmed glasses, quirking an eyebrow at me. "Perhaps you need a job, Mr Wolf?" she suggests smoothly.

I scoff. "I'm a billionaire. I don't need a job."

She blinks at me. "You poor thing. I'm so sorry for you," she says, completely deadpan.

I huff, rising from the sofa where we've been discussing business, and march over to my liquor cabinet, pouring myself a decent measure of whiskey. "I'm just in a rut," I grumble.

"You have plenty of board meetings, charity galas, and pitches from start-up companies to fill your next week with," Harris says, focusing once more on the iPad that's always glued to her hands. "If you're complaining because you haven't got a new product of your own to work on, I believe that's no one's fault but yours."

I snort, both annoyed by and welcoming her bluntness at the same time. I'm fully aware that our relationship is a professional one, but that doesn't stop her from being the closest thing I have to a best friend.

I stare out over the grey skies of London, appreciating the lofty view from my penthouse. Ever since I sold the app I developed in my early thirties, I haven't had to give a single worry about financial matters. Now I just occasionally invest in other people's dreams, and watch my percentages roll in. It's easy.

It's boring.

For a while, I'd lived large. But the constant partying has somewhat lost its charm. I want to be useful again, and not just as someone who says yay or nay on other companies' boards.

I want my *own* company again. My own passion to pursue. I miss the joy of creating something innovative. My app has touched millions of lives around the globe. It helps everyone from self-employed businesses to global companies sort out their taxes more efficiently. I poured years into developing and growing it, creating a company of my own that employs hundreds. I *mattered*.

Now I find myself watching the clock, wondering when's an acceptable time to start getting shitfaced.

Harris is right, of course. I have plenty of ways to fill my day. But nothing is really inspiring me right now.

"I'll know the right idea when it hits me," I grumble, sipping the dry, spicy drink.

She hums noncommittally.

"What?" I demand.

"You need some good sex," she says plainly.

I scoff again. "I get plenty of sex," I say, trying not to sound defensive. Because I do. I can click my fingers and have any number of sugar babies at my beck and call, ready to be fucked into the next century.

Harris doesn't need to know that it's been months—

maybe years—since fucking hasn't left me feeling completely hollow the moment the orgasmic high has faded.

"I'm not talking about a quick fuck," she says, tilting her head to stare accusingly at me with her bright green eyes. Along with her shining red hair, it's not hard to see her Irish heritage. Not that you could miss it with her sharp Belfast accent. "You need a boy to boss around all the time," she tells me smugly.

I've never asked, but I strongly suspect that Harris has a boy of her own, no doubt happily chained to a bed desperate for his mistress to come home and peg him senseless. She's certainly no stranger to kink.

Once, after far too many Jägerbombs, I confessed to her that it was a relief to finally get old enough where men actually took me seriously as a Daddy. In my twenties, I tried a few boys who were older than me, as well as some my own age or a bit younger, but nothing ever clicked.

Then I became obsessed with work, and settled for mostly vanilla sex with no strings attached. Now I'm approaching forty and have some silver creeping into my dark hair, I'm finally starting to find the dynamic I crave more.

But in that time, I also got really rich. It's easy to find sugar babies. Boys who are confident and sassy who know they're worth spoiling and aren't afraid to ask for it. Over the past few years, I've been able to scratch some of my Daddy Dom itches, but something is definitely still missing.

"And where would I find such a boy?" I ask her nonchalantly. I know she sees right through my bullshit, but I keep up the pretence anyway.

She taps something on her iPad, then smirks at me. "Check your phone."

I do. There's an email inviting me to join something called Collr. "And this is?"

"An app for kinky fucks to find one another," she says smugly. "A buffet of boys just waiting for you to go and judge the hell out of their profiles. But I'm betting there's at least *one* boy lurking in there that might tickle your fancy."

I scoff sceptically. "Online dating? Really?"

"Join the twenty-first century," she snaps at me. "You're one of the only people I know who insists on picking hook-ups in person. It's embarrassing. You're a tech billionaire who barely uses his phone for anything more than *calling* people." She makes a face to illustrate how distasteful she finds that.

I roll my eyes. "I'm rich, hot, and fit as an ox. I do just fine in bars," I inform her.

I should have known better than to walk into her trap.

"Oh, really," she says with a false air of optimism. "Please show me where you're hiding all these long-term relationships! Are they in the bathroom with all of your other ox shit?"

I feign a laugh and trudge back over to sit on the other corner of the couch to her. "Dating apps are for people who are either ugly or have no personality. I am neither."

"Try again," she says without pause.

I sigh and rub my eyes. "Okay! People just want me for my money, and it's getting stale. Sure, I want to spoil my boy rotten. But I don't want that to be the main reason he wants *me*. Does that make sense?"

Does that make me a spineless whelp?

Honestly, having feelings is exhausting. But as I get older, I can't seem to shoo them away like I used to.

Harris snorts and actually locks the screen on her iPad. She rises gracefully to walk over to my fridge, retrieving the chilled bottle of Champagne she knew would just be sitting in there, waiting for a special occasion.

Like a Thursday afternoon where I start moaning about

my dating life. That's typically the kind of occasion that warrants opening a two-hundred-quid bottle of bubbles.

"You know I don't like to get...squishy," she says, wrinkling her nose. "But you are—as you say—seriously hot. If you're into that sort of thing." She waves her hand up and down in my general direction, and gives me a grimace as the Champagne pops loudly.

I arch an eyebrow. "I'm sorry my six-pack is such a turn-off for you," I say dryly.

She smirks. "I like them small and soft. But that's not the point. *Objectively* speaking, you're a stud muffin."

"Thank you," I grumble, accepting the tall glass she's handing me. I'm not that insecure. I know I'm a ten, so I don't need her approval. Besides, she's right. I like them small and soft as well.

"And being rich protects you in so many ways," she continues, pouring her own drink and settling beside me again. "It's not like you're going to get swindled by anyone, after all. You're too savvy. However, you are also *kind*, Jacob. I know you hate people seeing that, but it's true. You are kind and generous and caring. You're dying for a sweet boy to dote on or a naughty boy to spank and spoil or something else in between. But you have got to stop with these superficial little hoes with pound signs in their eyes."

I shake my head and throw my free hand out. "Exactly! So how will removing the personal interaction help with that?"

She quirks an eyebrow. "I know this isn't a foreign concept to you, but obviously in this instance you're a little blinded. *Bend* the truth, Jacob. Can you not lie, just this once? Or not even lie! Simply don't mention money in your profile. Then see what kind of results you get."

I rub my chin before cautiously looking at her. "If I say that without my money, I'm wondering what kind of person I even am...will you judge me?"

She giggle-snorts, the bitch. I slap her leg, and she just cackles even more. "You superficial twat," she goads. "Of course I'm going to judge you." She winks at me. "But that's why I love you. Okay. You quite rightly see your wealth as a sign of working really fucking hard, and being a hard worker is something you admire."

"Yes," I agree with a nod followed by a big swig of Champagne. It's a bit too sweet to me after the whiskey, but I can tell drinking this bottle with Harris is a bonding experience she's devised. So I'm not going to snub it.

"But you agree that the likes of nurses and teachers work their arses off, yeah?"

"Of course," I say hotly. "My mother was a teacher."

She grins, biting the tip of her tongue between her teeth and shaking a pointed finger at me. "But they don't get paid fuck all now, do they?"

I chew my lip. "No," I admit.

"Look," she says, sounding dangerously close to something like sympathetic. "I'm not saying you should live a fucking lie with someone. I'm just saying you should make a profile on the stupid app, and don't advertise that you're filthy rich. Put everything *else* in there and see who wants you for you. Ah, go on. Will you do it, just for me?"

I scowl at her, but I can't stop the smile from creeping onto my lips. "I do like a challenge," I admit.

"Yes!" she crows. "Good man."

I arch my eyebrow. "You just want to fob me off on a boy so you get more time to yourself, don't you?"

"Abso-fucking-lutely," she says with a feral grin as she snatches up her iPad once again. "Now, let's get you signed up to this app, shall we?"

3

———

LUKE

"Sammi?" I say as I gently knock on his door. "Have you got a sec?"

He looks up at me from the book he's studying, and smiles. He's juggling a part-time degree in primary education with work as an office assistant, and never seems to stop for fun unless we make him. He's so dedicated. "Of course, babe. What's up?"

I'm so nervous, but I trust Sam and Callum more than anyone else in the world. I know it's unfair, but I look to Sam for advice probably more often than I should. Out of all of us, he's the most decisive, though, and it makes me feel better to run things by him.

Especially something as important as this.

He beams at me and closes the book, making me feel like I'm welcome and not intruding. So I walk a few more steps into his bedroom, clutching my phone to my chest.

"I think I found someone. A Daddy. A good one."

"Really! That's amazing!" He pats his bed from where he's sitting at the cramped desk, inviting me to sit down. "Tell me all about him!"

I swallow, still not quite believing I've had the guts to even think about doing this. But I meant what I said the other night. I'm sick of the anticipation. I want to get this over with. After the disaster date, though, I feel I have a right to be wary. That's why I need a second opinion before I muster up the courage to make a move.

I perch on the bed and give Sam a small smile. He's so genuinely enthusiastic, so I steel myself. It feels ridiculously scary to admit out loud that I like someone, however. Even if it's just an online profile.

"So I'm still not really sure what exactly I'm looking for on this app," I confess as I fiddle with my phone. "But I've been looking at a lot of profiles on Collr to see if any of them jump out."

"That's a good idea," Sam says warmly, and I relax just a fraction at the simple praise. It's kind of a shame that Sam doesn't want to be a Daddy. I mean, I totally understand wanting to be a boy, but he'd make a pretty good Daddy, too. At least I think so.

"There are lots of nice looking and sounding Daddies," I explain, not sure how much Sam has looked at the app himself yet. "I'd probably be okay to message a lot of them. Especially the Daddies who say their top priority is to spoil and care for their boys."

Sam squeezes my knee. "That sounds perfect for you."

I don't know why, but that makes me a bit emotional, and I have to take a breath. We all have different needs and kinks. But Sam's right. After growing up with my terrible parents, I crave a lot of love and fuss, but also someone to just take charge. I've never found anyone like that yet, but in my fantasies, that's what my Daddy would be like. I'm not sure if wanting that makes me selfish, though.

Before I can lose myself in a downward spiral of anxiety, I rally myself and focus. Sam has assured me on countless occasions that it is *not* selfish to be clear about my needs and boundaries. This is kind of what joining this app and finally losing my virginity is all about. Moving beyond the demons that have haunted me for so long.

"But there's this one Daddy," I hedge, trying not to squirm where I sit. "He's uh, a bit different."

"Oh?" Sam prompts.

I swallow, trying not to let my fingers tremble as I unlock my phone screen. "His profile is kind of, uhh, *exciting.*"

I figured I was supposed to be looking for a Daddy who would make me feel safe and secure. And I do want that. I *do.* But this guy is sort of, well…scary. Intimidating. The kind of man I should probably run a mile from, but instead, I'm finding myself drawn all the more to him.

"You can't really see his face in the profile," I explain, opening the app up.

You're allowed to upload a maximum of five pictures. There's one of him in swimming trunks, then the others are of him hiking or wearing a fancy suit. But in all of them, his face is turned away or cropped off.

"Is that a bad thing?" Sam asks.

I shake my head. "No. It doesn't feel like he's doing it because he's ashamed of how he looks. It's more like, uh, mystery? That's what makes him different. Hot. You can see his body is amazing in the swimming trunks one." I blush, realising what I'm saying. "Oh, who am I to judge anyone's hotness?"

"Luke," Sam says firmly. "You're allowed to be attracted to people or not." He raises his eyebrows. "So, have you messaged him yet?"

"Oh, no!" I splutter and laugh. "No, no. I had to check with you first. Could I, um, read you out his bio?"

"Sure," Sam says warmly. "I'm all ears."

I'm not very confident reading aloud, but it's just Sammi,

who I know loves me. So I clear my throat and skim the first few words before I begin.

"I'm a D-D-Daddy who gets what I want. What I want is a good boy to sp-p-poil. Good boys can be naughty or nice, so long as they know that Daddy's in charge. With the right boy to keep my bed warm at night, I would be happy to spend my days skydiving or curled up by the fire. The right boy will have his own passions and dreams for me to nurture with him. He will be honest and hard working. He will be kind. Time wasters need not apply."

This Daddy sounds kind of *scary*, but I can't help but be drawn to him like a moth to a flame. I've got butterflies in my tummy again just reading the profile out loud. I managed it, though, without tripping over my words too much, and I look up at Sam to gauge his reaction.

He's got a strange expression on his face.

My heart drops. "What?" I say, starting to panic, and immediately feel relieved that I haven't messaged him yet. "What's wrong with him? I know he sounds a bit fierce, but I like that he wants a kind and honest boy. There are much safer sounding Daddies, but, well, I feel like the point of this new pact is to push ourselves, right?"

Sam shakes his hands and smiles at me, but it doesn't quite reach his eyes. "No, no! There's nothing wrong with him. He actually sounds great. Nice. I mean—exciting—like you said!"

I can feel the lump rising in my throat and tears gathering in my eyes. Why would Sam lie to me? He *never* lies to me. It's one of the things I can rely most on me in this world. So why...?

He sighs, and I look eagerly up, waiting for him to fix this. If he doesn't think I should message this guy, that would be understandable. I'd just want to hear why. "The thing is, babe —" he begins.

"Hang on," Callum's voice comes from farther in the flat. He appears at the door, leaning on the frame with his own phone in his hand and a confused expression on his face. "Were you just reading WolfDaddy84's profile?"

My entire insides drop. "Uh, yeah," I say softly. "Why?"

Callum chews his lip and comes in to sit beside me, facing Sam. He's got some material draped over his shoulder with several pins holding the pattern together, no doubt from one of his latest projects.

"Have you messaged him yet?" Callum asks, his eyes wide.

I shake my head. "No," I admit.

Callum nods. "It would be okay if you have," he assures me, grabbing my hand. "It's just…it's kind of funny. That's the guy I've been looking at all day, working up the nerve to message."

"Oh," I squeak. I try not to feel immediately crushed. "Well, you *should* message him. I meant it. I haven't talked to anyone yet. I don't mind." I try my best to smile, but Callum knows me better than anyone. Well, aside from Sam.

He shakes his head. "No…no, Luke. You should be the one to message him if you think he's special. Because *I* think he's special, and you deserve someone amazing."

I bite my lip, tempted. But then I look at my other best friend, who's watching us intently. "It's okay. Sam didn't approve of him anyway."

"Why not?" Callum asks, hurt, and I can't help but squeeze his hand.

"It's all right. Sam knows best, I'm sure."

Except Sam sighs and rubs his eyes before pulling out his own phone. "WolfDaddy84, you say?" He opens up the Collr app on a familiar looking profile. "I've been obsessing over him all day, too. His profile went up last night, I think. I've drafted several messages but haven't sent any. But…that was what my face was for, Luke. I didn't disapprove. It was the opposite. I approved *too much.*"

"Oh," I say. *"Oh.* So…we all like the same guy?" That sucks. A lot. Immediately, my need to make peace overwhelms me. "It's fine. I'll just forget about him. It's not like I know him or anything. Those bios are a five-hundred-word character limit, anyway. How much can you really tell about a person from that?" I laugh nervously and look at my besties to make sure they don't hate me.

Sam sighs and looks between me and Callum, and Callum squeezes my hand. "That hardly seems fair," Sam says. "He's the only guy you liked enough to want to message."

I shake my head. "I said there were *lots* of nice Daddies."

Sam arches an eyebrow at me, making my insides flip guiltily. Of course he sees right through me. "You said they were all *nice.* But he was the one you came in here excited enough to share his profile with me."

I shrug. "Well, what are you saying?"

"Maybe you should be the one to message him," suggests Callum gently.

I laugh.

"What? No! You guys have *way* more of a chance with him than I do. One of you should message him."

"Luke," Sam growls in a warning tone. I know he's going to tell me off for putting myself down, but I don't let him get the words out. I know I'm right.

"No, seriously," I say. "It was crazy to think I'd ever have the nerve to message someone that hot and cool and interesting-sounding. One of you should. I mean it."

"Why don't we all message him?" Callum says. "He's the only one who's really grabbed my interest in this app. How about you, Sam?" Callum raises his eyebrows. *"Or* none of us message him. I love you two more than some nameless cock I may or may not get."

That gets a laugh out of me, but I'm still not entirely sure what to say. I don't want to upset my friends and I want to be fair. But I *really* like the sound of this Daddy.

"Perhaps he just writes a great bio," I say with a shrug of my shoulders. "Maybe he's not really all that?"

Callum tilts his head and looks at me, asking if I actually believe that. I'm not sure I do. Whoever could write something like that must have *something* interesting going for them. I at least want to talk to the guy.

"What if…no," Sam says, shaking his head. "Callum's right. We should maybe just forget about him."

"No, what were you going to say?" I ask. I always want to hear Sam's suggestions.

He bites his lip. "Well…what if we were honest with him. Explain that we're all best friends looking to lose our V-cards. We all fancy him but we're not looking for forever Daddies, are we? We can ask him which one of us he'd prefer?"

I consider his idea. It hurts knowing that Daddy Wolf would never pick me over my friends…but, wait. This isn't just about me. I'm never going to get them to contact him if I don't. Perhaps this is the best option to get at least *one* of them in with a shot.

"I don't know," Callum begins sceptically, but I shake my head.

"I think that's the fairest way. We all like this guy, and we all want the others to be happy. He'll pick who he feels he's more compatible with, and then there will be no hard feelings between the rest of us."

"And what if he picks none of us?" Callum asks.

I hadn't thought of that.

"Then we get really drunk and watch Love Actually in our PJs with ice cream," says Sam firmly. I laugh. No matter what time of year, that's our go-to comfort night in.

"That would be a good consolation prize," says Callum as if Sam has suggested something very wise.

I giggle. I'm still sad, because I really let myself get carried away thinking I had a shot with Daddy Wolf. But there's nothing more important to me than my besties. Hopefully, he'll match with one of them, and whoever the other rejected one is can watch Love Actually with me.

This is just a pact to lose our virginity, not a wedding market. We're not looking for each of our happily ever afters. We're just trying to find someone to help us move into the next stages of our lives.

I genuinely hope Callum or Sam might find that with WolfDaddy84.

I'll just have to keep searching a little longer.

4

JACOB

"Any joy, then?"

I look at Harris with a raised eyebrow as we approach the car that's just pulled up outside the hotel. The concierge steps forward without hesitation to open the back door for us, and I slide in first so Harris doesn't have to go quite so far in her fancy dress.

"With what?" I ask, playing dumb.

I've had just enough to drink at this charity gala that I'm feeling suitably reckless to goad her. Besides, all that money I dropped into the coffers for the sick little kiddies has left me feeling disgustingly saintly, and I need some devilment to balance my soul out again.

"You know what," she says with an arched eyebrow as she buckles up. I do the same. Otherwise, my driver, Gerard, won't move, and I'd really rather like to get home now.

"If you're asking if I submitted a profile to that ridiculous app you suggested, then, yes," I say petulantly.

She grins triumphantly. "And?"

"And there are a lot of sugar babies, just as I predicted."

She narrows her eyes at me. "I thought you were going to

leave your net worth out of your description," she says accusingly.

I shrug. "What can I say? It's like they sniff it out."

I only feel a little bit bad lying to her.

The truth is I submitted a profile a couple of evenings ago, but I haven't had the energy to open any of the many messages I've since received. I'm honestly surprised at the sheer quantity of them. Are good Daddies in short supply? Who are all these boys?

I'm probably being massively unfair, but I can't imagine any of them are any more interesting than the boys I've met in bars over the past few years. Sure, I had a lot of fun with them at the time. But the idea of meaningless one-night stands right now is decidedly boring me.

I can feel Harris's gaze on me as we travel through the night-time streets of London, but I'm not one to ever cave in and break an uncomfortable silence. Besides, I don't actually want to disappoint her. I'll look at my inbox when I'm good and ready.

I don't particularly care about hurting the feelings of strangers I'll likely never meet, either. But I am aware that ignoring that many messages is bad business practice. *Fine.* I'll crack open a bottle of something vintage once I'm back home and tackle whatever tedium awaits me before it can grow into something even larger.

We spend the rest of the drive discussing my schedule for the rest of the week. I can tell Harris knows I'm purposefully ignoring the subject, but she's humouring me for now, so we both go along with the pretence.

I bid her good night after we arrive at my building, watching as the car moves on to take her to her own home. Then I greet the doorman in my lobby and head straight for the private lift, sighing as the doors slide shut behind me. I turn around to face them, then gratefully press the button to the penthouse.

Peace, at last.

I get my phone out and toy with it. What am I even hoping for by joining this damnable app? I could get casual sex easily from using it—or hell, just popping down to Soho. There are plenty of guys around looking for a good time, and some of them might even be into kink.

What I *want* is something more meaningful. Long-lasting. I want to be someone's Daddy both in and out of the bedroom. Harris is certainly right about one thing. I'm craving a sweet soul to boss around. I need someone who needs *me*. Desperately. For everything. Even just thinking about it makes my skin tingle.

So why am I resisting a chance to possibly find that?

Am I scared?

Of what?

It's not like me to hide from my fears. Usually, I rush at them, head-on. Have I spent so long wanting to be a Dom and a Daddy, now that I'm finally old enough to be easily accepted in that role, I'm worried I'll fuck it up? I chew my lip as I step out into the hallway on the top floor, key in hand to let myself in. No, I don't think that's it. Slipping into those kinds of roles has come naturally over the past few years, and I feel extremely confident in my abilities.

Yes, I know how to dominate.

But do I know how to *love*?

I grit my teeth as I shrug off my tailored suit jacket and toss it over a chair, heading straight for my drinks cabinet. I'm pretty certain I'm getting to the heart of the matter, and I can't say I'm particularly pleased about it.

I'm not sure I do know how to love. I push people away. It's easier like that, safer. That way I don't have to rely on anyone. I trust myself to get things done. I always have. Other people let you down.

But it can get lonely.

I look around my enormous penthouse, and feel the isolation keenly. It's silent and still and it makes me wonder what the hell I've worked so hard for if there's no one to share it all with now. I want a boy to spoil the crap out of. I want someone I can proudly explain my ideas to when I finally start working on something new. I want someone who can't wait for me to come home.

But is there actually someone like that out there? Who's going to care if I'm home or not?

Feeling frustrated at myself, I snatch up a bottle of red wine without even checking the label, marching over to the kitchen, where I fetch a bottle opener and a glass. Once I've poured a healthy measure, I activate my music streaming service via my phone and put an angry rock mix on, confident that the sound-proofing will mean my downstairs neighbours aren't disturbed.

Fuck this. I'm Jacob Wolf. I'm not frightened of anything. Not even of my own stupid insecurities.

"Let's be having you," I grumble as I log into Collr and navigate to the inbox.

There are over fifty unread messages. Bloody hell.

I drop into an armchair and dangle one of my legs over the side. I place my wine down on a small coffee table beside me and loosen my tie. Might as well get comfortable, I guess.

As it turns out, I was right. There are a *lot* of sugar babies here. Almost none of them come out and say that they've sussed I'm rich, but there's a lot of talk from good or naughty boys who are looking to be spoiled.

Am I a hypocrite? That's pretty much what I said in my profile. I *want* a boy to spoil. But it feels like it ruins the illusion if he downright comes to me begging for it. My money should be a secondary perk they get to enjoy once we've already built a relationship. Right?

I'm almost tempted to give up. But instead, I pick up my wine and persevere. I make myself promise not to stop until I've properly read every damned one of these messages.

That doesn't mean I can't read them fast.

I don't bother replying to any of them to let them down. After all, I could get to the end of this depressing list and start all over with lower standards. But also, I feel like seeing that I've read their message and not replied should ultimately be clear enough.

I bite my lip and sip more wine, inhaling deeply and closing my eyes for a second. Am I being unfair? Could my bad-temperedness be unjustly clouding my judgement? I shake my head and reopen my eyes. If so, sober me can decide tomorrow when I take a second run at my inbox, if I even want to. But right now, the whole point is to try and find someone new and different. If none of these boys are exciting me, it wouldn't be fair to start a conversation with them, even if they seem nice enough.

I'm not looking for nice. I'm looking for extraordinary.

A couple of the more bratty messages stir my interest a little, but I just mentally bookmark them. This has become more of a race to the finish more than anything else now, and I'm eager to get it over with. I feel like a fool, chasing rainbows instead of accepting there's going to be a thunderstorm.

Did I really think I'd join one stupid app and find true love, just because my EA has had enough of my moping and wished it so?

Just as I'm about to claim a bittersweet victory, a brand-new message appears at the top. I'd started with the oldest ones at the bottom of the list, so the new message headline taunts me at the start where I can't avoid seeing it. Logically,

I know that's the point, but I'm ready to ignore the damn thing on principle. I'd decided I was going to give up for the evening and sulk into the rest of my bottle of wine, but the perfectionist in me demands that I finish what I started and open this last-minute missive.

Then I read the title.

Unusual request – we need your help, Daddy!

My eyebrows raise, and something strange unfurls from within my heart. I'm not sure if it's the 'we' or 'need your help' that grabs me more. And it's not like plenty of the other boys didn't call me Daddy in their titles or the body of the messages themselves, but for some reason seeing the name at the end of this plea makes it read differently.

Feeling more intrigued than I have for any other message, I click to open it.

Dear Daddy Wolf, it begins. *We need your help!*

We are three best friends looking for a special Daddy. We promised ourselves that by the end of the year we would each lose our virginity, so we turned to Collr to find our perfect matches.

The trouble is, we each picked a favourite, but all three of us picked you. To keep things fair, we have agreed to let you decide who you like best, and then the other two will keep hunting for their first time Daddy elsewhere.

If you are interested, here's a little bit more about each of us. We've enclosed a photo to help you decide.

I glance down to the bottom of the message and can't help but smile. There are three young men sat closely side by side, but they've done what I've done in all my photos and hidden their faces by looking down into their laps. The reason they're looking that way is because they are each holding a matching stuffed piggy, each with different clothes on to discern them. The first has a rainbow bow tie and a tutu, the second a smart black suit, and the third a knitted pink jumper and magic wand in its hand.

From left to right, the photo explains, starting with the sparkly rainbow one.

Snazzy Pants is a loud, fun-loving boy who can be a bit of a handful. He's a good boy, but sometimes, likes to be bad and bratty first.

Mr Bacon is thoughtful and gentle, but he needs a Daddy who's going to care for his boy like he's the most important thing in the world.

Squish is a shy boy who worries he's not going to be good enough for a Daddy, so he's hoping for lots of praise and cuddles.

If none of us take your fancy, that's okay! We all liked you so much we wanted to give it a shot, but if it's not meant to be, we'll be all right. We have each other, after all.

We look forward to hearing from you,

With love,

The Three Little Piggies

I blink and read the message a couple more times. There were definitely other boys who were sweet and vulnerable in their messages, but I'm locked into the idea of these three best friends all laying their hearts on the line, not to mention their virginity. No other boy mentioned that in their messages. In fact, most bragged about their extensive experience. These three are shiny and new, looking for their first times.

And they chose me to ask.

Me, who's so bloody grumpy he's been resenting all his other messages until now.

Well, I have been honest with myself. I was looking for something extraordinary.

Have I just found it?

I check the username, which is BacOnRa$h3rs, so I assume the message has come from the middle boy's account. But I keep reading back over all three of the little bios they've sent me. Except every time I just try and read the bios, I end up reading the entire thing again. And when I look at the photo, my eyes keep darting back and forth across all three laps.

Each boy seems enticing on their own. But it's the *whole* package that's really stopped me in my tracks. So what does that mean? What am I going to do? Should I meet them all in person and then make a decision? These are the only profiles that have intrigued me enough that I feel compelled to ask for a face-to-face, after all.

Hang on. What the *fuck* am I thinking? One bloody message from these boys, and I've turned into some sort of wet blanket. I know what I want. I *always* know what I want.

And that's *everything*.

5

LUKE

I PUT MY KEY INTO OUR FLIMSY FRONT DOOR AND LET OUT A sigh in an attempt to rally my spirits before I enter. I had a particularly draining shift at the pub from people shouting orders at me, and I'm covered in at least two pints of beer.

I just want to get into the shower and then crawl into bed. But I also want to make sure I'm happy and smiling for my besties if they're still up. I don't like them worrying about me.

Especially when I know I've been fighting to stay cheerful ever since we decided to message Daddy Wolf as a threesome and ask him to pick the one he'd like to meet—if any of us. Sam said he was going to send the message sometime this evening after spending all day with us drafting it. I'm half dreading finding out if he's already got a reply and half just wanting to get it over with.

"I will be happy for whichever one gets chosen," I whisper to myself, holding the key steady in the lock. "Or I will be there to look after them if all three of us have been rejected."

There we go. Decision made. I take another breath and enter our crummy flat. It's best not to hang around in the hallway. Our awful landlord tends to lurk in the shadows, waiting to yell at us for the most ridiculous things. He loves a surprise inspection, as well, so it's best not to antagonise him. He once threatened to evict us because the bin was a bit too full.

Usually, after I get back from a late shift, the place is pretty dark. Either the other two have already gone to bed, or one of them is still awake in their room watching TV quietly with the lights out.

But right now, the lights in the living room are on full blast, and both Sam and Callum are fully awake. I can tell this from the way they both leap up from my bed the second I get through the door. They've both got a glass of that terrible cheap rosé from the local corner shop that we can't seem to stop ourselves buying, and before I can even process what's happening, Sam is thrusting a full glass into my hand.

"W-what—?" I manage to stammer.

"Luke!" Callum cries, practically dancing on the spot. *"Luke!"*

"Yes?" I reply nervously.

Sam places a hand on my arm and gently guides me towards the bed. We sit with Callum, who is still vibrating with excitement. That's not entirely unusual for him, but Sam is also beaming like he can barely contain himself.

My nerves are becoming panicky. I don't like surprises.

"W-w-what's going on?" I say more urgently.

Sam immediately chills out, probably sensing my distress. "It's okay," he says, touching my knee. "It's good news." That helps relax me a little. He wouldn't lie to me.

"You'll never believe what's happened," Callum hisses.

I shake my head and let out an anxious laugh. "I don't know. Has one of you won the lottery?"

"Kind of," Sam says, his grin only getting wider. "We got a response from WolfDaddy84."

I can't help it. My stomach drops. "Oh," I say, forcing myself to sound as cheerful as I can muster. "Did he pick one of you, then?"

They shake their heads, but they look so happy about it I'm completely confused. I take a gulp of wine, not sure if it helps or not.

"He wants all three of us," Sam says, practically quivering next to me.

I'm still confused. "A-a-all three?" My heart rate spikes. "At once?"

Sometimes—when we've had a lot to drink and are feeling naughty—we get into bed and *do* things. Together. It's always in the dark, and we never talk about it when we're sober in the morning. But I'm not sure if it's okay how much I *love* it when we do those things.

Sure, we kiss each other casually all the time and there is never a shortage of hugs. But those nights we get *naked,* and I just love the feel of my best friends' bodies next to mine, our happy laughs and messy kisses as we touch ourselves…as we make ourselves *come.*

There have been times when I'm having a late-night wank that I allow myself to imagine that we touch *each other* and make *each other* come. I'm pretty sure that would be crossing a line, though. I'd never, *ever* want to lose my bestest friends in the whole world because things got weird.

But it's like I can't help myself. I think it would feel so nice. I've never let *anyone* else touch me down there. However, I think Sam and Callum would be a good kind of touch.

Not like how I imagine a Daddy would feel, though. I yank my many thoughts back to the here and now, trying to work out what's happening.

Sam shakes his head, and for a second I almost become disappointed. But he doesn't give me the chance.

"Why don't you read the message?" he suggests, thrusting his phone into my free hand. I nervously sip some more wine and hungrily scan the words.

My dear little piggies,

I'm honoured by your message. In fact, I'm delighted and intrigued by it. But you are very naughty boys for trying to make Daddy choose between you when you're all so lovely.

Here is my proposal. I want you all. You are offering me the gift of your first times. I'm not sure what that means to you exactly, but I know I want them all. I want to spoil you like you've never dreamed of.

You are to decide an order amongst yourselves. Then I will treat you each in turn to a magical, intimate weekend that you will remember for the rest of your lives.

You indicate in your message that you're not searching for forever Daddies, and that's okay. I'm not offering that. I'm offering a no-strings-attached time of all your lives to allow you to continue your Daddy searches, knowing exactly just how specially you should be treated.

Don't keep your Daddy waiting. Let me know soon who I will get to devour first.

Yours,

Wolf

I gulp, and my entire body shudders as the implications of the message sink in.

Daddy Wolf wants all of us. *That includes me.* Me. I'd written myself off the moment I'd realised my best friends had also fallen for this enigmatic stranger. But…

"Oh my god," I whisper.

Callum shakes my knee and squeals. "I know, right? Isn't it crazy?"

"I-I don't…" I stammer, feeling a little faint. I thrust Sam's phone back at him and take another big glug of wine. "He c-c-can't…no…I…"

I'm shaking my head, and I realise with horror I'm getting tearful.

Sam and Callum's expressions drop, and Sam throws his phone onto the bed so he has a free hand to cup the side of my face. That immediately helps me to calm a little, but I'm still quaking.

"Babe, what's wrong?" he asks. "I thought you'd be happy."

"You said you liked him so much," Callum adds, clearly confused.

I pause a second, then nod. "I did. I do." I suck in a breath and try and find the right words. "But he can't really want *me*, can he? He'll be so disappointed. You guys should meet him, though!" I add in a rush. "His message is so, uh, I mean, it's really…sexy."

I'm blushing as I mumble the last words into my wine glass. If I wasn't on the verge of an anxiety attack, I'd be able to appreciate how turned on it made me. It was just so *commanding*.

"Oh, *Luke*," Sam says sadly. "Babe. I wish you could see yourself like we see you." Callum nods eagerly, and I look between them. "You're gorgeous," Sam continues. "Sweet. Talented. Sexy."

I scoff loudly, even managing a laugh. "I am *not—*"

Sam grabs my chin and kisses me firmly on the mouth, startling me out of my protests. *"Sexy,"* he insists.

Callum throws his arm around my shoulders and smacks a big kiss on my cheek. "Sexy AF, squishy baby boy. Of course Daddy Wolf is as interested in you as he is in us."

"I think we should all meet him, like he suggested," Sam says, nodding as he looks between us. "We all liked him, and this is basically the dream response, right? We can *all* have an amazing time with him."

I bite my lip. "I did *really* like his profile," I whisper. "But I didn't think…I never thought he'd pick me."

Sam sighs fondly and caresses the side of my face. "Maybe this will help you see how beautiful you are, babe. How special. And it's no strings attached! So there's no pressure. But he says he wants to spoil us, so hopefully, we won't be dropping our standards either."

"Definitely not," Callum scoffs. "He better *Pretty Woman* the shit out of all of us."

That manages to make me laugh. "Oh my god, is this really happening?"

My friends laugh as well, the mood finally lifting. "It seems so," Sam says, raising his wine glass. "I think that deserves a toast."

"I think that deserves another bottle of terrible wine," Callum says jovially as we all clink glasses.

"There's one already in the fridge!" Sam announces, much to our delight.

He dashes into the kitchen, and Callum puts some party music on. I finally take my shoes and coat off, feeling slightly dizzy as I snuggle against my pillows and drink more pink wine.

It's a good kind of dizzy. I can't believe this is real, but apparently, it is.

Daddy Wolf wants us all.

Now we just have to decide in what order.

6

―――――

JACOB

"Let me get this straight," Harris says. I hear her scepticism, but if I don't look up from my laptop screen, I don't have to *see* it, and therefore it doesn't really exist.

"Hmm?"

"I told you to go find a boy to have a relationship with, and instead you found *three* to have one-night stands with?"

I scratch my jaw. "It's not like that."

"Then by all means, explain it to me," she says.

I can at least hear the humour in her words now, so I know she's not really pissed at me. In fact, I'm pretty sure she's impressed that I'm engaged in a project I'm passionate about for once. It's been a long time since I bound out of bed well before midday in order to do some work.

It doesn't matter that I'm not getting paid for this. There are *spreadsheets* and they're *colour-coded,* so that means it's work.

And I'm having fun. A lot of it.

"They aren't one-night stands," I say, aware that I'm being picky. "I've offered them two nights each, like a weekend. But they all do shift work or are at uni, so we've worked out when I can see them over the course of around ten days. Oh, that reminds me. I'm going to need to clear my calendar for ten days."

She doesn't reply, so I finally look up to see her narrowing her eyes at me. I don't care. My mood is too good. I just grin at her, then go back to the dozen or so tabs I currently have open.

"Why three?" she asks, exasperated. "Are you hoping to audition them down and find just one to date for real?"

I shake my head. I'm aware that my last several messages to her about this have not been coherent at all. I'm...*giddy*. Like a child. I can't remember the last time I felt such genuine joy.

"No, they don't want that," I explain. I'm sure I've told her all this already, but perhaps that was one of the imaginary conversations I had with myself in the shower. "They're best friends who all want to lose their virginities. If you read their messages, you'd understand. Harris—they're *adorable* and they *need* me. They all liked me so much they asked me to choose, but I didn't want to. Don't you see? This is a challenge. It's fun! I get to take the V cards of three boys—but that's not the actual challenge. Any idiot could do that."

The idea of just any man deflowering these boys sets my teeth on edge. They're vulnerable. They need someone who's going to give them the care and attention they deserve. And that's *me*. Not some arsehole off the street.

It's ridiculous, but I'm already starting to think of them as *my* boys. I guess in a way they are, though. They're trusting me.

"I have the chance to give them each the most unforgettable experience. It's a big responsibility."

"Ah," she says with a knowing nod. "So it's a competition. That I understand."

I frown at her. "Who am I competing with?"

"Every other Daddy out there," she says with a smirk. "You want to ruin them for anyone else."

I huff. "No," I say. "Look, they were very clear they're not looking for a relationship. I am, but this came up instead, so I figured…well, it's a change of pace for me from the obnoxious sugar babies. I'm thinking of it like a palate cleanser. I'll have some fun with them, get back in the game, then look for something long term."

In the messages we've shared so far, I've made it seem like I'm not looking for a forever boy either so as not to put any pressure on them. If we all agree to a no-strings-attached deal, then we can all have fun before going our separate ways.

Simple.

"And these aren't sugar babies?" Harris asks.

It's a fair question. But I shake my head. "I really don't think so."

"Based on what?"

I wince and sneak a look over at her on the other side of the couch. "I…have a good feeling?" I say weakly.

She tries to keep a straight face, but then she snorts and rolls her eyes. "I'd call you an idiot, but unfortunately I'm fully aware that your gut instinct has earned you millions before breakfast on more than one occasion."

I grin cockily at her. "They just don't have that vibe. I know I'm right. And I'm not planning anything ridiculously extravagant for them." I nod towards all my tabs and spreadsheets. "Just three simple little getaways where we can have some peace and quiet."

She arches a red eyebrow. "With private catering, chauffeurs, extravagant gifts, and lord knows what else."

I frown at her then at my laptop screen, wondering if she's somehow acquired X-ray vision in the past five minutes. "I haven't booked a single international flight!" I say defensively. "We'll need to eat, so that means caterers, and I'll have to get them to the properties, which Gerard can do. So, yes. Food and transportation will have to be taken care of. And I figured a gift or two would set them at ease. Maybe give them something to remember me by."

"Yes, that sounds all very sensible," she says, using her mean sarcastic voice. "Might I suggest throwing in a personal appearance by their favourite pop stars? How about a petting zoo?"

I have the numbers of over half of Below Zero sitting in my phone, but I dismiss that idea. I want these nights to be about just the two of us. And I wouldn't want a whole zoo, but considering they are my little piggies, some animal companions might not be—

"I was kidding!" Harris calls out loudly, pulling me from my spiralling thoughts. I blink at her but realise she's laughing. "However, you know what? This is great. I haven't seen this side of you since we first met."

"What side of me?" I ask, genuinely not sure what she means.

I could accuse her next smile of actually being kind. "The child-like tech genius who wasn't afraid to be a geek. The man who was so filled with optimism. I still think this whole venture is hare-brained, but if this is the effect three adorable boys are going to have on you before you've even met them in real life, then I'm on board. I'll clear your calendar. Go nuts." She holds a finger up and crooks an eyebrow. "So long as you promise me you won't give up after this. You'll keep looking. Because there's a guy out there who could make you happy for the rest of your life if you'd let him."

I grunt and look back at my screen. I want to deny that there's any truth to her words, but I can't. I've grown into this sophisticated, cold playboy. I've been doing it so long that it feels natural now. But she's right. For the past couple of days, it's like I've slipped back into the person I was at university. So alive with possibilities and hope. I was more carefree and easy-going.

It's kind of scary. I'd get eaten alive if any of my competitors saw me like this, but...well, I don't have competitors anymore, do I? I sold everything. I have peers instead, and they can't take my money away from me. So I don't care what they think.

I care what my boys think.

I don't want to intimidate them, especially if they actually *haven't* clocked that I'm Mr Moneybags. But I want to spoil them rotten, for sure. What's the point of being rich otherwise? I can't take it with me when I die. I've promised my little piggies the best nights of their lives, with first times that will be so memorable maybe it *will* ruin them a bit for other guys. Like I said, I want to show them how they should expect to be treated.

And yeah, sure. Once I've seen through this little project, I'll turn my efforts to finding someone long-term. I'm hoping being with three different types of boys in such a short time might make me consider what I'm looking for the most, then I can adjust my Collr profile accordingly. Maybe I'll prefer the bratty boy or the gentler one? Who knows?

"I won't give up," I say to Harris eventually with a wink. "I can't promise that Mr Happy Go Lucky is here to stay. I'm sure the novelty will wear off soon enough. But this has at least reminded me how much I need new challenges in my life. Whether that's dating or work. I'm done sitting on my arse moping."

She nods. "That's all I want to hear."

And I mean it. But right now, I can't seem to care about

anything beyond my three little piggies. I want each of these getaways to be absolutely perfect for them. And for me. I want us all to have the times of our lives.

After that, I promise myself I'll think about the future. But right now, it just doesn't seem important at all.

7

———

SAM

"Are you sure you packed your toothbrush?" Luke asks for the second time.

"Never mind that. Have you got enough lube?" Callum asks, wagging his eyebrows.

"Guys," I say firmly. I don't want to show how nervous I am by snapping at them. They're just being thoughtful friends, after all. But I volunteered to go first to make sure that Daddy Wolf is legit.

So not only am I fretting about possibly getting murdered by a serial killer, but I also have the little matter of worrying about finally losing my virginity.

So you know, nothing big going on.

I can't stop imagining what it will be like to open up and be vulnerable with someone like that. Will I feel different afterwards? I know that virginity is a social construct, and technically I've already lost it with the blow jobs and wanking off I've done with other guys. Hell, what I've done with my besties might even constitute doing the deed.

But try as I might to be modern and progressive, there's

41

something within me that's clinging on to the importance of penetrative sex. Of letting another man *inside me.* It's thrilling and terrifying in equal measures. Daddy Wolf also asked us to get tested before we see him, and so has he, so there's literally going to be nothing between us.

Therefore, I've got enough on my mind without having my best friends winding me up, no matter how good their intentions are.

"Daddy Wolf gave me a list, remember?" I say, wagging my phone at them. "Clothes for walking and being comfy in. Pyjamas and wash kit. It's not rocket science."

"And Mr Bacon!" Luke says, grabbing him from my bed and thrusting him into my hands. I hadn't forgotten him, but I think it's sweet that Luke wants to make sure he's not left behind.

"Yeah, is that weird?" Callum asks, scrunching up his nose. "I know we used the piggies in our photo, but why would he want you to bring him for your date? He's going to see your face."

I shrug and toy with the edge of Mr Bacon's jacket. "I don't know. But it was on the list to bring, so that's what I'll do. I don't want to disappoint him before we've even begun."

I try and keep a brave face on for the others, but I can't help the insecurities that sneak their way in. What if he *doesn't* like me? I've hardly had men falling over themselves to be with me until this point.

Callum sees right through me, however. "He's going to *love* you," he says firmly, squeezing my arm.

"Just like we love you," Luke agrees.

Callum shakes his head, though. "No, different to us. He's going to love you like a Daddy, and it's going to be *amazing.*" He waggles his eyebrows. "And so is the sex, *oh* my god."

I laugh and hug Mr Bacon to my chest. It feels really weird making an arrangement like this specifically to have sex. I always thought it would be something that would happen naturally once I started dating someone special. But perhaps that's where I've gone wrong. By putting so much pressure on myself for it to be perfect, I've ended up in a situation where I'm making a more formal arrangement.

Oh, for goodness sake. I'm not paying a gigolo. Not that it would be wrong if I was. People arrange for hook-ups all the time on all the different dating apps—especially the gay ones. A lot of men have crazy high sex drives, and where's the harm in setting something up to everyone's mutual satisfaction?

At least, I hope everyone's going to be satisfied.

Oh, god.

Right, no more second-guessing. The car is going to be here any minute.

"It's kind of weird that he's sending a car, right?" I say as I close up my small suitcase. "He must have a lot of money."

"That's not weird. That's awesome," Callum says, indicating our small flat as they walk with me towards the front door.

I also indicate the flat. "That's what I mean. We're poor. If he's rich enough to send a fancy car, he might be disappointed with us." *Me*, is what I really mean.

For once, it's Luke who narrows his eyes questioningly at me. "I know none of us has actually had a Daddy yet, but doesn't it make sense that they'd want to spoil their boys? Why would he need us to be rich?"

I consider him a moment, then smile as something lightens in my chest. "You have a really good point there," I admit.

Callum nods. "So *enjoy* being spoiled. I bet he's going to take you to a fancy hotel or something."

"And a posh dinner!" Luke adds.

The truth is, we have no idea where I'm going. I know all

the advice says to never meet a stranger in private, but he has given my best friends all the information they need about where I'm going in a sealed envelope that was posted to us yesterday. But he's told them not to ruin the surprise, and to only open the package if they don't hear from me regularly. The same will go for all three of us.

This is why I think we were all drawn to Daddy Wolf. He gives off this aura of mystery, like an international spy or something.

So I'm aware I'm taking a risk, but the excitement is too much to ignore. I just hope it doesn't blow up in my face.

"I'll be back soon," I promise the others as I hug them at the front door.

They wanted to follow me all the way down to the street level, but Daddy Wolf thought of that, too. He said that each boy should have a special, unique experience from the moment we leave our flat. Therefore, we say our goodbyes here, and I'm to go down alone.

"Have an *amazing* time," Callum says.

"We'll be waiting for your text, so don't forget," Luke adds.

"I won't," I say. I give them each a kiss—just little pecks on the mouths—but it gives me the confidence to take a deep breath and walk away from them. "I love you both," I call over my shoulder with a wave.

"We love you, too!" they cry enthusiastically from the threshold of the door.

Honestly, you'd think I was boarding a ship to cross the Atlantic. I laugh at how stupid we all are, then push through the fire door to jog down the stairs.

I wanted to be early, but there's already a sleek black limo parked by the kerb with a driver waiting for me. He's got a completely straight face, even though the sign he's holding up says 'Mr Bacon'.

I swallow down a snort.

This is pretty ridiculous.

It's also extremely exciting. My whole body tingles as I wave over to him, and I have to resist a squeak as he actually bows and tips his driver's cap at me.

"Good afternoon, sir," he says.

"Oh, um. Hi. I'm Sam." I indicate the sign. "I mean—Mr Bacon. I assume Mr Wolf sent you?"

He nods again, reaching for my wheely suitcase. "He did indeed, sir. My name is Gerard. Please make yourself comfortable, and we'll be on our way shortly."

He takes my case to put in the boot whilst I settle in the back of the limo. It feels crazy big as I'm all by myself, but I'm soon distracted by the snack bar on display. There's water and fizzy drinks, chocolate and sweets, but also sliced veggies and dips. I'm glad. I'm nervous, so my instinct would be to snack on sugar, but the crunchy carrots and hummus settle my tummy much better. At least to start with.

It's kind of slow going getting out of London, but that's to be expected. However, the limo has an entertainment system, so I can listen to music, watch TV, or even play video games. I decide on a music playlist to start with, then allow myself to stare out of the window as the world goes by.

The windows are tinted, so no one can see me. But I can see them, and it's kind of thrilling seeing how many people are staring. Obviously, it's the limo they're looking at, probably curious as to who's inside. They'd most likely be very unimpressed if they knew it was a nobody like me, but I can't deny the delight I get anyway.

I've never done anything like this before in my life.

It was early afternoon when we left our flat. After an hour or so, London starts to slip away, and we enter one of the surrounding home counties. I keep an eye on the maps app on my phone so I'm not completely in the dark. We're heading east into Essex.

A lot of people have set ideas of what kind of a place Essex is and the kind of people that live there thanks to a lot of different reality TV shows. But it's not all fake tans, nails, and eyelashes. In fact, it's got a lot of beautiful countryside, as I'm now seeing.

We stop off at a fancy VIP service station, and that's when I realise the car is an electric one. I should have known from the lack of engine noise, but I guess I was too distracted by everything else going on. Whilst it charges, I use the facilities and stretch my legs, doing my best to keep my nerves at bay.

The chauffeur told me it wouldn't be long now.

Sure enough, we only drive for about another half an hour before we come off the main roads and start travelling down lots of twisty, turny lanes. The only ones here gawking at the limo are cows and sheep.

I take a few deep breaths, telling myself that just because we're in the middle of nowhere doesn't mean I'm going to get murdered. It'll all be fine.

Hopefully.

Nearly there, I text my besties, keeping them in the loop.

One of Daddy Wolf's instructions was that I wasn't allowed to give them any details or send them any photos. He says he wants us all to have a big surprise. I assume that means he's going to bring us all to the same place, and I'd hate to ruin anything for the others, so I'm determined not to give too much away. I'll give them just enough so they know I'm safe and (hopefully) having a good time.

When I look up from my phone, I see that we're driving down a winding road lined with oak trees. There are fields either side, and between the branches I can see fluffy white clouds in the periwinkle blue sky. It's the middle of spring— my favourite time of year. The days are getting much longer, but the weather isn't so hot yet that it's got uncomfortable.

Then up ahead, I see it.

I gasp.

There's no other building in the area, so this has to be where we're headed. At a glance, I'd guess it's a converted barn. The L-shaped building has a real thatched roof, but the two storeys are made of floor-to-ceiling windows, the glass glinting in the sunshine. We turn off the road onto a gravel driveway, and there's a bubbling fountain between us and the front door. It looks like a fancy wedding venue or something.

"This can't be happening," I whisper to myself.

But sure enough, the limo swings around and comes to a halt. I gulp and reach for the door with a shaking hand. However, Gerard has already sprung out and opened it for me before I get the chance.

"Thank you," I manage to say without stammering.

As I'm standing there admiring the building, he retrieves my bag, then hands me a key. "There you are, sir. If you need anything, there are emergency numbers in the kitchen. Otherwise, Mr Wolf will be with you shortly."

I nod and say my thanks again, waiting for him to get in the car. But then I realise he's waiting for *me*, so I take a breath and march up to the front door, opening it easily with the key.

I close the door and look out of the side window to finally wait for the driver to leave. It's not that I found him creepy or anything. He was absolutely fine. I just want to savour this moment in private and not feel like I'm being watched or judged.

I'm glad because when I walk down the short hallway into the main area, I definitely make some sort of gurgling spluttery noise.

Holy. *Fuck.*

The floors are gorgeous wooden panelling, and the ceiling has vaulted wooden beams. There's a split level, and I can see that upstairs on the mezzanine is a massive open double bedroom behind a balcony rail and a door that I guess leads to an en suite. Downstairs, there are exposed brick parts of the walls mixed in with plastered white paint. Expertly distressed, I guess is how I'd describe it. All the furnishings are modern designs, with a lot of glass and chrome, and I know nothing about artwork, but the pieces on the walls seem pretty funky to me.

Then I see the garden.

I leave my suitcase in the middle of the open-plan living room to slide open the French doors. The patio is a mixture of grey slate and wooden decking. Evening hasn't begun to fall yet, but I see a lot of fancy light fixtures dotted around that I'm sure will make a cosy atmosphere later. Several cobblestone walls create various levels of descending grassy areas, and then there's a wooden fence with a cute gate that leads right out into the adjoining field.

But there are two things that have made my jaw drop. First, there's a hot tub sunken into the decking that's already bubbling with its lights on that's making me desperately wish I'd brought my swim trunks.

The second thing is that strutting around the grass are three honest-to-god peacocks.

They're beyond stunning. Their bodies are a bright royal blue, and their feathery tails trail behind them like a bridal train with a hundred eyes. I step closer to one, but immediately stop as he shakes himself all over…and then his tail begins to rise.

I know I can't tell my besties anything yet about what's happening, but I can damn well take photos now to show them later when this is all over. Very carefully, I slip my phone from my pocket, capturing several shots of the magnificent bird before he wanders off, his tail gently dropping down again.

"Wow," I whisper to myself.

My throat feels dry from all this excitement, so I head back inside and make my way to the kitchen area. I plan to just get a glass of water, but curiosity urges me to open the fridge. I'm not sure what I'm expecting to find, but it's not to see it fully stocked with all kinds of mouth-watering things.

I blink as I take in the assortment of meats, cheeses, olives, fruits, and other little bits to make up a serious charcuterie board. I look around at the central island in the space, and realise there's also a basket of bread, crackers, butter, jam, and slabs of different kinds of chocolate. Daddy Wolf asked us all if we had any dietary preferences in one of his messages, as well as our favourite cuisines, and now I know why.

This is mine. Now the crudities in the limo also make sense. I love lots of nice picky bits, but usually that means splashing out on a fancy cheese every now and then from the supermarket, then everything else is as cheap as I can make it.

Nothing about this is cheap. In fact, I'd guess it was all extremely fresh and organic. Farm-to-table type stuff.

I'm not sure if I should start eating anything yet before Daddy gets here, though. But I'm still thirsty. That's when I spot a shelf in the fridge that's filled with a number of bottles. Without thinking, I assume they're wine, but when I pull one out, I realise they're various sparkling fruit cocktails. Non-alcoholic—because you don't mix drink with kink.

Holy shit, this is really happening.

I slide the bottle back in and stick to my plan to just get a glass of water. Once that's in hand, I continue exploring this incredible property that's going to be my home for the next couple of days. Daddy Wolf must have rented it just for us, and I think Callum must have been right.

He's pretty rich.

The way I see it, I can either be intimidated or enjoy it. I'm still worried he's not going to like *me* as a person. We've had so little interaction, after all, so I don't feel that's unreasonable. But I think Luke was also right. Daddies like spoiling their boys. So it would be ungrateful of me not to appreciate the gift he's given me.

A laugh bubbles up in my throat. I really do feel like Julia Roberts in *Pretty Woman*. This is like another world.

I get my next surprise when I reach the bedroom upstairs. There are a few different towelled robes hanging up, and on the bed are several different swimming shorts. Some are trunks, some are boxers, and there's a selection of sizes. Then it dawns on me.

These are for me to choose from.

"Oh, wow," I say, reaching out to touch the slippery material of the closest one. I so wanted to get in the hot tub, and Daddy Wolf made sure that's exactly what I could do.

I bite my lip, only hesitating for a second before tearing all my clothes off. The house is ridiculously exposed with all the huge windows, but there's also not another soul out here for miles. Unless you count the peacocks, but I'm sure they won't mind seeing a quick flash of my bum.

I throw on the right sized dressing gown (because there's a selection of those as well) and find flip-flops in the bathroom. Daddy Wolf has really thought of everything.

The water is just as amazing as I imagined. I've never been in a hot tub before, and there's something magical about it. I love the cool evening breeze on my skin as I watch the sun just starting to slip behind the tree line. I make sure to text my besties again to assure them that I got here and am okay, then I sit back and relax, soaking everything up.

This is some kind of paradise.

I'm not sure how much time passes, but for once, I'm not rushing anywhere or worrying about anyone but myself. It's strange but also wonderful. And that's when the doorbell rings through the grounds of the house. I sit up suddenly, jerking my head back towards the front door.

"Daddy," I whisper.

8

JACOB

I DON'T WORRY THAT IT TAKES A WHILE FOR ANY SIGN OF movement to appear beyond the door. I instructed for the swimming trunks to be left out so that my little Mr Bacon could hopefully take some time to relax and unwind before my arrival. Of course I have my own key, but I want him to let me in. He's in charge, after all.

Anticipation is fluttering like butterflies in my stomach as I wait patiently for him to make an appearance. Good lord, I don't remember the last time I was this excited when it didn't involve watching the stock market. I've been wondering what my first little piggy is going to be like all day, and now the moment is finally here.

"Hello?" a confident voice comes through the intercom.

I don't bother to try hiding my grin. "Hello?" I say back.

"Oh, um, what's the passphrase?"

Good boy, I think to myself. I was worried for a second that he was going to forget. I have to keep my boys safe, and that means not letting any old stranger in off the street.

"Little piggy, be a good boy and let Daddy in," I murmur against the speaker.

I wonder if it's my imagination, but I think I hear a faint whimper.

My grin only gets more feral, I'm sure.

There are a couple of clicks, and slowly the door of the property opens, and I get my first glimpse of my first boy.

I'm not disappointed.

In fact, he quite takes my breath away.

He's wrapped up in one of the towelled robes I had delivered, so I assume he's delved straight into the hot tub, which makes me extremely happy. His cheeks are slightly flushed, and the floor has some wet splatters on it, so I must be right.

The boy himself is of a stocky build, and only slightly shorter than me. Despite his youth, he has a dark, neatly trimmed beard that suits him very nicely. I have a little bear cub on my hands, and I couldn't be happier.

"Hello, gorgeous," I say, leaning against the door frame. "I'm Jacob, but please feel free to call me Daddy. It's a pleasure to finally meet you."

The boy blinks a couple of times. "I'm Sam," he says eventually. Then he shakes himself and opens the door fully. "I'm being rude. I'm sorry. Please come in."

I don't have any luggage with me, as everything's already been delivered that I'll need. So nothing encumbers me as I step up towards him, bringing us very close together. "Thank you, good boy. I'm not done saying hello yet, though. May I hug you?" I ask.

This time, he definitely lets out a happy little whimper, and his eyes have gone ever so slightly unfocused. "Uh-huh," he utters.

I slip my arms around him, feeling his solid body under the dressing gown. He easily hugs me back, and I breathe in deeply. He mostly smells of chlorine, but I've always enjoyed that smell. There's something that's uniquely him as well, however. It's warm, like sunshine and freshly baked bread.

I'm taking a huge risk agreeing to see all three of these boys. All the planning in the world can't anticipate whether or not there's going to be real chemistry between us when we finally meet. Luckily, I'm certain that's not going to be a problem with boy number one.

I nuzzle my nose against his cheek and kiss him chastely. "I'm so happy to meet you, Sam," I say. I lean back and caress my fingers around the back of his neck and up into his short hairs. His shiver under my touch is addictive. Holy fuck have I missed sweet, submissive boys. "Shall we head inside now? Perhaps you can give me a tour."

He licks his lips then nods as a small smile creeps onto his face. "Of course, Daddy."

Urgh, that makes my heart swoop and my cock throb all at once. Yes, I am Daddy, and this gorgeous boy is all mine for the next two days.

It's very natural as we turn, and our hands slide together. I allow Sam to lead me into the main room of the property. I've only seen photos online before, even though I've arranged for many deliveries to be brought here and put away to my very specific instructions. I wonder just how much exploring Sam has actually done.

"Do you like the house?" I ask. That's all I really care about. I'm happy wherever so long as my boy is satisfied.

His nod is unabashedly eager. "It's incredible!" he gushes, and his cheeks go that beautiful light pink again. "Thank you so much for organising this for us, Daddy. It's already very special." His eyebrows shoot up. "Did you know there are real live *peacocks* in the garden?"

I grin, more than a little smug that my instincts seem to have been on the money. I figured Mr Bacon and his fancy suit might appreciate such beautiful creatures. "Really?" I say, feigning ignorance.

"Do we need to feed them or anything?" he asks sincerely.

Something unexpected flips in my chest. I'll confess, I organised them as an extravagant bit of ornamentation. But this young man is automatically thinking of their well-being.

"Their handlers assured me that they'd left out a trough of food and water for them and that they'd also forage for themselves," I explain. "But it wouldn't hurt for us to keep an eye on them, I'm sure."

Sam beams and nods, looking out over the gardens and at our colourful guests. I remember that he was the one to write to me in the first place, and he also insisted on meeting me first out of the three. I thought perhaps that was because he was bossy and bratty, which would have been fine. But I'm starting to get a different impression of him now.

He's got a big heart. He's worried about the birds, and I'll bet that he wanted to meet me first to make sure everything was on the level before the other boys came away with me. His concern touches something soft in me that I haven't felt in a long while.

We find where the peacock feeding station is and see that it's indeed well stocked. Still hand in hand, we take a walk around the garden as the sun dips lower and the outdoor lights start coming on. I notice when he shivers, and my protective instincts immediately go into overdrive.

"It's getting chilly. Would you like to get back in the hot tub, or perhaps head inside to have some dinner?"

He considers for a moment. Good, I like that he's thinking about what he really wants. "I'm quite hungry," he admits. "So dinner sounds lovely."

I smile and lift his hand to kiss the back of it before we start heading back to the house. "Of course. Why don't you shower and get changed into something comfy? Feel free to wear your own clothes or rummage through the drawers and wardrobe. I have several options available for you if you want to enjoy something new and different."

He bites his lip as we pause in the living room. We're out of the evening breeze now, so I don't feel the need to hurry him along. "Is anything in my size?"

Ah. I sense a bit of hesitation there. I was wondering if that was going to be an issue. I think he's gorgeous, but people can be very cruel regarding body types, especially online.

However, I studied the photo they sent me of the three of them very closely. I did everything I could to ensure the comfort of all my boys.

"There absolutely should be options in your size, gorgeous boy. I had to guess, but I have quite a good eye for these things."

He swallows, then looks me in the eye. There's a hint of defiance there. "Does it bother you that I'm not small?"

I know this isn't the time, but I find his confidence in this moment very attractive.

"I think you are extremely handsome," I say, not wavering from his gaze. "You are a big boy with a big heart. The question is, does it bother you? Because if it does, I won't compliment you on such things or mention it again."

He licks his lips, not blinking as he continues to hold my gaze with his lovely brown eyes. "I love the way I look," he says eventually. "It's an important part of who I am. But other people see it as a flaw or something to be fixed."

I sigh happily and slip my hands either side of his face. "My first thought when I saw you was how perfect you are and how lucky I am to spend this time with you. We still have some getting to know each other to do, but please be in no doubt that you're stunning and I'm very drawn to you."

His smile is full of relief. "I, um, think you're really hot as well, Daddy."

I laugh and rub my thumbs gently against his cheekbones. "Thank you, sweetheart. I want to give you a special name for our little holiday. I'd love for you to be my big boy. Are you happy with that?"

He searches my face for a second. I wonder if I've made an error. But then he nods, his eyes a little glassy but his smile is happy. "I'd really love that, Daddy," he whispers. "That makes me feel good."

I want him to feel fucking cherished, so this is a good start. "Thank you for being honest and communicating with me, big boy. I'm proud of you. So much so, that I'd really love to kiss you right now. Would that be okay?"

He utters that little whimper again that's quickly becoming my favourite sound. He doesn't manage to speak, but he nods eagerly at me.

I lean closer, hesitating just as our lips are about to touch. His breath ghosts over my skin, ragged and warm. *Delicious.* I don't tease him for long, though, as I'm just as eager to taste him for the first time. I press my mouth against his, sweeping my tongue out to demand entrance, which he grants me right away. He melts against me, slipping his arms around my waist.

He might be a virgin, but he's not shy or inexperienced, as far as I can tell. He kisses me desperately, like he's been waiting a long time for this.

In a way, I feel exactly the same.

I let the kiss go on for a little longer, then hum as I gently wind it down. My boy said he was hungry, so he needs feeding before the evening can get much heavier. I caress his neck and cheeks, giving him a couple of sweet extra kisses to end on.

"Go have a shower, big boy," I murmur. "Make yourself

nice and fresh and comfy, and by the time you come back, everything will all be ready for dinner."

He takes a deep breath. His skin is flushed, and his eyes are blown, making him look absolutely delectable. I can't wait to give him all that again and more later.

"Yes, Daddy. Thank you."

Those words make me feel content down to my bones. I hug him to me, kissing his cheek and squeezing his bum through the dressing gown. That makes him squeak and giggle, which I absolutely love. I tap his behind as well for good measure, then run my hands up his thick body, showing him how much I want him.

"Now, off you go."

"I'll hurry back," he promises.

"Good," I tell him.

Suddenly two days don't seem all that long, and I'm going to want to spend every minute I can with this precious boy.

9

CALLUM

"So, Sam's said that Daddy Wolf—Jacob—has arrived and everything's going well," I announce to Luke as I read the message in our group chat. Luke's hands are wet, and he won't be able to check his phone for a while, so I thought I'd fill him in.

The lack of details is frustrating me, but I do know those are the rules. Daddy Wolf said we weren't even supposed to talk about specifics until all three of us have met him. I think I'm going to combust before then. Part of me would have preferred to go last rather than have to keep my mouth zipped any longer than necessary, but I know Luke will need assurances from both me and Sammi. Otherwise, he'll never go.

My best friend is in the kitchen, cleaning up after dinner. I made us fajitas, so in theory, I should leave him to do the dishes, but I grab a tea towel anyway. My mum taught me it was rude not to help out. And besides, the sooner he's done, the sooner we can enjoy the rest of our evening.

There's a strange sort of vibe. I know we're both a little apprehensive about what's going on with Sam. That's why I got some of the slightly terrible rosé in so we could distract ourselves. Luke often needs a drink or two in him to make himself stop worrying.

"Thank you," he says, handing me one of the plates. The kitchen is small, so we only have a few of everything, and that makes it easier to manage.

Our arsehole landlord loves to let himself in and give us surprise inspections, so we always try and keep the place as tidy as possible at all times. I'm very bad at leaving things to do 'tomorrow', but with Sam and Luke's help, I'm getting better at putting systems in place that ensure things more manageable for me in the long run.

That's why I love my BFFs so much. The three of us are really good at bringing out the best in each other. I know that's going to change when one or more of us finds Daddies, but for now, I'm enjoying it whilst it lasts.

"Do you think Sam is okay?" Luke asks as we finish up the last of the dishes.

I shrug and hand his wine glass back to him, picking up my own and the rest of the bottle as well. "He says so," I tell him as we head back to his room. He doesn't seem to mind that we use it as the communal room. I like having a space that's just mine, but I think it makes him feel more included that he sleeps in the living room.

He's so silly. We'd include him no matter what.

"Do you think he's nervous?" Luke asks as we sit down on his bed. We've got a movie on, but it's one we've both seen a lot so we're not really paying attention to it. It's more just to have something on in the background.

I shrug. "Maybe a little. I hope he's enjoying himself, though. That's the point for all of us. To have fun."

Luke gulps and fiddles with his pyjama cuff. "I'm so scared I'm going to do everything wrong," he blurts out.

"Oh, hun, no!" I cry. I put my wine down so I can hug

him. "You're so sweet. Daddy Wolf is going to love you. I bet you'll be the best-behaved, loveliest boy he's ever met! He's going to eat you up!"

Thankfully, that gets a small laugh from him. "Any boy would look well behaved next to you," he teases.

I tickle his side, making him yelp. "I am a fucking delight," I say with a huge grin.

We made sure Daddy Wolf knew what each of us was like before we all agreed to this, so dealing with naughty brats must be something he enjoys. If I'm honest, I get tingly all over just thinking about it. I just wonder if he'll be able to fulfil any of my *really* secret fantasies. Talk to me and treat me the way I want.

Like I'm not only a naughty brat, but *bad.*

I'll have to wait and see, I guess.

I've had some guys in the past who thought that I was cute or whatever, but I never felt I could ask for what I really wanted from any of them. I don't think they were old enough, maybe? I need a Daddy with experience and a firm hand.

Luke needs a Daddy with patience and complete confidence that he knows what's best, so he can take care of my sweet friend. I worry that we're not going to get all that from the same person, but if I had to choose, I hope that Luke gets everything he wants. He deserves it.

I'll be happy just to finally have a real cock up my arse. Toys only do so much. Oh *god* I want to be pinned down and fucked so badly. If Daddy Wolf can give me that, I will be more than happy.

"Callum," Luke whispers. "What if...what if I can't speak properly? That last guy—"

"Was a grade A arsehole," I interrupt firmly. "He didn't deserve a second of your time."

Honestly, thinking of someone making fun of Luke's

stutter is enough to push me over the edge into a homicidal rage. Nobody is allowed to talk to my bestie like that.

Luke offers me a small smile. "Still, I struggle when it's not you or Sam. And then there's the other big problem…"

Ah. Yeah. I've been worrying about this, although I haven't admitted it out loud. Not even to Sam. But Luke isn't great with being touched. His dad was an abusive bully, who hit him a lot. It took Luke a whole two years to admit that to us after we met at school, but as we were all turning eighteen and getting jobs, it was the easiest decision to find a place to live together and get him out of that hell. After that, he gradually got better at letting us cuddle him. Now we do it all the time.

That's why out of all of us, he's the one who's had the least hook-ups. I'm not sure he's even done much more than kiss another guy, if I'm honest. He can get triggered by things even he doesn't anticipate. I'm pretty sure Sam will have mentioned something about this to Daddy Wolf, so he's not going in blind, but I can understand Luke's fears.

An idea flashes into my brain, and I down the rest of my wine before grinning at Luke. "Let's practice!" I say, bouncing on the bed.

Luke licks his lips and raises his eyebrows. "Practice?"

"Yeah," I say enthusiastically. "I'll be Daddy, and we can have a kiss and a cuddle. Like roleplaying. People do it in real proper therapy!" I've read about it online. I think I'm really onto something here. "We kiss and cuddle all the time. This will show you that it'll be the same with Daddy Wolf, just a little different!"

Honestly, sometimes I think it's sad that we're all so painfully submissive. If not, maybe we could have dated each other. I know I love Sam and Luke more than anyone else on the planet. But we all know there's something missing that we crave. A different kind of energy that comes from being dominated.

Regardless, I feel completely at ease as I throw myself down on the bed and open my arms out for Luke to join me. "Come here, baby boy," I say, getting into the role. I can pretend to be a Daddy for a little while, especially if it'll help my bestie face some of his fears.

"Callum, I…" he says, sounding hesitant.

"Baby boy," I say firmly, raising my eyebrows. "You're a good boy, aren't you? Come here to Daddy."

That does the trick. He also hastily chugs his wine and snuggles up next to me.

Something else I'm worried about is that I'm sure Daddy Wolf won't want us to drink if we're going to be doing scenes together for the first time. Luke's going to have to find a way to be brave whilst sober. I hope that's not going to be an issue for him. But for tonight, I'm going to use it to my advantage whilst his inhibitions are down.

"How's this?" I ask, skimming my hand under his T-shirt, feeling his smooth skin.

He shivers against me. "It's nice."

"It's nice…?" I try and prompt him. I really want him to get into this game. From everything I know about headspace, he needs to let go and trust the person he's with. If he can't trust me, how's he going to trust a near stranger?

"It's nice, Daddy," he says with a giggle.

"That's it, good boy," I say, really getting into character. We snuggle down against the pillows, and I kiss his neck, finding one of his nipples to stroke. "Just keep calling me Daddy. You'll forget to worry about anything."

He gasps, and I hope that means I'm doing a good job.

It's not like we haven't fooled around before. I remember the first time we were all intimate together. We'd been drunkenly play-fighting, and I announced that I was horny as fuck and needed to go and have a wank. It had been Sam who pointed out we were all hard, so why didn't we just wank off together. It had been so fucking *hot*, but it only seems to happen when we're really drunk.

Right now, Luke and I are just a little tipsy. But with me pretending to be his Daddy, it's making me feel freer. Like it would be okay to go further than we usually do. All in the name of helping Luke overcome his fears, of course.

But there's no reason we can't enjoy ourselves as well, right?

"How are you feeling?" I ask.

We're kissing on the mouth now, and I don't just mean the usual sweet pecks on the lips. There's something a bit messy happening right now. Good! Luke needs to let loose! He's also kind of grinding against my thigh, and I'm pretty sure he's getting hard.

I know I am.

"Good, Cal—Daddy," he says, correcting himself. Then he laughs. "Daddy Callum."

"Damn right," I say, puffing out my chest. "I'm Daddy and I'm in charge, so I get what I want, yeah?" I think this is how Daddying works, right? I certainly want to be bossed around. "Oh, shit," I add as a thought pops into my head. "Let's do red, yellow, and green checks, yeah? If something gets weird, Luke, just tell me red, okay?"

He bites his lip. "*Is* this weird? We're kind of making out."

I shrug. "I'm having fun," I say honestly. "And I love helping you get more confident. I don't think we're crossing too much of a line." I waggle my eyebrows. "Besides, if Daddy Wolf is going to fuck both of us anyway, that's only one degree of separation. I bet he'll be *happy* if we practice for him."

"Practice fucking?" Luke asks dubiously, and I quickly shake my head.

"No, sorry, I don't want to do that."

Thankfully, he sighs in relief. "No, me neither."

"But I thought we could practice touching," I say, stroking his side. "Good touching. So your brain gets used to feeling someone else there and doesn't panic."

He swallows and raises his eyebrows. "Good touching?"

I nod, then carefully trail my hand down between us… before rubbing my palm against the bulge in his pyjamas. They aren't doing much to hide that he's half-hard, and his cock practically jumps into my grip.

"Oh, fuck!" he cries.

"Is that okay?" I ask, stilling my hand. "What's your colour?"

"Uh…uh. It's green," he says a little frantically. "That's good, right? It feels pretty amazing to have someone else touching it."

That makes me wonder how far Luke's *ever* gone with another guy. He's been on dates and kissed men, I'm sure. But is he more of a virgin than me? I've never pried.

Now's not the time. Now, we're busy.

I can't help but grin as I resume my stroking again. "Do you want to touch me as well?"

"Yes, Daddy," he says.

Oh, fuck, yeah! My science is working! And, huge bonus point, he really does reach out and palm me through my jogging bottoms as well. Yes, this is so fun!

This is the big difference between me and Luke. He overthinks everything. Whereas I often jump into things with not enough thought at all. But together, we often work really well, and I feel like this is one of these occasions. I'm not worrying that we're going to ruin our friendship, because I just don't think that's possible. But he's just cautious enough that it's helping me to think like a real Daddy and make me consider his needs and emotional state.

I definitely don't think I could do it in the long run. I'm not made to dominate. But for a one-off, I'm having a great time.

I kiss my best friend as we both fondle each other's dicks. "Good boy," I murmur, because I know Luke craves a lot of praise and affirmation. "Good boy, that feels amazing. Daddy likes that."

"Daddy, oh, Daddy," Luke says, getting more flustered.

I know not to push him to get naked. I don't care myself. I think I'm pretty hot. I also think Luke has a lovely body. But I know my limits. I don't want to push him too far or too fast. I think he can cope with a *little* bit more excitement, however.

We've all wanked off together several times. But I've always wondered what it would be like to get each other off.

I hope at least two of us are going to find out.

I pause and slip my hand underneath the elasticated waist of Luke's pyjama bottoms, feeling his hard shaft under my fingers. He's already leaking pre-cum, and his skin is hot to the touch.

He takes his hand off my dick for a second, and I panic. But then I realise it's because he's shoving down his bottoms to his thighs. Hell yeah! I like where this is going! I copy him, wiggling to push my joggers down, and then we're each tugging at each other's cocks again.

"Colour, baby boy?" I ask.

"Green, Daddy," Luke says as he kisses me hungrily again.

I've had quite a few hand and blow jobs before. My own hand is more skilled at doing exactly what I like. But there's such a fucking thrill to have someone else touching me, even if it is a bit clumsy or awkward.

Besides, it feels like there's a lot of pent-up energy between us. I wonder if Luke's thought about doing this together as well. I'm kind of sad that Sam isn't here to join in, but he's with a *real* Daddy right now, so I can't feel too sorry for him.

It's probably also some of Luke's nerves relaxing about the whole Daddy Wolf situation, which is absolutely what I wanted. He needs to be brave and trust that a Daddy can touch him like this and not hurt him. A good Daddy will take care of him properly and make up for some of the awful hurt his actual parents put him through.

Luke deserves all the wonderful things. Including orgasms. I deserve them, too. So all in all, this was an excellent plan!

"Who am I, baby boy?" I ask as I rut against him. My hand is flying over his cock, and I look down to see just how mesmerising and fucking hot it is.

"Daddy," Luke whimpers against my mouth. "Daddy, Daddy."

"Good boy," I gasp, feeling myself coming undone. "Oh, fuck—*yes!*"

I try and hold on, but I start to release, spurting thick ropes between us. It's okay, though, as I manage to keep my hand moving, and in a few seconds Luke's jizzing, too.

We make a pretty big mess.

We ride out the high, and our hands eventually still. I'm panting for air and that gradually becomes a laugh. I feel amazing. But I'm also still pretending to be Daddy, so I remember what aftercare is.

"Was that good? Are you okay?"

Luke takes a few breaths, then looks into my eyes. "I'm okay if we're okay?"

"Of course we're okay," I say without hesitation. I kiss his mouth and grin at him. "That was fun, right? And you did so well! You didn't freak out at all! I'm so proud."

Luke gives me a nervous laugh, but his smile is big. "Thank you, Callum," he says with genuine affection. "I do think that's going to help me, but it was also, um, just nice on its own. Between us."

"Right?" I say excitedly. "I know it's not *everything*, but it was nice. Fun. More friends should just wank each other off. Everyone needs stress relief, yeah?"

Luke snorts and slaps my arm. "You're too much."

"You wouldn't have me any other way, though," I say saucily.

His expression softens. "No, I wouldn't."

For a second, we share a calmer moment in each other's arms, just smiling at each other. But we can't stay like this.

"Right!" I announce. "I say we clean ourselves up and go sleep in my room. We can sort out all this mess in the morning."

"Can we have ice cream and *then* sleep?" Luke asks.

I blow a raspberry. "There's no Daddy here," I say playfully. "We can do whatever we *want*. How about we put sprinkles *and* chocolate buttons on the ice cream?"

"And strawberry sauce?" he asks.

I kiss him and nod. "Sounds perfect."

10

SAM

MY HEART IS FLUTTERING IN MY CHEST AS I HEAD BACK downstairs. I so desperately wanted to video call Callum and Luke, but that's against the rules. So I managed to resist by talking to myself in the shower instead, imagining the conversation I'd have.

I'd start by telling them how ridiculously *hot* Daddy Wolf is. When he arrived, he was in a classic black suit that was absolutely tailored to fit him like a glove. I'd guess he was in his late thirties, and the body under the suit is strong and hard. I liked being hugged by him a *lot*.

I could go on about his dreamy golden eyes or the ball-tingling low timbre of his voice, but I know exactly what's made me fall head-over-heels for him.

The man knows how to *talk*.

Don't get me wrong. The rock-hard abs and chiselled jaw are definitely not turn *offs*. But I melted when he asked me how I felt and what I wanted as if I was the most important person in the world. Like he desired nothing more than to listen to my every need and make it a reality.

I also loved how he treated me in my own skin. He said I

was perfect just as I am. I'm so sick of getting messages from guys saying, 'you're cute, *but you'd be even cuter if you lost weight'.* Urgh. Fuck them. The way Daddy ran his hands over my body when we kissed left me in no doubt that he meant what he said.

He thinks I'm gorgeous.

I take a deep breath as I reach the bottom of the stairs. I'm excited for what's to come but still a bit nervous. It's kind of like being in the presence of a celebrity. He's so together and authoritative. Exactly what I'd hoped for in a Daddy.

I turn the corner into the open living area and stop in my tracks. I assumed when Daddy said he was going to sort dinner out that he'd just get some things out of the fridge and put them on the kitchen island.

It looks like we will be eating all the delicious goodies I found earlier. That's not what's surprised me. It's that Daddy has laid out a picnic blanket on the floor, complete with throw pillows and lit candles in hurricane jars. The food has been taken out of all its packaging and displayed prettily on plates and in bowls. He's got one of the sparkling fruit concoctions chilling in an ice bucket with two Champagne flutes. Daddy was resting on the corner of the blanket, but as I've entered the room, he's risen to his feet, a single red rose held delicately between his fingers.

"There's my big boy. Looking gorgeous, as usual."

It's like I can't move a muscle as he saunters over to me. He's taken his suit jacket off and unbuttoned the top of his white shirt. I have a whole folder on my laptop filled with photos of men who look just like that which I've used as— *ahem*—personal motivation many a night. Except this is something only I will ever get to see.

Holy fuck.

It's only then that I register that he called me gorgeous. But he told me to get comfortable, so I'm just wearing jogging bottoms and a super soft long-sleeved T-shirt that I found amongst the clothes he'd bought for me. (And he was right. There were a few different options, but my sizes were all there.)

"No, *you* look amazing," I manage to croak. "This is all amazing. I should get changed…"

I try and turn to run back upstairs to see if there was perhaps a tuxedo that I missed hanging in the wardrobe, but he grabs my arm with a laugh. "You look refreshed and beautiful, big boy. Exactly what I wanted. You can change your attire if you feel uncomfortable, but I think you look very cuddly and delectable."

I swallow. As much as I like being smart, this dinner is hardly black tie. The rug and pillows all look soft and snuggly, so I'd prefer not to feel restricted by my clothes.

Daddy is waiting and watching me. I'm suddenly overwhelmed. He did all this just for me. He wants me to be happy and at ease. He thinks I'm special and gorgeous…

I can't remember the last time anyone looked after me. And I don't mean *cared* for me, because Luke and Callum do that all the time. But they always look to me to take charge. It's just our dynamic. And I love making sure they're happy and healthy. But bloody hell, I'm *tired*. It's not like my parents were abusive like Luke's, but they were definitely absent. I've been fending for myself since I became a teenager.

And now here is this stunning man, catering to my every whim, lavishing me with time and attention and decadence.

It's almost a bit too much.

"Sweetheart?" Daddy says, cupping my chin to get me to look at him. "Is something wrong?"

I shake my head and try and swallow down the lump in my throat. "No—no. Nothing's wrong. The opposite. It's unbelievable. I'm so touched."

I'm glad when the concern falls away from Daddy's face.

"That's all I wanted. To spoil you rotten. So, are you happy with your clothes, or would you prefer to change?"

I manage to smile, blinking away my tears before they've had a chance to spill. "I'm really comfy as I am."

"Excellent." He traces the full, red head of the rose along my jaw then twirls it, offering it for me to take, which I do. "Then may I please take you to your table, sir?"

I laugh and let him lead me over to the picnic blanket. I end up sitting with my back to Daddy's chest. He encourages me to load a plate up with everything that looks tastiest, but then—*ohmygod*—he plucks little morsels from the plate as I hold it and then *feeds them to me*. From his fingers. It's ridiculously sexy, especially when he pauses to brush a crumb loose or leans in for a quick kiss.

This is like something out of a movie.

He's eating as well, but he seems more interested in me. In between bites, he asks me about my life, my job, my hopes and dreams. I tell him all about how I'm training to be a primary school teacher, but that it's taking a while as I have to work part-time to be able to afford it. I just adore the idea of moulding tiny minds, though. I know it will be really fulfilling if I ever graduate.

I try a couple of times to ask about his work, but he shrugs it off saying it's not nearly as interesting as me. I at least get him to confess that he loves his job, however he's between projects now and that seemed to get him a little down.

All things considered, I am more than happy to be his distraction if work isn't going so great right now. I will distract him *all night long*. Because I'm a good person like that.

Judging by the way he's rubbing his hand in circles on my tummy, I think I've got a good hold on his attention. The food is so unbelievably yummy, and usually nothing would distract me from sampling everything. However, I've got something on offer I've never had before, and I'm not talking about the white alba truffles.

My heart rate is picking up again as I turn my head. I've just swallowed some chocolate fondue that Daddy scooped up with a couple of his fingers, and now as I look at him, he's sucking the last of it off himself.

My heart skips a beat and my cock jumps. That's probably quite obvious underneath the cotton of my joggers.

Good. I've got no intention of playing coy right now.

"Daddy?" I whisper.

He doesn't ask what. He just leans in and kisses me on the mouth. It's filthy and tastes sweet from the chocolate, but there are also hints of salt from what we've eaten before.

"I'd like to take you up to bed now, big boy," he murmurs against my lips. "And I'd like to bring the chocolate. How does that sound?"

I think I do very well not to splutter right into his mouth. Instead, I manage a little whimper as I nod. Smiling, he helps me to stand, then leans down to blow out the candles, then pick up the fondue pot and a bowl of strawberries.

I make myself focus on how hot this is and how good I'm feeling, and not the more overwhelming realisation that I'm finally going to have full-on naked man sex. *With* chocolate. Not even in my wildest dreams did I think things would turn out this way.

Our hands are linked as he leads me up the stairs. I've also brought the rose with me. It feels like a good luck charm. I'm glad I left the bedroom tidy after I had my shower and got changed. It might have ruined the mood a little if I'd left my old pants lying around. Maybe I don't entirely suck at this romance thing?

As it is, the lighting is low, and the large bed looks about a million times comfier than my crappy mattress back at the flat. Our skinflint landlord refuses to supply new ones, even though the springs are almost poking through in some places, and I've had many sleepless nights.

Sleep isn't exactly on my list of priorities now, though. I'm hoping Daddy has many more exciting ways that he wants to test the mattress out.

He sits on the side of the bed and places the strawberries and chocolate on the nightstand. Then he guides me to kneel at his feet. I place the rose by my side. My heart is hammering as I look up at him, and I feel myself practically quivering in excitement.

"I'm going to ask you some questions, big boy," Daddy says, caressing the side of my jaw. "Every time you answer a question honestly and openly, you will get a treat. Do you understand?"

"Yes, Daddy," I say without hesitation.

He smiles and takes a strawberry piece from the bowl. They've been topped and quartered, so it's not too big. It's still juicy and sweet, though, as he dips the end in chocolate and offers it out for me to eat.

How am I ever going to use a fork again? His fingers are *everything*.

"Good boy. Now, I'm right that you are a good boy, yes? You want to do what you're told and make Daddy happy?"

I nod eagerly. "Yes, Daddy."

"Remind me what you wanted most from your Daddy in the sweet letter you wrote."

I take a deep breath and lick my lips. For some reason, emotion suddenly pricks at my eyes and makes my throat thick. For a second, I'm not sure I can get the words out. But I have to be good for Daddy and answer his question.

"I want to be taken care of," I manage to whisper. "I want to be…um…spoiled. Like I'm special."

He immediately touches his thumb and finger to my chin

to make me look at him. "You *are* special, my big boy. Thank you for your good answer. That's exactly what I wanted to hear."

I let out a shaky nod and smile. "Um, thank you."

Normally I take charge in everything. I'm not hesitant. But I guess this is what happens when I let go. When I get what I want. I have to trust that Daddy is in charge, and that will give me the freedom to relax. Be uncertain. Not have to be responsible and decide everything.

He feeds me another nibble of chocolate and strawberry, and I take a moment to enjoy the burst of flavour on my tongue.

"I'm going to use standard red, yellow, and green check-ins. Are you comfortable with that?"

"Yes, Daddy." I've read a lot about the traffic light system.

"Your safeword will be Mr Bacon. Did you bring him with you like I asked?"

I nod eagerly. "He's in my suitcase."

"May I fetch him?" Daddy asks. I nod again, so he stands up and opens my case. My stuffed piggy is on the top where I left him. Daddy returns to sit in front of me, carefully placing Mr Bacon by the pot of chocolate fondue. "He's here to protect you. So if you're not happy or don't feel safe, you call out for him, understand? I will never, *ever* be cross with you for using your safeword."

I look at my treasured piggy and nod. There's something completely new and warm in my chest. I feel cared for in a way I don't think I'd imagined I could be before now. I turn my gaze back to Daddy and smile.

"I understand, Daddy. Thank you."

"Good boy," he praises me, feeding me another strawberry. "Have you ever been spanked?" he asks as I swallow.

I blink up at him. He's caressing the side of my neck, waiting patiently for my answer.

"No," I say slowly.

"Not for punishment," Daddy clarifies. "For pleasure. I think you might enjoy it. What do you think?"

I chew on my lip. "I don't know," I say honestly, because that's what he asked me to do. "I've never really thought about it."

Callum jokes a lot about it. 'Spank me, Daddy!' is one of his favourite jokey lines when he's being bratty. But I always thought of it as a consequence.

Then I have a sudden thought. I have a particularly sharp comb that I use on my beard, and I really *like* it when the teeth scrape over my skin. I thought I as being weird, but…

"Can it be nice?" I ask, feeling tingly.

"*Very* nice," Daddy says. "We can try it if you like? I'll just be using my hand."

I was prepared to give all kinds of new things a go over these couple of days. I'd not imagined this in particular, but I don't feel afraid as I nod. I trust Daddy. If he thinks it might be something I enjoy, I'll keep an open mind.

"Good boy," Daddy says, giving me another strawberry. Then he takes my hands and helps me to my feet. We carefully place the rose by Mr Bacon. "It's best on a bare bottom. I'm going to ask you to lie across my lap. So either we can pull your joggers down, or you can take all your clothes off. Which would you prefer?"

My breath hitches. For just a second, I want to stay covered up. But Daddy already told me that he thinks I'm gorgeous, and I wasn't lying when I said that I like the way I look. I sometimes wish it was *easier* to be a bigger boy. But I wouldn't change anything about my appearance.

So I pull my top off before I can second-guess myself, then wriggle out of my jogging bottoms and underwear.

Daddy grins and immediately reaches forward to run his hands over my belly and down my hips and the tops of my thighs. He drinks me all in—including my half-hard cock—then looks back up approvingly.

"You are *beautiful*, big boy. Let's get you comfy."

He arranges some pillows for my head, and then I lay across his lap with my face turned to the side. I let out an involuntary gasp when I realise that we're reflected in the wardrobe door mirror.

"See?" Daddy says. "Beautiful."

It kind of is. I mean…*I* kind of am. Beautiful. I look like a cherub. Daddy sort of looks like a wicked modern-day devil in his suit with his glinting eyes. He gently rubs my bum, and I shiver.

"Now, it's up to you if you want to close your eyes," he says. "But to start with, I'd like you to keep them open. Just for the first few times. I want you to see how gorgeous you are and what it is that you're enjoying. Then, if you want to lose yourself in the sensation, it might help to close your eyes and drift away. Do you understand?"

"Yes, Daddy."

"What's your colour?"

"Green," I say with a happy sigh. I fluff up the pillow under my head, taking in everything about this unbelievable scene.

"I'm going to start with five smacks," he explains. "I'll ask your colour, then give you another five. If you are green both times, I will then continue for as long as I think you need. If you get tired or too sore, you must use your colours or safeword. Do you understand, big boy?"

"Yes, Daddy."

If you'd have told me yesterday that I would be trembling with excitement in anticipation of being hit, I'd have called you crazy. But as the first blow lands on my right cheek, something blossoms in me that I've never felt before. There's a jolt of surprise and a spike of adrenaline, but then it's like it melts inside me into something warm and delicious.

Daddy rubs the slightly sensitive spot with one hand and cards his fingers through my hair with the other. "It's okay if you want to cry out. Letting everything go is good for you. Just do what feels natural, big boy."

I nod to show I've understood, but I don't feel like I have any words right now. Thankfully, Daddy doesn't seem to expect them. Instead, the second blow from his hand comes down in a different place on my other cheek, and I groan happily.

I don't hesitate to tell him I'm feeling green when he first asks after five. At ten, I barely hear him. I just murmur 'green' and let myself slip further away as he carries on with his firm hand.

I'm not sure where I go exactly, but it's somewhere dreamy and far away. The sharp stings keep my blood pumping, and I have no idea if I make any noise out loud or if it's all in my head. Either way, I think maybe this is what people mean when they talk about bliss.

"Big boy?"

I blink my eyes. I have a feeling that isn't the first time he's called out to me, but maybe I was just dreaming. Then I realise the spanking has stopped, and Daddy is rubbing a soothing lotion over my bum and the tops of my thighs.

"Daddy?"

"Good boy." I'm still resting my head on the pillow, but I see his smile in the mirror. "You were so very good for Daddy. I hope you liked your treat."

"I loved it," I manage to rasp. I shift a little on his lap as I'm coming back to my senses, then I gasp in surprise discomfort.

I have a *raging* erection.

Daddy laughs softly. "I can tell you loved it. Come here. I'm not done spoiling you yet."

I'm groggy, but he helps me to get on all fours. Then he shifts up the bed so he's resting his head on the pillows before encouraging me to snuggle up against him. It's kind of weird with me being naked and him being fully clothed, but I discover that for whatever reason, I like it. In fact, even in my sleepy state, it's a turn-on.

Which is a good thing, because Daddy squeezes another dollop of the pretty smelling lotion on his palm, then reaches down and...*oh fuck*...wraps his hand around my throbbing cock.

I cry out and flinch into him. Wow, I'm sensitive, and his firm touch feels so fucking good. I also roll onto my bum a bit, and that makes me wince in pain as well. So many sensations and emotions bombard me at once, I can't help the sob that escapes my chest.

"That's it, good boy," Daddy murmurs. He doesn't let up, however, as he starts to stroke me with fervour. "You deserve this. Let Daddy take care of you. It's okay to let go. I'm right here. I'll look after you."

I gasp and shake and cling to him, my orgasm rushing up to crash into me like a high-speed train. *"Daddy,"* I manage to utter, screwing my eyes shut and falling over the edge.

I don't think I've ever come so hard in my life. It's like my entire body shatters into a million stars. I'm not sure where I begin or end.

All I know is I'm safe in Daddy's arms, and that's all that matters.

11

JACOB

I AM…UNNERVED.

Sam fell fast asleep almost as soon as our scene ended. I managed to get a glass of water in him, and he was mumbling sweet little things as I cleaned him up. Mostly, he just kept saying 'thank you, Daddy'. But as soon as I got him into some pyjama bottoms and under the bedcovers, he was out like a light.

Unlike me, who is now wired and antsy but not sure what the hell to do about it.

I've gone to the red wine I had stashed in a specific drawer in the kitchen. There would never be any drinking involved whilst I'm playing with a boy. But right now, I'm glad that I anticipated there might be situations outside of that.

What the hell just happened?

Obviously, it was a highly successful scene. Sam is a beautifully behaved boy that took to my instructions like a duck to water. Seeing him thrive under my care was immensely rewarding.

But it's more than that.

So much more.

I rub my chest and take myself outside to sit on the patio. The night air is cool as it's still spring, but there are heaters incorporated cleverly into the décor. Besides, I'm still so hot and bothered, regulating my temperature probably wouldn't be a problem anyway.

I take out my phone, very tempted to message Harris. But I'm not entirely sure what to say.

Hey, I'm freaking out because this boy is kind of too perfect —maybe?

I scratch the edge of my phone against my chin, then sip my wine instead. Perhaps it's just because this is different to the interactions I've had before. I've certainly changed myself in the past couple of decades. And the only boys I've made time for recently have been brats who saunter in and out of my life like all they see are pound signs, a big cock, and a firm hand.

Sam isn't like that.

He was so…*adoring*. And he felt like he was melting under my care more than that damn chocolate. There is something frighteningly precious about him that I have to admit I'm finding a little scary.

For a moment, I regret this whole arrangement. Why didn't I just pick one boy like Harris told me to? Then I could have picked Sam. And…

And what? The message was very clear that these boys are just looking for experience from a caring hand. That's all. Not a full-time Daddy. And I'd be crazy to jump into something long-term with the first boy to fall into my bed in as many months.

This isn't just 'any boy', though. I've been with enough boys (and men) to know when something's special.

How Sam could be oblivious to just how special he is astounds me.

I rub the scuff on my chin, feeling the prickles against my fingertips. I guess I'm trying to deny this instant chemistry because it's so fucking alarming. I feel vulnerable, not something I'm used to, nor is it something I want to *get* used to.

But then again, the thought of letting Sam go…

No. I have to keep a grip on myself. We laid out the terms of agreement, and I'm going to stick to them. Money might not be changing hands, but this is a business arrangement, nonetheless. There's no harm in everyone enjoying their time to the fullest, but then we are going to part ways. That was what we committed to.

I'm probably just in the throes of the high I got from Dominating with such good results. Sam was truly stunning. Once that fades, I'll be able to see more clearly.

The next boy should cure me of that, I'm certain. Remembering what's in store makes me feel like I can breathe again. Snazzy Pants—Callum, Sam said—is a self-confessed brat and therefore should be much more like my usual flavour of boys. I wouldn't be surprised if he's more of a sugar baby as well, impressed by the fancy surroundings far more than worrying about any peacocks' well-being or whatever.

I'll probably end up tying him up and fucking him, and that will be that. No complicated feelings or strange aching sensations in my chest. After that will be the delicate seeming Squish—Luke. I feel like I'm going to have to be very careful with him, and that will undoubtedly take a lot of effort that won't hold my interest in the long run.

So, there we go. I'm overthinking this. I've spent my whole adult life in control and in charge, so it's only natural that I'd want to keep a handle on all the variables. But I know in business as much as in life that's not possible. I'm simply out of practice keeping a lid on the stress that comes from high-risk situations.

And this *is* high-risk. I mustn't forget that. All three of these boys are trusting me with an extremely important rite of passage. Something they've guarded fiercely until now. These trysts aren't about me at all, in fact. The only thing that matters is their comfort and enjoyment.

I exhale and finally put my phone back in my pocket before taking a long drink of wine. There we go. I'm simply an instrument in this scenario. By removing myself emotionally, it's going to make letting Sam go that much easier. I can do this. It's my job as his Daddy to put his needs before anything else.

Tomorrow, I will treat him like the prince he is. We'll have another night together, and then I will set him free like a bird whose wing I've healed. I hope he will always treasure our time together, but I *know* that he'll go out into the world that much better for it. He won't accept anything less than the highest standards from any future relationships.

I try to ignore how just thinking about him with another man makes my fist curl into a ball.

I'll simply have to preserve the memory of our rendezvous as well, like a photograph in a frame, perfect in its frozen state for evermore.

More alcohol should help with accepting that.

Because as much as I want to convince myself that I'm a neutral party, that I'm doing this as an act of charity, that it won't mean anything once he's walked out the door…there's a part of me that realises my heart is going to break just a little knowing that he's out in the world and not a part of my life.

Maybe I will text Harris after all and ask her why the hell she let me agree to this lunacy in the first place.

1 2

SAM

When I wake up, it's morning, and I have no idea what's going on.

But I work out pretty quickly that whatever bed I'm in... I'm not alone.

I turn around to see who it is—because I'm not at home, and this definitely isn't Callum or Luke—but as I move, my bum lights up with a strange kind of pain, and I gasp.

Finally, my memories come flooding back to me. I'm with Jacob—Daddy Wolf. And yesterday was one of the best days of my life. But if it's morning...

"Oh, no," I whisper.

"Big boy? What's the matter?"

Daddy is still blinking sleep from his eyes, and yet he's immediately alert and awake, honed in on my needs. A lump rises in my throat. This is too much to deal with before I've even had a cup of tea.

"Uh..." I almost say 'nothing', but Daddy told me last night how important honesty is. So I lick my lips and rub the side of my neck. "I can't believe I fell asleep and wasted a whole night of our time together."

Daddy's face melts from concern into a warm smile. I realise he's shirtless, and *fuck a duck,* yep, I was right about those abs.

He opens his arms out and pulls me to him. "You didn't waste any time at all, big boy. You were perfect for me, and then you slept so soundly I realised you obviously needed it badly. This is why I booked for us to have forty-eight hours together. We've still got all of today, tonight, and tomorrow morning to make the most of."

I bite my lip and relax into the hug. I vaguely recall Daddy helping me to get my pyjama bottoms on to sleep in, and it appears that he's just in his boxers.

I was naked whilst he spanked me last night, and yet this seems so much more intimate.

We spend a few quiet minutes in each other's arms. Daddy gently runs his fingers along my side and occasionally kisses my hair. Our peace is interrupted by my stomach rumbling.

"Oops," I say with a wince.

Daddy just laughs, though. "Why don't you take a quick shower, and I'll whip us up some breakfast. Are eggs okay?"

"They sound great," I say genuinely. "Don't you need to shower as well?"

He beams and kisses my forehead. "So thoughtful," he muses. "I had a shower before bed, big boy. Thank you for worrying about me, though."

Technically, I had one after my time in the hot tub. However, I've had an orgasm since then. I sort of remember Daddy cleaning me up with a warm flannel, but after all that excitement, another quick rinse isn't a bad idea.

Besides, I want to be fresh as a daisy for whatever Daddy has in mind.

By the time I get downstairs, he's not only made a batch of scrambled eggs that look creamy and divine but also buttered toast, crispy bacon, baked beans, and fried mushrooms. Somehow it's all still hot, and he's timed it just right so he starts plating up as I sit at the breakfast bar. My bum is still a little tender on the hard seat, but it's not too bad.

"Wow," I say, genuinely impressed. "You didn't have to do all this, really. I usually eat cereal," I add with a laugh.

Daddy pauses in his dishing up to lean down and capture my mouth for a hot, possessive kiss. My heart flips. "I'm spoiling you, remember?" he mumbles against my skin as he trails a couple more kisses along my jaw.

I shiver and giggle a little as a shiver runs down my spine. "Oh, um, okay then."

He sets our plates down, as well as two mugs of tea and a sugar bowl. Then he sits next to me and leans over to nuzzle his nose against my cheek and rub my back. My heart does a couple more somersaults, and I resist the urge to sigh. I could get used to this.

But I can't.

Fucking hell, what am I doing? I'm becoming an absolute puddle of goo for this man and seem to be forgetting that this is simply my turn. He's not mine. This is lovely, but it's all been arranged for a purpose.

He's not my actual Daddy.

I need to remember that, or at this rate I'm going to get burned.

"So, um, you like cooking?" I ask to break the moment. It works. He pulls away from me with a smile, and we tuck into our breakfasts.

Daddy shrugs. "I *can* cook. I haven't got the patience to do anything particularly complicated or long-winded, especially just for myself. But I enjoy cooking for other people a lot."

I nod. "I do, too. Food brings people together. I never really have enough money to do anything fancy like I'd want to, though. I don't mind spending time on something if it's going to be appreciated…"

I trail off. *Shit.* I swore I wouldn't bring up money before I even got here. But now I've seen a hint of just how rich Daddy is, I didn't want him to know how poor my besties and I really are, no matter what Luke said.

I don't want anyone's pity.

"What's your favourite big meal you've ever cooked for other people?" Daddy asks warmly, pulling me from my thoughts. He doesn't appear to have reacted to my comment at all, but I'm sure he didn't miss it. I'm happy to pretend like it never happened, however.

I swallow a bite of food as I consider. "Maybe Christmas dinner for me and the other piggies this past year," I say.

I don't want to go into how Luke can't go home and how my parents thought it was fine to take themselves off on a cruise around the Bahamas without me. Needless to say, Callum announced that he'd visit his family between Christmas and New Year's and made out like it would be no big deal to spend the holiday with us. The presents were small, and the meal was on a budget, but it was genuinely one of the best days of my life.

Instead of going into all that, I smile at Daddy. "It's complicated managing all the different parts of a roast—plus Luke is vegan—so I enjoyed the challenge. And it's just a really happy day to spend with the people you love."

Daddy hums.

I wonder who he spent his last Christmas with.

We finish our breakfast discussing our favourite dishes to make. I notice all the picnic stuff has been tidied away from last night, and it makes me ponder what we're going to have for dinner later.

In the meantime, we come up with a plan for the day. Daddy says there's a lovely nature trail we can follow, which sounds great to me. Then we have a loose itinerary of getting in the hot tub, lunch, cracking out a board game, and watching a movie.

And that's pretty much how the day goes. I enjoy pointing out some of the plant life I know to Daddy as we walk hand in hand along winding country paths for a couple of hours. We get less talking done in the hot tub. There's a lot more kissing and heavy petting that leads to him giving me another hand job in the shower afterwards.

It's funny, but even though I can see he's turned on as well, he insists that he's fine and doesn't want anything from me in return. It makes me feel like I'm being a pillow princess, but the way he phrases it makes it seem like a *good* thing. So I roll with it.

After a lunch of spiced parsnip soup and soft buttered rolls, we put a film on the big telly. But then Daddy insists we snuggle down on the couch with him spooning me from behind, so I fall asleep for quite a while. I wonder if he nodded off as well, or if he just held me the whole time.

We play a couple of games that he produces from a drawer in the living room that get my blood pumping again. I love a bit of competition, even when Daddy beats me. Because losing doesn't matter when I've got his happy smile and eyes crinkled with laughter as a reward.

As Daddy starts to make dinner, the nerves flutter in my belly. We had a pretty flirty day, but now evening is drawing in.

He must have plans for tonight. He *must.* That's the whole point of this getaway.

There's a danger I could retreat more into my thoughts. But Daddy is very good at asking me questions about myself. I feel a little bit selfish, but it's so nice to have someone so genuinely interested in what I have to say that I don't think too hard about it. Therefore, by the time he serves up the pasta dish he's made, I realise I haven't had much time to worry too badly after all.

He puts some quiet background music on, and we eat at the dining table which is tucked in the corner. Again, he lights candles and even scatters actual rose petals in between our plates. I feel like we could be in some fancy restaurant in Rome, but upon reflection, this is even better because it's just the two of us.

There's something electric between us as we gradually stop eating and conversation eases off. Daddy's looking at me like I'm all he wants for dessert.

As it turns out, I'm right.

Without a word, he takes my hand and guides me to stand up from the table. He makes sure the candles are blown out before leading me to the bottom of the stairs. He cups his hands either side of my face and looks into my eyes.

"Big boy. Please head up to the bedroom and take off all your clothes. I want you on the bed on your knees with your head comfy on a pillow. Can you do that for me?"

For a second, I forget how the English language works. But then I manage to nod enthusiastically. "Y-yes, Daddy," I rasp.

"Good boy," he says, then kisses me sweetly on the lips.

I rush as fast as I can up the stairs without actually running. My heart is pounding. I don't know how long I have, but I don't want to disappoint Daddy. I want to give my nether regions a very quick freshen-up before anything important happens down there, so I strip in the en suite, then just use a little water and my hand to rinse the bits that matter.

After hastily drying off, I rush back into the bedroom, relieved that he's not there already. In fact, I can hear him doing something downstairs still, so I have a good few moments to arrange myself how he asked me to.

And—*ohmygod*—it feels so wanton and delicious to expose myself like this. Daddy would never make me feel cheap, I know. But there's something debauched about this that is really enticing. Like…like in that moment I was *made for him to fuck.*

He doesn't leave me waiting long.

I've got my head turned to the mirrored wardrobe doors again, so not only do I hear him approaching, but I also see when he enters the room.

Stark bollock naked.

I bite my lip so I don't do something embarrassing like choke on my own spit. But Daddy is ripped with muscular thighs and a dusting of hair all over his body. His cock is hard and stands proudly out from the neatly trimmed thatch of hair between his legs.

He got himself hard for me.

That's not all. He's got a bowl of something in his hand with a spoon or fork handle sticking out, and I figure we're going to have some more fun with food.

He grins as he places the bowl down, but his eyes are fixed on my exposed hole, and *holy shit* if that doesn't make my balls tingle and my growing cock jump underneath me. It's like he's inspecting me, but it's okay because he likes what he sees.

"Good boy," he murmurs, sliding a hand up my thigh, along my bum cheek, and then down my back.

I'm not really sore from the spanking at all anymore. I wonder if a different part of me is soon going to be sore, though…

"I'm going to get you ready for Daddy now, so you just relax."

I hum some kind of noise in agreement as I don't trust myself to speak coherently.

And that's before Daddy spreads my cheeks apart, then

uses the spoon in the bowl to drop a dollop of fresh cream right on my hole.

It's cold, and I squeal, but then I laugh. "I'm okay," I say quickly.

I love that Daddy laughs as well. I don't want this to be too serious. But I certainly stop laughing when he kneels down behind me and *starts licking out the cream.*

I have no idea what noises I start making then, but I'm sure they're obscene. I've had a few blow jobs before, but I've never been rimmed. No one's certainly ever used their tongue to stretch me out, but that's what Daddy's doing.

The cold cream and his hot mouth are a crazy combination that drives me wild. I'm mewling into the pillow and scrunching up the bedcovers in my hands. I'm not sure how much more I can take of this, but at the same time, I'm also not sure I ever want it to end.

After some time, though, Daddy pauses, and I hear some rustling around. I don't want to open my eyes because I'm totally lost in this moment, so it's a bit of a surprise when I feel slippery fingers pressing against my entrance. Daddy has been working hard, however, so the two digits slip in quite quickly.

I've fingered myself at home and played with toys, but this is a whole other level having someone else do it to me. I tremble and whimper as Daddy crooks his fingers and strokes my prostate. The bundle of nerves sing like a choir from within me, the aftershocks rushing all the way to my fingers and toes.

"Good boy," Daddy keeps saying, his voice even more gravelly than usual. "That's my big boy. Like that. So good for Daddy."

It's like I'm starring in a porno. I never thought I'd have sex that was this exciting, let alone for my first time. I'd expected some guy to get me drunk, stuff it in, and then kick me out of his flat without exchanging phone numbers.

Right now, I'm a prince in my own gay fairy tale, except instead of trying to get a glass slipper to fit, it's going to be Daddy's big, fat cock.

He kisses down my back as he adds a third finger, and pulses inside me. But before I can start humiliating myself by babbling nonsense in my desperation, he pulls his hand free. There's more lube drizzled against my crack, and then...

Oh shit...

My eyes are still closed, so I feel rather than see Daddy press the end of his dick against my entrance. He rubs my hole with it for a moment, but then he presses it against the ring of muscle, stopping just as he's about to penetrate.

"Are you ready, big boy?"

"Yes, Daddy," I practically sob. "Yes, please. Holy fuck I want you so badly."

"Good," he grunts, holding my hip hard enough to leave bruises. "Because Daddy needs your tight, sweet hole. He's going to be the first to take you and spoil you and make you scream like you've never screamed before."

I do cry out as he forces his way inside me. It burns like nothing I've ever felt before, but kind of like the spanking, it's actually not unpleasant. Especially as he eases in farther and my body gets used to him. Then it starts to feel pretty amazing.

"Oh, god. Oh my god," I ramble.

I want to try and be the best I can be for him, but it's like I've boarded a roller coaster and now it's all I can do to hold on until my knuckles turn white. I cling to the duvet as he bottoms out, touching that magic spot that makes fireworks explode before my eyes, even when I open them.

And I do open them, because I have to prove to myself that this is real as he begins to thrust majestically into me. I watch us in the mirror. His body is glistening with perspiration and moves like a well-oiled machine as he fucks me. I feel impossibly full, but it's glorious and I cry and grunt every time he slams forwards.

"Daddy, Daddy, Daddy." I'm gasping, feeling like I'm building up to a spectacular combustion. I don't even think about touching my own cock until he reaches forwards and does it for me, and then—*fuckity fuck*—there's no way I can last much longer.

"Good boy," Daddy pants, picking up his pace. "Big, beautiful boy. Come for Daddy."

Those words flick a switch inside me. In a matter of seconds, I'm blowing my load all over the bedsheets, bellowing like some sort of animal. Daddy keeps pounding me relentlessly, until finally he goes all stiff, clinging to my hips as his cock throbs and spurts inside me.

And then it's over.

Except it's not.

I don't know if I expected to feel like A Man™ once I'd been fucked for the first time, but I certainly feel a kind of euphoria like I've never experienced before. I'm sore and trembling but also light and dreamy. I'm aware as Daddy eases his way out of me, then gently wipes me down with a warm cloth like the night before. I think he cleans some of the mess from under me as well, but it's like I'm locked into place with my eyes shut.

Then his hands are there, rubbing my back and thighs with long, sturdy strokes. He massages my shoulders and arms before gradually getting me to move with him. He pulls the covers back, and then I'm snuggled against his hot, naked body, protected by the blankets, as I rest my head on his chest.

"Good boy," he's murmuring. "You were so good for

Daddy." I mumble my reply, but he doesn't hear me. "What was that, big boy?"

"Perfect," I manage to say with a loud sigh. My hands cling to his shoulders, and I try and nuzzle my face closer to his hard chest. "That was perfect."

It was everything I could have ever dreamed of for my first time.

It's not until I wake the next day that I mourn the fact that it will never happen again.

13

LUKE

The front door finally rattles, and I can't help but jump to my feet from my bed. *"Callum!"* I whisper as loud as I dare. *"He's back!"*

I worry that I'm not acting casual enough, but Callum full on runs out of his room and slides to a halt by my side before crossing his arms and leaning against me.

"Subtle," I say with a laugh.

But as soon as Sam eventually gets his key to work and the door opens, Callum drops his arms and starts dancing on his toes.

"Ohmygodhowwasit?!" he squeals. He launches himself at our other best friend. Sam jerks in surprise and lets his suitcase go just in time for Callum to throw himself on him, practically knocking him off his feet.

"I missed you, too," Sam says with a laugh. He pats Callum on the back before untangling himself and shutting the front door. We never know when our landlord is going to be snooping around, so it's always a good idea to keep it closed and locked at all times.

"Did you have fun?" I ask as I approach him with slightly less hysteria. "I know you can't give us any details, but—"

I'm cut off as Sam grins and envelops me in a massive hug. "It was amazing," he says. "Unbelievable. I can't wait to tell you guys every detail. But until then, I'll just say how excited I am that you're going to get to meet Daddy Wolf too and be just as spoiled."

He leans back to smile at me, and I feel my eyebrows raise. "Wow," I say quietly. "That good, huh?"

He presses his lips together as if he's physically trying to stop himself from spilling the beans.

I know the feeling.

"It was more than I could have dreamed of," he says with a sigh.

Callum groans and spins in a circle, his hands clasped to his chest. "I'm so *jealous*. I can't believe I have to wait another couple of days!"

"I have to wait almost a week," I say, doing my best to ignore the swoop of nerves in my belly.

Sam hugs me again and waves his hand for Callum to join us in a cuddle, which he does. "It will be worth it," Sam says, his voice heavy with sincerity. "I'm *so* glad we're doing this together. The only thing that could make this experience better is knowing I'll be able to share it with you both after."

I tilt my head and look at him. "Are you sad?"

He blinks then smiles brightly. "What? No! Of course not. I'm just tired. Let me get unpacked, and we can grab some lunch or something."

He kisses both of us on our heads, then moves into his bedroom.

I glance at Callum. We both agreed that we'd tell Sam what happened between us right away because it's no big deal and we don't keep secrets between the three of us. But… I'm not a dummy. Something's not quite right with Sam.

"Shall we wait?" I ask.

"Hm?" He turns and blinks at me.

Of course he didn't notice. I have to laugh. Bless my adorable Callum. "Sam seems a bit…distracted. Maybe we should wait to tell him what happened between us until he's more himself?"

Callum frowns, then looks between me and Sam's room. "Oh, you think?" Then he hugs me to him and kisses my cheek. "Okay. If you reckon so, I won't say a word until you say he's ready. I'd *hate* to spoil his moment. He deserves to bask in the glory of losing his V-card."

I snort and kiss him back on the lips. It's so easy, like always, but there's just a little something more now than there was before.

I like it.

So it pains me to keep it hidden from Sam, but Callum's right. This is his moment, and he should get to revel in it. We're not keeping a secret. We're being respectful.

The problem is it leaves us in kind of a stalemate. Sam can't tell us anything about his time with Daddy Wolf, and the only interesting thing that occurred for Callum and me was that we tossed each other off.

And it was so hot I haven't been able to stop thinking about it for two days straight.

I appreciate what he was trying to do by getting me to call him Daddy and everything. But that was only a little part of it for me. I have no idea if that's going to make me less nervous when I meet Daddy Wolf for real or not.

What I do know is that I've wanted to touch Callum and Sam like that for a long time. If we're going to start dating other men and moving on with our lives, I feared the window I had to try anything like that was closing. But then Callum just made it happen for me. I know it was only role-playing, but I think that's probably as good as it will ever get between us, so I'm determined to treasure what happened.

It's different to what I crave from a Daddy, but it was still wonderful. Everything is just so easy with my besties. I'm scared of how hard I'm going to have to work to trust a stranger to get that close to me.

In fact, I'm starting to really worry that I don't want to go through with meeting Daddy Wolf at all. I'm desperate for details from Sam to reassure me, but that's against the rules. He's said that it was amazing, and he's certainly got a glow about him, but I know what I saw.

There's something else going on.

I trust that if he felt like I shouldn't go—that I wouldn't be safe or I wouldn't enjoy it—he'd tell me. I absolutely know he would. But my brain hates a void, and it's impossible to stop myself from thinking up all kinds of reasons for his hint of melancholy.

The main thought I keep coming back to is that it was a hollow experience. In our haste to lose our virginities, we've put ourselves in a situation where we're going to have meaningless sex with a stranger, and I'll be honest, that very idea brings me out in a cold sweat.

So when Sam comes back out from his room and we cram into the kitchen to make sandwiches for lunch, I smile and talk about anything and everything other than what's really on my mind. I natter about customers at the pub and my annoying manager. I tell him about a silly comedy gameshow I watched on the telly last night whilst Callum was at work. I even tell him about the new cat on the street that I've made friends with.

I don't tell either of them that I'm starting to regret taking this risk. I don't say that I've got all the love I need right here and that I want things to stay as they are.

Because neither of them does.

They need to move on, start grown-up relationships. And if that means leaving me behind, then I'll just have to find some way to live with that.

Even if it's going to break my heart.

1 4

CALLUM

I can't believe that Sam really didn't spill one single bean the past couple of days. I'm shocked that for once my powers of persuasion failed me.

I know that those are the rules that Daddy Wolf set, and I'm not sure I actually wanted to break them. But I still tried. Hard. Sam didn't budge.

Therefore, I'm absolutely clueless as I head downstairs from our tiny flat to the street below. Of course I'm late, but I'm hoping I won't get in trouble. Or if I do, it'll be the good kind, mwahaha. It's not like I did it on purpose. I really tried to be packed and ready on time. But it's like when I'm not looking the hands on the clock just leap forwards.

Anyway, I'm here now. I see the limo waiting by the kerb and think that's an oddity. However, it honestly doesn't click that it's for me until I realise the sign the driver is holding up has 'Snazzy Pants' written on it.

"Oh, shit!" I cry, bounding over to the guy and sticking my hand out. "That's me! Are you my ride? Holy crap, I've never been in a limo before! This is so fancy."

The driver's mouth twitches, and I get the feeling that he's resisting a smile. "Good afternoon, sir," he says with a slight nod of his head. "Mr Wolf is looking forward to meeting you. My name is Gerard. Would you allow me to take you bag?"

I look up and down the limo again and shake my head in disbelief. Sam really was holding out on us. "Yeah, of course. Thank you. Oh! Wait. Can I just grab…"

I tear open the battered small case and grab my bottle of water and earbuds. My phone is in my pocket already, and for once I remembered to charge it. I hope I packed my charger for later, as I need to text the boys, but that's a problem for Future Callum. Right now, I grab Snazzy Pants as well to keep me company, then hastily shut the bag back up again.

"There you go," I say proudly, offering the handle out to the driver. "Thank you. Am I all right to get in the back, then?"

He fights off a smile again and nods. Yeah, I know, I'm A Lot™ even when I'm not so excited I could burst. I can't help it, though. Today is dick o'clock, and I am *long* overdue. I've been doing the 'Callum's Getting Fucked' dance all morning and driving the others mental.

We're soon driving through London, and I work out that this bitchin' ride has a bloody entertainment centre in the back. I completely lose track of time as I preoccupy myself killing zombies. I think we maybe stop at a service station at some point, but I'm too busy trying not to get my head gnawed off.

I don't even realise the damn car has stopped until the driver opens the door and scares the holy bejesus out of me. I drop the controller with a shriek then look sadly over at the screen as the horde of undead descend on me.

"Well, that's one way to end the game," I lament.

But then I realise that if we've stopped…*fucking fuck, that means we're here!*

I jump out of the car (then promptly have to jump back in again to pick up all my things). By the time I get out for real, Gerard has fetched my suitcase from the boot. "Thank you!" I say cheerfully and offer him a tenner. I thought you were supposed to tip limo drivers, but he folds his hands behind his back and inclines his head.

"I assure you, that won't be necessary, sir. But thank you for the kind offer."

"Oh," I say, putting the money back in my pocket. I feel a bit put out, but I guess it would be rude to push it if he doesn't want it. I don't wish to insult the man. Besides, there's a lot I can do with ten quid, so I don't mind keeping it.

"Here is your key," he says, producing one from his pocket. "If you let yourself in and make yourself at home, Mr Wolf will be with you shortly."

"Oh, right. Okay, then," I say, taking the key and giving him a little salute with it. "Thanks again. Safe drive back!"

I wait and watch him leave. It's only then do I finally look around at where the hell I am.

Sam told me to check where I was on the maps app on my phone. It seems I'm somewhere south in a foresty part of Surrey. Ooh, posh. Yep, that would make sense. I'm completely surrounded by trees. It's so quiet it's eerie. I'm a city boy, through and through, used to a lifetime in London.

But as a change, I have to admit this is pretty bloody nice. I turn and look at the massive log cabin, and figure we're staying in a bed and breakfast. It's not a five-star hotel like I was imagining, but it looks like it's been done up all modern and fancy still. Besides, compared to our rubbish flat, pretty much anything's a palace.

Rather than head straight in and have to deal with whoever's on reception, I take a minute to walk around the place. We're on a reasonably steep hill, so half the building goes down to a lower level whilst the ground floor is held up on sturdy looking columns. On the lower level is a patio with a sunken fire pit. It's filled with wooden logs but it's not lit. I'd have thought there would be other guests out here enjoying the stunning view.

I'm drawn by the sound of running water, so I drag my suitcase around to the other side of the cabin to where a stream is running alongside the property. I'd think that was pretty cool anyway, but hot damn there's a real-life water wheel attached to the cabin that's turning in the stream! I don't know if it's powering anything anymore—maybe it's been repurposed to produce electricity? But it looks so old I wonder if this cabin was once a mill or something.

I love history. It's so fascinating to think about all the people who came before us. I imagine who stood on the very spot I'm in right now and looked around this place. I think about who built the wheel and if it ground flour. Who sold it? Who ate that bread?

My brain is buzzing so much with all these questions I don't realise there's a field with a little barn beyond the stream until I notice movement.

I jump back in shock. I'm not sure where the other guests at this B&B are, but I'm definitely not alone.

I leave my suitcase where it's standing and go up to the small bridge that crosses the water, leading to a fence by a field. At first, I thought the three animals were sheep, but their necks are too long. Then I realise what I'm looking at are alpacas.

I *love* alpacas!

Of course, I've never met one in real life before, but they just look as cute and friendly as they do in photos. These three are different colours—one black, one white, and one caramel. I wonder what their names are as they come trotting over to me, clearly interested. Aww, they're so fluffy, and their bottom teeth stick out, making them look all goofy.

"Hello, hello!" I cry in delight as they let me pet them. They're so soft and they surprisingly don't smell bad like I thought they might.

I think about if Sam learned their names whilst he was here, and I pull out my phone to ask him. But just in time, I remember that's against the rules. I'm not supposed to tell the others *anything*, not even Sam, even though he's already been here. I am supposed to check in with them and prove that I'm alive, though, so I fire off a message to the group chat letting them know that I've arrived and that it's awesome.

Since my phone is in my hand, I look up what alpacas eat. They've got plenty of grass, so I figure they're not hungry out here, but the article I find says that they also like snacks like apples and carrots.

"I wonder if there's anything like that inside?" I say to my new friends.

There's bound to be a kitchen I could ask in. I bet guests frequently want to feed these beauties. Oh, then I should probably also check if I'm allowed to give them anything. I don't want to spoil their diet if they're on one.

"I'll be back soon!" I tell them with a wave, hurrying back across the bridge.

I fetch my suitcase and make my way once more in front of the house. I try and push through the door, but then I remember the key I was given. It takes me a second to find which pocket I stashed it in, but then I'm making my way inside.

I stop at the threshold as my jaw drops open.

The floor and ceiling are wooden boards. The walls are a mixture of wood and regular painted plasterboard, except the one on the left, which is comprised of huge grey stones. A fireplace is built into it as well, although like the pit outside, it's not lit.

Actual wood and metal chandeliers hang above me. There are thick rugs on the floor, loads of squishy armchairs and sofas, a dining table big enough for eight, and a kitchen with another partial stone wall and cabinets painted black. I feel like I'm in a modern medieval tavern or something.

Then I realise what this place is lacking.

A receptionist.

"Hello?" I call out. But it seems completely deserted.

I leave my suitcase standing where it is and go to open every door. I find three bedrooms and a bathroom, but no other human beings.

Then it dawns on me. This isn't a bed and breakfast. Daddy Wolf has hired out the entire place for us. I'm all alone.

"No shit?" I say out loud with a slightly hysterical giggle. I cover my mouth and look around the huge house again with fresh eyes.

This is incredible.

It's only because I spot the fruit bowl on the kitchen island that I remember why I came inside in the first place. The alpacas, right! I dash over there and start pulling drawers open, looking for a knife. I get a good-sized one and a chopping board, then put some music on to fill the silence before setting about making a snack for my new friends. I figure if there's no one else up here they probably aren't being over-fed, so a few apple slices won't harm them.

I'm busy making a nice pile of snacks when there's a knock at the door, and my heart almost jumps clean out of my chest. I'm lucky I don't accidentally slice a finger off. "Bloody hell," I say, clutching my chest with the hand that doesn't have the knife in it.

Then I come to my senses.

That was a knock at the door.

That means Daddy's finally here.

15

JACOB

I think I hear some yelping beyond the door as I wait patiently for boy number two. A couple of days alone have given me some perspective since I said goodbye to Sam.

He was incredibly special, no doubt. It's kind of startling how much I've missed him after only spending forty-eight hours together. But I'll always cherish the time we spent together, and I'm sure in time the pain of letting him go will fade.

For now, I have a new challenge to keep me preoccupied.

In fact, as soon as the door flies open, I know I'm going to have my hands full.

This boy is a few inches shorter than me, but his body is lean and muscular for his age. He must spend an awful lot of time working out, judging by the way the slinky V-neck clings to his torso. He's got a tousle of strawberry-blond curls and bright blue eyes that shine like the ocean.

"Daddy?" he squeaks in excitement. He's holding the edge of the door with one hand, but in the other, he's wielding a sodding knife.

I raise my eyebrows. "You were supposed to ask for a

passphrase before you opened that," I growl. Honestly, I could have been anyone out here in the middle of nowhere.

"Oh, shit, yeah," he cries before slamming the door in my face. "What's the passphrase, Daddy?"

I struggle to keep the amusement off my face. I was expecting a self-assured little brat. Not a human hurricane.

"Little piggy, be a good boy and let Daddy in," I say.

He opens the door again with a grin. "Hi, Daddy," he says breathlessly. "I'm Callum. Sam said you were really nice."

I wasn't expecting to hear Sam's name either. It feels like a fissure cracks through my heart. I was trying to pretend that these boys were isolated, but we got into this situation exactly because they're best friends.

I smile, though, and try and put my big boy from my mind. It's Callum's turn now, and I need to give him everything he deserves.

Good and bad.

"Yes, but Sam was a good boy," I say in a low voice, fixing Callum with a fierce stare. "He didn't open the door to a stranger before he checked who it was."

Callum bites his lip, but he can't hide his grin. "Oh, um. Oops. Sorry, Daddy. I was just so excited. Have you seen this place? It's *amazing!*"

To my astonishment, he grabs my hand and yanks me inside. I barely get to shut the door before he's pulling me into the middle of the open space. "We've got it all to ourselves," he cries in wonder as he twirls on the spot, still with the damn knife in his hand. "I mean, you probably know that. You booked the place. But did you know there are *alpacas* in the field next door?" He finally seems to realise that he's got the knife still in his grip, and he waves it at me. "I was just making them a snack! I hope that's okay. I assume the food here is for us?"

For a second, I just blink. Are these boys all fucking

Disney princesses or something? God damn it. This was supposed to be the boy like the ones I'm used to. Self-centred and bratty. The first thing that he's done is look after the bloody animals. I wasn't sure he'd even notice them. I'd have thought he would have entertained himself trying on the clothes waiting for him in the bedroom. I wonder if he's even seen those?

"Everything here is for you, naughty boy," I say. The name just slips out after his stunt at the front door, but the way he blushes and grins bashfully makes it immediately stick.

"Um, do you want to feed the alpacas with me?" he asks. "I know you're wearing a fancy suit, so if you don't want to—"

I step up to him and slip my hand against his face, cradling his jaw. "Of course. I'd love to," I tell him sincerely. "Why don't we finish chopping up the fruit and take it out to them now."

He breathes out and beams at me. "Yes, Daddy," he says reverently.

I notice he's got music playing quietly from his phone that's resting on the kitchen island. He's…a lot. But not in an annoying way. In fact, his high energy is charming.

"I've never met alpacas before," he chatters away as he finishes slicing up the apples. "I've seen lots of photos, but they're even cuter in real life. Is there someone who looks after them usually?"

"There is," I say as I fetch him a bowl to place the fruit in. "No one will be disturbing us whilst we're here, though. We have the place to ourselves."

"That's bonkers," he says, shaking his head. "I thought this was a bed and breakfast when I arrived! You must have a really great job to afford all these things. That must be nice. I feel like I'm always scrambling around doing odds and sods just to make sure I've got rent money each month."

He laughs like he's not especially bothered by that. I recall

Sam's words about their financial situation. He didn't seem to want to delve too deep into it, so I let it slide, but Callum seems less embarrassed by it.

I don't want either of them to be anxious about money. In fact, my knee-jerk reaction is to write them a big cheque. But that's too much, and I know it. I'm not here to fix their lives. I'm here to give them each the most memorable and special first times I can.

"What do you do?" I ask as we head outside. He marches confidently towards the little bridge that will take us across the water.

"Hustle," he says with another laugh, and grins at me. "I studied fashion design at sixth form, and that's what I love the most—making clothes. But it's really hard to get into without a degree. I'd love to start up my own little boutique or something, but that would be a *lot* of time and money and stuff, so...I don't know. Maybe one day. I also love pole dancing, so I teach that now as well as giving sewing lessons to baby drag queens. I make okay money from posting videos online as well. I film myself making pretty things then modelling them." He shrugs. "I just kind of do whatever. Sometimes I pick up work in restaurants or supermarkets, especially around Christmas. It's a nightmare when I have to do my taxes, but I figure I'm still working myself out and what I want to do, so...why stress about it now, you know?"

We get to the alpacas, and he turns to look at me. He's so expressive it takes my breath away. He'd be handsome anyway with his features, but it's the way his personality shines through that makes him truly beautiful.

Fuck.

Fuck, fuck, *fuck.* I was hoping to ease the pain I felt after getting too close to Sam, but here I am, falling head over heels for Callum as well.

"Yeah. Why stress?" I agree absently. I also remind myself

to introduce him to a certain app I know that might just help him with his taxes in the future…

I try not to, but I feel some stress of my own creeping in anyway.

I'm an instrument, I remind myself firmly. *I'm just here for Callum. This is all about him and his experience. Get a grip on yourself, Wolf.*

Callum gets me to hold my palm out flat then places some apple on it. The black alpaca comes and snuffles it right out of my hand, their lips grazing gently over my skin. It's a strange sensation but charming.

For a while, we stand quietly side by side, taking it in turns to feed the sweet creatures. Once we're out of apple, they allow us to pet them for a little bit longer.

"Have you explored the house much?" I ask.

Callum shakes his head. "I had a quick look around, inside and out, but I was more concerned about making their snack."

I glance over at him, seeing how absorbed he is stroking the caramel one's head. So he doesn't see me gazing at him. That's probably for the best.

In a way, I'm pleased he hasn't torn through the house opening every cupboard and drawer. I'd quite like to see the look on his face when he realises I've got a wardrobe full of designer labels waiting for him. I thought I'd detected a bit of a fashionista in the photo the three boys sent me, but I'm thrilled to discover that clothes are his passion. Sam seemed more touched that his clothes fit. I'm hoping Callum will get a real kick out of the up-and-coming designers I selected.

"Does that mean you don't have a favourite part of the cabin yet?" I prompt him.

He scrunches up his nose. "Well, I love the water wheel," he says. "Oh, and the patio with the fire pit looked super cool with that view."

Perfect.

I slip my hand into his and meet his eyes, which have gone wide at the contact. "Let's go there, then."

"Can you light the fire?" Callum asks excitedly.

"I'm sure we can try," I say. After all, I want him to stay warm with what I've got in mind.

He leads me to the other side of the house and down the steps to a lower level. As it turns out, there's a very easy operating system to get the fire pit burning. Good. I don't want to be wasting time on that when I've got much more important things to concern myself with.

I sit myself in one of the big wicker chairs with a large cushion to make it comfortable. It's more like an egg-shaped oval that's been cut in half at an angle, giving me plenty of room to spread my legs out. I stand Callum between them, holding his hands as he looks down at me with wonderous eyes.

"What kind of boy are you?" I ask.

He frowns and thinks for a second before working out what I mean. "A naughty boy," he says quietly, biting his lip and grinning shyly.

"Yes, you are," I say, rubbing my thumbs against the backs of his fingers. I can feel he's started to tremble, which gets my blood racing. "Why were you naughty?"

"Because I opened the door without asking for the passphrase," he says, looking into my eyes through his long golden lashes.

"Good boy," I say. "So you understand I need to punish you for that, don't I?"

His throat bobs and he swallows and nods, and his breath speeds up a little. Good. I thought he'd want disciplining, and I was right.

"Yes, Daddy. I'm sorry, Daddy. I'm sorry," he says breathlessly.

"Do you understand your colours, naughty boy?"

He nods quickly. "Green is good, yellow means pause, and then red is bad."

I bring his fingers to my lips and kiss them. "That's good, yes. Your safeword is going to be Snazzy Pants. Did you bring him like I asked you to?"

"Yes, yes, Daddy," he says eagerly. "I had him in the car with me, then I think I left him on the dining table." His face drops. "At least, I think I did. I hope I didn't leave him in the car."

I kiss his knuckles again and rub the backs of his hands. I hope that's not the case, but if it is, I'll have Gerard drive here right away and reunite the boy with his piggy. "Why don't you run back into the house and find him. If he's there, bring him out here. If he's not, I promise I'll get him delivered back here as soon as possible, okay?"

Callum takes a shaky breath. He's genuinely distressed, and I hate that. "Yes, Daddy," he whispers.

I squeeze his hands. "Go now. Hurry back to your Daddy."

He nods, then dashes back up the stairs on his long, lean legs. I rub my chin and wonder if it's even worth trying to fight the ache in my chest.

Well, fuck. It seems I've fallen for two out of the three boys I'm just supposed to be fucking.

But…nope. There's absolutely no use resisting the way my heart swoops when Callum comes running back to me waving his stuffed piggy in his hand. "It's okay. He was in the kitchen," he says breathlessly, skidding to a halt back in front of me. "No need to call the police."

I can't help but smile at him as I gently take the colourful piggy from him. "That's good, naughty boy. Next time, try and be more careful with your precious things so Daddy doesn't have to worry about you."

He nods eagerly. "I will, Daddy. I promise."

"Good boy." I place the piggy on the small table beside me. "What's your safeword?"

"Snazzy Pants," Callum replies right away.

"Good boy," I say again. "That's because Snazzy Pants will always be looking out for you and keeping you safe. You will never, *ever* get in trouble for using your safewords. If for some reason you can't use your safeword, you will raise your hand. Do you understand?"

"Yes, Daddy," he says. His cheeks are flushed from the running, but I think me talking about starting our scene is also exciting him. Excellent.

"Now, naughty boys have to be punished, don't they?" I ask and he nods. "So now you're going to take all your clothes off for Daddy."

"Here?" he squeaks, looking around.

We're completely alone but also very exposed to the elements. The view of the hill unfolding below us does give the impression that we could be seen from very far away.

I watch him as he snaps his head back to look at me, even more colour in his cheeks. But there's a thrill dancing in his eyes that makes me almost certain that I'm right. He's got a bit of an exhibition kink, whether he knew it before or not.

I arch an eyebrow at him. "Am I going to have to ask you twice, naughty boy?"

He stares for just a moment, then he's whipping off his clothes like they're on fire. Within seconds, he's standing before me with all his luscious skin on display. He's smooth and waxed with just a neat little patch of hair between his legs where his cock is proudly jutting out.

I like that he's already hard. This will make this punishment even better.

"Get a pillow," I instruct him. He hurriedly grabs one from the nearest stool. "Good. Drop it at my feet and kneel."

He does that lightning-fast as well. He rests his hands on his thighs and looks up adoringly, waiting for my next command.

He's so achingly beautiful and submissive that I have to stop and caress his jaw. "Good boy," I murmur. "For your punishment, you're going to get Daddy's cock out and suck him until he comes down your throat. You are not to touch yourself. You are *certainly* not allowed to come. Do you understand?"

"Y-yes, Daddy," he says. "I promise. I'll be good."

I narrow my eyes, debating which direction to take this. "No," I say. "You're a naughty boy. That's what got you into this situation in the first place."

"I'm sorry, Daddy," he rasps, placing his hands on my knees and looking up at me with pleading eyes. "I'm sorry. It won't happen again. I'll be good, I swear."

He's panting and sweating and possibly even harder than before, despite doing what he's told and not touching himself at all. Yes, I think he's a very naughty boy who likes being punished quite a lot.

"We'll see," I say, palming myself. I've certainly started thickening thanks to this little interaction. "Show Daddy how good you can be. Make him happy."

He practically smacks my hand out of the way in his desperation to get to my fly. He makes short work of dragging the zip down and fishing his hand through my briefs. As soon as he frees my cock, he's sitting up on his knees and swallowing me whole. I grip the sides of the wicker chair, so I don't thrust my hips forward and choke the poor boy, but fuck his mouth feels good.

He's not shy. And I'm sure he's had plenty of practice at this. He opens his throat wonderfully and gets right to work twisting his hand at the base of my length. He uses his other hand to fumble inside my underwear and massage my heavy balls. *Fuck*, that's amazing.

"Good boy," I say, petting his hair like he was petting those alpacas. He keeps bobbing his head, but he looks up at me with those big blue eyes. "That feels so good. You're making Daddy very happy."

He moans and doubles his efforts. I grunt and bite my lip. My eyes want to flutter closed, but there's no way I'm missing a second of this erotic sight. He's devouring me with gusto, and he's hard as a diamond, too. His leaking tip dances as he works on me, but as instructed, his hands never leave me to touch it.

"That's it, good boy," I encourage him. "Naughty boys can be good sometimes. I bet you wish you could come. But you're taking your punishment beautifully."

He whimpers and pops off my cock. His lips are swollen and wet. "I'm sorry, Daddy. Please, Daddy."

I tighten my hand in his hair, making him gasp. "Please, what?"

"Please let me touch myself. I'm so hard. You're so hot, and your cock is so yummy."

Ah, here's that little brat. I knew he was lurking somewhere. "No," I say with a smirk. "Naughty boys only give orgasms. They don't get them. Now, what did Daddy tell you to do?"

"Suck his cock and make him come," he rasps. "I'm sorry. I'll do it now. I'll be good."

"You will be good," I say, pushing his head back down to where it belongs. He takes me hungrily, using his tongue, lips, and the back of his throat to do everything he can to drive me wild.

It's working.

"So gorgeous, naughty boy," I say as my climax builds. "That's it. You love Daddy's big cock, don't you?"

He whimpers and blinks wet eyes. His hand is a blur and he's fondling my balls like he can squeeze the orgasm right out like a tube of toothpaste.

He's not far off.

I tighten my hand around his hair as I start coming without warning. He gags and splutters, but I hold him in place, making him take everything I'm giving him. I groan as I spurt again and again, but gradually I empty out and start to soften.

When I ease his head back, he releases my member from his mouth and gasps for air, tears clinging to his lashes. "Stunning," I murmur, gently rubbing my thumb over his swollen lower lip. "Absolutely stunning, naughty boy. You were so good for your Daddy. Do you think you can stand up?"

He's shaky as he gets to his feet, but I help him by holding his hands. I release him so I can slip my cock back inside my underwear and do up my trousers. Then I entwine our fingers and tug him to sit in my lap with his legs draped over the arm of the chair.

"Come here, good boy," I say as I cradle him to me. He's still shaking and panting, his gaze struggling to focus. "You were absolutely perfect. Can I kiss you, please?"

He blinks, then manages to look at me. He gives the tiniest of nods, so I lean down and gently press our lips together. He melts under my touch, and I rub his arm as the kiss deepens. I taste my own intimate flavour on his lips, and I lap it up like cream.

"Naughty boys get punished," I mumble into his mouth. "But good boys get spoiled. Daddy's going to spoil you now, okay?"

"Okay," he whispers back.

I rest our foreheads together as I reach down and wrap

my hand around his poor, neglected cock. He jerks and yelps out, but I hug him tighter to me and comfort him.

"Shhh. It's okay," I assure him. "Daddy's got you. You're all right. Just relax. Let go, my naughty boy."

He whimpers and clings to my shirt with his eyes screwed up. But his swollen lips are parted as he pants out little breaths and thrusts his hips just a little in rhythm with my hand.

"Good boy," I tell him. "Good boy. Let go."

It takes a few more moments, but then he's arching his back and spurting all over my hand. I keep tugging him, milking every last drop from his balls, emptying him out down to his toes.

"Daddy, Daddy, Daddy," he cries, burying his face against my chest.

I wipe my hand on my trousers. He's already splattered my shirt, so a wardrobe change will be necessary anyway. But I don't want to be any stickier than I have to be as I hug him closer to me.

"Daddy's got you," I say as I kiss his hair. "You were so very good for Daddy. I'm proud of you."

"Thank you," he whispers, sounding so tired with relief.

There it is again. That crack in my heart, widening just a little more.

How I ever thought I could just fuck these boys and walk away unscathed, I'll never know.

16

CALLUM

I'M HONESTLY WONDERING IF I'VE MADE DADDY UP IN MY head. How else would he know the right exact things to say to me to make my blood race like it never has before? How else would he know how to treat me the way I've craved?

I've asked guys before to tell me I'm bad or whatever, but they never really got it. Sometimes I'd leave a hook-up feeling cheap and nasty, even though they did what I thought I wanted.

I didn't even have to ask Daddy. He just knew, like magic. But the biggest difference is that now I've been left feeling *amazing*.

I loved gagging on his cock. I loved being punished. I don't feel ashamed. I just feel centred and right. Like I'm at peace with myself when I didn't even realise I was unsettled. I kind of already knew I was a kinky fuck, but this is by far the furthest I've ever gone, and we're only just getting started.

At least, that's what I hope.

He's laid me down on the sofa and snuggled me up in blankets. I'm still naked, which is kind of thrilling but comforting at the same time. The material is so soft on my skin, it's like I'm being hugged all over.

Daddy got me a sugary drink that he made sure I started sipping right away, and put the TV on for me so I could find something I wanted to stream. He also fetched me my phone and Snazzy Pants, all without me asking. I've put something on the screen just so there's background noise and movement, and I'm absently scrolling through Instagram, wishing I could post photos of this place on there.

But mostly, I'm just letting my thoughts wander. I'm in a kind of sleepy, floaty state of mind, but I'm also wired and excited for more.

There's got to be more, right?

Of course there will be. Daddy promised.

I'm vaguely aware that Daddy's been cooking, but I'm not really sure what. In fact, I'm totally lost in my own thoughts until he comes over, mutes the TV, then crouches in front of the sofa to look me in the eyes.

"You've been a very good boy for Daddy," he says, caressing the side of my face. "Would you like to keep with the scene or break out for dinner?"

I blink at him. "What does that mean?"

He smiles. "Good boy for asking. If you want to keep playing, I was thinking you could kneel beside me, and I could feed you. You'd be naked. Or if you need a break, you can put whatever clothes you want on and sit at the table to feed yourself. Which would you enjoy?"

My heart has leaped into my chest. I'd have never thought about it before, but I know exactly what I want. "I'll kneel," I say hurriedly. "I want Daddy to feed me."

His smile gets bigger. "Lovely. Dinner's ready. Can I help you over to the table?"

He holds his hand out for me to take. As I stand, the blankets fall away from me and I pause, a sudden shiver rippling through me. I bite my lip and look down at them. "Could…could I keep one of them over my shoulders?" I ask.

"Of course," Daddy says. "Which one would you prefer?"

I point to the softest one, and he bends down to scoop it up and then drape it around my shoulders. *There.* That feels better. I'm still naked and exposed, but the comfort from the blanket does something to settle me.

I hold it closed around me with one hand and cling to Daddy with the other as he leads me to the big dining table. He pulls out a chair, then guides me to kneel next to it. My soft cock lies between my thighs, like an unspoken promise of things to come.

The blanket stays in place without my help, so I rest my hands on my knees. Daddy has gone back into the kitchen area, but then he returns with a single plate of food. I'm not entirely sure what it is, but it smells really good.

Daddy concerns himself with sitting down and then picking up his knife and fork to start cutting into something. He's not looking at me, and my heart rate picks up. Is he ignoring me? Why is that exciting?

Sure enough, he raises a bit of red meat on his fork and puts it in his mouth, chewing thoughtfully. Then another. Finally, with the third piece, he turns to me and holds out what looks to be beef.

I open my mouth obediently, letting him feed it to me. And—*ohmygod*—it's steak and it's really fucking good. I make myself chew it properly, so I don't choke, watching Daddy as he watches me. His lips twitch in the corner, then after I've swallowed, he rubs his thumb over my lower lip.

"Does that taste nice?" he asked.

I nod. "Yes, Daddy. It's delicious."

He doesn't speak again for a while. I get lost in the silence, my whole world narrowed down to the movements of Daddy's hands as he feeds us both bits of steak dipped in peppercorn sauce, crispy chips, and spears of tender stem broccoli. He's even got more of the same sugary fruit drink in a glass with a bent metal straw that he offers me regularly to take sips of.

Ordinarily, I have to have music on whenever I do anything. But right now, I don't feel the need for it. My only concern is Daddy, anticipating when he's going to deign me with a look again and something to put in my mouth.

He doesn't ask what I want, he just decides. Normally I'd be pretty unimpressed with anyone getting between me and my food. Don't get me wrong, this isn't something I'd want to do all the time. But for a treat—and it *does* feel like a treat—I'm finding it all rather thrilling.

In fact, I slip into a kind of light floaty headspace. I don't need to worry about anything. Daddy is taking care of it all.

So I'm not sure how much time has passed before he places his knife and fork down. The clink of the cutlery on the plate makes me blink and brings me somewhat back to reality. He offers the cup again and I take a long drink through the straw, then he puts it down before extending his hand out to me.

I accept it and stand, allowing the blanket to fall. The atmosphere has changed, and I know I don't need it anymore.

Wordlessly, he takes my hand. We walk across the cabin towards the biggest of the bedrooms, and I realise I'm trembling. I don't know what he has in mind. I just know I need more of what I've already had.

I also realise I have the power to *ask* for what I want. Daddy's done such a good job so far, but I don't want to be passive in this. I get a kick from causing a fuss. I know I do, that.

So as we get to the threshold of the door, I plant my feet

and stop. Daddy also pauses and turns to look at me, our hands still connected. "No, Daddy," I whisper.

He raises his eyebrows at me.

"No," I repeat, my heart rate quickening. I can feel my pulse trying to jump out of my throat. "I won't do as I'm told. I'm bad and naughty, and I do what I want!"

He blinks at me…then drops my hand as he steps closer to me again. He takes my chin between his thumb and finger. "You're right. You are a bad, naughty little boy, aren't you?"

I gulp. "I'm sorry," I hiss. "Daddy, I'm sorry. I need to be punished. I'm bad. I…"

I close my eyes searching for the right words to ask for what I want. What I *need*.

"You should laugh at me. I'm pathetic."

There's a beat of silence, and I wonder if I'm going to pass out. I'm suddenly overcome with nerves, worrying that I've messed all this up. Or—even worse—that my fears are true. That I'm actually fucked up and what I'm asking for is wrong. That I've crossed a line. I've never dared ask anyone for this before.

He pinches my chin tighter and I gasp, my eyes flying open.

"You *are* pathetic," Daddy sneers, his eyes blazing. A shiver flies through my body. *Yes.* I think he understands. "A silly little virgin who's come crawling at my door. A bad boy, wasting my time." He laughs and—*ohmyfuckinggod*—my balls tighten like I'm going to explode on the spot. "Why the fuck should I give you my cock? You don't deserve it."

I let out a sob. I'm shaking all over and panting, my gaze locked with his as he looms over me. "I'm sorry, Daddy. I'm so sorry. You're right, I don't deserve it. I'm sorry. I just want it so badly."

"That's because you're a desperate little slut, aren't you?" He digs the nail of his thumb under my chin, and I whimper.

"It's a good thing for you that I'm already hard and need a tight hole to satisfy me. I think you'll make a good little cum bucket, won't you? You're not worth anything more."

"I'm nothing," I say with a shaking voice. "I'm so sorry. I'm just a hole. Use me, Daddy. I'm just a cheap little slut."

He wraps his hand around my throat and steers me backwards towards the bed, shoving me down on the mattress. I blink and stare at him as he starts to strip his clothes, revealing a god-like body of tanned skin, muscles, a delicious dusting of hair all over, and an angry red, throbbing cock.

"You're going to lie there and you're going to take what I give you. Do you understand? Bad little sluts don't get a say. They just get fucked. Hard. Daddy's in charge."

"Yes, Daddy. Yes," I babble. I cling to the bedsheets, not sure if I should move or not. I wait for Daddy to tell me what I should do, and I'm not disappointed.

He smacks the side of my leg, and I gasp. "Get up the bed. I need room to work. Hold your knees up. Your hole belongs to me, naughty boy."

I scuttle like a crab in my eagerness to follow his orders. I grip my knees as hard as I can and hug them to my shoulders, stretching out my most intimate area for him to see. My cock is hard and leaking, but I don't even think about touching it. That belongs to Daddy as well. He decides if I get to come or not. I am very bad. Maybe he won't let me.

Watching me with narrowed eyes, Daddy stalks around the bed and yanks open the bedside drawer. He removes a bottle of lube that he throws onto the bed beside me before he slams the drawer shut again, making me jump. As he crawls over the bed to me, his stare is feral.

"Look at you," he scoffs as he moves between my legs. "So desperate. It's pathetic. No wonder you're still a virgin. Well, not for long. I'm going to ravage you until you can't see straight. I'm going to use you to pleasure my cock. You can cry all you want. I don't care. You're mine now."

"Yes, Daddy," I gasp, nodding frantically. "I'm yours. You can do what you want with me. I'll be good, I promise."

He lunges forward and grabs my jaw, squeezing my cheeks. "I don't need your permission, boy. You're mine, so I can do what I want. I don't care about your feelings. You're nothing but a hole to me."

"I'm sorry," I choke out, a couple of tears sliding down the sides of my face. My heart is racing, and my cock is throbbing. I feel dizzy, I'm so turned on.

It's kind of like at the dinner table. My whole world was reduced down to Daddy and the food on his fork. That was it. The simplicity held a kind of bliss.

This is the same.

Right now, I'm nothing more than a hole to be used for his pleasure. A needy, greedy little virgin who's rightly ashamed of how badly he needs to get fucked. I don't have to think about whether it's right or wrong. Daddy's in charge and he'll make all the decisions. I don't have a say. I just need to lie back and enjoy what's about to happen.

He snaps the cap on the lube bottle, squeezing out a good dollop on his fingers, then he shoves the middle one against my pucker, forcing his way inside as I cry out.

"That's it," he growls, pushing his knuckle past the tight ring of muscle. "Look at you. You love it, don't you?"

"I'm sorry, Daddy," I squeak. "I can't help it!"

He hums and pulls the finger out so he can add more lube then—*ohshit*—he adds another finger. It burns as he makes me stretch around the digits, and I have to grit my teeth as a keening noise escapes my throat. He gets them all the way in then pulses, stroking my prostate.

For some reason, it feels a hundred times better than

when I prod it with a dildo. A real live man has his fingers up my arse, and it's like I'm being jolted with electricity.

"Fuck, shit, yes!" I ramble, screwing up my eyes.

"Look at me, slut," Daddy commands. My eyes fly open, and he grins at me like he really is a wild wolf.

And I'm his prey.

"I think that's all you deserve," he says, pulling his fingers out. He adds more lube on his hand and between my open arse cheeks, then he leisurely strokes his raging erection. "You looked so good sucking Daddy's cock earlier. I think that's all you're good for. My cock in your mouth or in your hole."

"Yes, Daddy, please!" I cry, sobs racking my chest.

He leans down and pushes the fat head against my entrance, making me hold his gaze as he drives past the tight ring to penetrate me. I'm dripping with sweat and trembling as I lie there and take it, just like he told me to. It hurts, but I love it and know that just makes me even more of a bad, naughty freak, but I can't help it.

He doesn't give me time to breathe when he's forced his way as far in as he can. He just starts fucking.

I'm being fucked.

I feel like I'm being split in two, but then the burn kind of changes into a different sort of sensation. It's like I'm flying in the clouds above, even though Daddy is very much pinning me down. I'm trapped, but I'm also the freest I've ever been in my life.

How crazy is that?

He drives me wild by changing the pace from slow to fast. Sometimes he thrusts hard, almost shoving me up the bed, but then he'll stop and inspect me for a second. As if he's got an insect in a jar that he's studying. I bite my lip and whimper and wail, having no clue how long it goes on for. Just that I'm in some kind of heaven.

Daddy picks up the pace. Holy shit, he's really pummelling me now, his hips ramming like pistons as he drives his cock as deep as possible inside me. It's relentless, and I almost want him to stop, but then I *never* want him to stop. I just cling to my knees and grit my teeth, my gaze never leaving his dark eyes.

And then he stiffens, the cords in his neck bulging out as he blows his load inside of me. I'm his dirty little cum bucket and I cry out with him, feeling his cock pulsing as he spills every last drop.

I'm breathing so hard I'm feeling light-headed. But I can't seem to help it. I'm wound up like a spring. I watch as he takes his time to come down from his climax, wiping his hand over his brow to catch the perspiration before pulling out of me.

He doesn't say a word as he shifts his weight, drops down, pushes my thighs so my legs jerk up higher than they already are, then…

Goodgodinheaven!

He starts licking his cum right out of my arse.

It's the filthiest thing that's ever happened to me by a long shot. My skin is tender against his tongue and lips, and the slurping noises he's making are fucking feral. I wrap my hands around the backs of my knees so I can try and open myself up even more than I already am. I have no idea what I'm saying. I'm just sort of wailing and crying out any old nonsense that's coming into my head. I'm sure there's a lot of 'Yes, Daddy!' and 'Don't stop!'

I don't think I'm in any danger of that.

When he does have his fill of my hole, he moves to suck on my balls and wrap his fingers around my neglected cock. I really scream at that, and he takes a second to release me and lean forwards so he can look me in the eyes.

"Don't you fucking come. Do you understand me, boy?"

"Yes, Daddy," I promise. But oh, fuck, it's a struggle. He sucks my balls for a while, but then he moves his mouth to my member, working like he's trying to suck my soul out of my body. I dig my fingers into my legs, sobbing. *"Please, Daddy, please."*

Just when I think I can't take it anymore, he lifts his head and wipes his mouth with the back of his hand. Then he starts wanking me off at a vicious pace.

"Come all over yourself, you dirty, naughty boy."

I let go.

I've never done a bungee jump or leaped out of a plane, but that's what I imagine this feels like. I shatter as lights explode in front of my closed eyes. I can't breathe. I can't see. All I am is his hand on my cock. That's all I'm worth. That's all I'm good for. It's simple and beautiful and perfect.

Then it's all over and I have no strength to hold myself up anymore. My arms and legs drop to the bed as I gasp for air. "I'm sorry," I whisper, my face wet with tears. "I'm sorry, Daddy. I'm sorry…"

17

JACOB

No.

Callum is not like any of the bratty sugar babies I've ever fucked before.

He's a precious angel.

He shakes and cries his way through his orgasm. My heart is still hammering in my chest from my own climax and the intensity of the scene. When he told me the direction that he wanted to take us in, I wasn't sure how far he'd really want to go with the humiliation. But the cathartic mess I'm currently witnessing tells me we did it just right.

I cuddle him to me as he cries, stroking his side and kissing his hair.

"Good boy," I murmur. "Good, sweet boy. You were perfect for Daddy. I'm so proud of you."

I quietly repeat these and similar other words until my naughty boy blinks and looks up at me, as if he's finally come back down to Earth. "Daddy?"

"Hi, naughty boy," I say fondly, brushing his curls back from his forehead. "You were magnificent. So perfect for your Daddy. Did you enjoy it?"

He bites his lip and looks worried for a second. I wait for his answer before jumping to any conclusions, but I can't deny it makes me anxious. Thankfully, he doesn't take too long to speak.

"I loved it," he whispers with wide eyes, like he's giving me a big confession. "Is that okay? I said…"

"Of course it's okay, sweet boy," I tell him with a fierce hug. "I'm so proud of you for asking for what you needed. I loved everything you did and said. That was a spectacular scene."

He nibbles his lip a little more. "So…you enjoyed it, too?"

Naturally he's worried about me, because apparently these boys exist to kill me over and over again.

"I adored it," I say with a growl, nuzzling my nose against his cheek. "But that doesn't matter. It was your first time. I just care that it was special for you."

He blinks sleepily at me. Then he reaches up to touch the side of my face. "It was beyond special. But of course it matters, Daddy," he says softly. "You have to be happy, too."

Fuck.

I don't want to press the point. Because I *don't* matter. My feelings are irrelevant. The fact that my heart wants to crack yet again is *irrelevant.* I'm an instrument here to deliver the best possible experiences for these boys.

"I'm happy," I assure him, because that's far easier than trying to unravel how I'm really feeling. "Come here."

I gather him up in my arms. I intended to hold him in a bridal carry, but he automatically wraps his legs around my waist and clings to me like he's a koala. I kiss his neck.

My sweet, naughty boy.

Whilst I run our bath, I sit him on the closed loo seat and hand him a toothbrush loaded with paste. He manages to give his mouth a thorough scrub, then leans over the sink to rinse and spit. We still have a few minutes before the tub is full enough, so I stand in front of him and cradle his head against my stomach, stroking his damp hair as he stares off into the middle distance. He seems deeply peaceful, and I only hope that's how he feels inside.

I add a rich, sweet-smelling bubble bath to the water, then I take Callum's hand and help guide him to sit in the suds with his back against my chest.

We're quiet as I wash him down. I'm extremely gentle with his hole because I know it must be sore. We probably won't be able to fuck again tomorrow, but I hope it was worth it for his first time. Besides, there are plenty of other things we can do, which is a good thing, because I have a feeling that this bratty boy is going to be after more orgasms before I know it.

We don't spend too long in the tub. I can tell how badly Callum needs to sleep. Point of fact, so do I. It was a reasonably physically exerting scene, but emotionally I'm wrung out like a washcloth.

Everything will feel better in the morning.

Or maybe it won't, but that's not Callum's problem. It's mine. So I'll continue to be here for him however he needs me.

I refuse to lament how little time we're going to have because that will only lead to it slipping away from me.

Instead, I dry my sweet boy off as well as myself. He's like a zombie, just standing there and waiting for me to do everything. It makes my heart swell with joy. He needs me so badly. This is why I want to be someone's Daddy all the time.

It's just so sad that I can't be that Daddy for Callum or Sam.

For tonight, though, I can be. I take his hand and lead him from the bathroom back out to the bedroom. The covers are hardly spoiled at all, which makes it much nicer as we prepare to climb under them.

"Naughty boy?" I say, caressing along his jaw. He blinks then focuses his eyes on mine.

"Hmm?"

I smile at how adorable he is. "Would you like pyjamas or would you prefer to sleep naked?"

He frowns a little. "Uhh…naked," he says with a nod. I'm not surprised. I suspect that will give him the chance to wake up doing something naughty, and I honestly can't wait.

"Good boy," I say, going to lead him to the bed, but he shakes his head.

"Snazzy Pants?"

For a second, my heart stops because I think he's safewording. But then I realise he's *asking* for his piggy. We left him in the living room from where Callum was watching TV.

"Of course, sweetheart," I assure him. "Let's get you into bed and then I'll fetch him for you."

"Daddy bed, too?" Callum asks as he slides under the duvet. His eyelids look so heavy, poor angel.

"Yes," I promise him.

I kiss the back of his hand before letting it go. Then I take myself out into the main body of the log cabin.

Snazzy Pants is sitting on the floor by the couch in his rainbow tutu and bow tie. I rub the silky material between my fingers and thumb, wondering if Callum made this for his piggy.

I'm wondering a lot of things about these best friends.

More than I should be, I know.

I shake my head and return to Callum before he can worry. He's already dozing off to sleep, but as I press Snazzy Pants against his hands, he automatically hugs him tightly to his chest. Equally, when I also get under the covers and snuggle up to him, he wriggles as close as he can get as the little spoon.

I guess the only upshot of not being able to stay with Sam or Callum is that it means I'm not forced to *choose*. Because I'm not sure I could. They're different, but they're both so lovable in their own ways.

That's the thought that sort of comforts me as I turn out the lights and try to get some sleep. But it's quite a while before I manage to nod off.

My heart is full but also heavy, and it's a terrible weight inside my chest.

SAM

"Callum finally messaged," Luke announces as he walks into my bedroom.

I look up from my textbook and smile. Luke has been very preoccupied between Callum's messages to our group chat. I tried to warn him that would probably be the case. Callum isn't renowned for his memory. In fact, I'm amazed that he's messaged as much as he has, and I wonder if Daddy has been reminding him.

Daddy.

Oh, dear. I can't let my mind go there, not in front of Luke. I'm just being ridiculous, after all. I couldn't *possibly* have fallen in love in only a couple of days. I've just imprinted on the first man to make love to me, like a baby bird that's fallen into the wrong nest.

"What's Callum said?" I ask before my thoughts can spiral much further out of control.

Luke shrugs and bites his nail. "Not much. Just that he's still alive and having an amazing time, but that he also misses us."

"Tell him we miss him, too," I suggest.

Luke's face lights up as he nods, then he concentrates on his phone for a few moments. I use the pause to mark my page by laying a pencil underneath the paragraph I was reading, then close the book. Something tells me that Luke wants to talk.

I'm right.

"Um, do you have a sec?" he asks.

"Of course," I say genuinely. "Do you want to sit on the bed?"

He exhales in relief and nods. Before I can get up from the chair by my desk, he's jumped on the mattress by the head of the bed and puts his back to the pillows. That's interesting. Normally, we sit on the side of the bed. I don't mind this development. I simply take note of it.

I don't say anything. I just act like this is totally normal as I sit beside him and drape my arm around his shoulders. He naturally snuggles under my wing. It feels nice.

"I want to tell you something," he blurts out. "I promised Callum that we'd talk to you together when he gets back, but it's eating me alive, and anyway, it was *my* problem. Callum just helped me with it, so really, I figure he'd be okay if I needed to t-t-talk about it with you. It's just you were so happy when you came back from seeing Daddy, but then you weren't, so I worried something might have been wrong, s-s-so—"

"Whoa, whoa," I interrupt. "Babe, slow down. First of all, everything's fine with me, I promise. So don't worry about that."

I've just fallen head over heels for a man who's going to fuck us all and never see us again. No biggie.

Luke takes a shaky breath in and hugs his phone to his chest. "Okay," he whispers.

I squeeze his leg. "You're kind of freaking me out,

though," I admit truthfully. "Are *you* okay? You and Callum? Did something bad happen?"

My heart is in my throat. I was only gone a couple of days. Everything seemed all right when I returned. What could he be talking about?

"No, no. It wasn't bad," he assured me. "It was pretty brilliant, actually. But...well, I'm worried you're going to be upset or feel left out."

I frown, honestly having no idea what he could be talking about. "It's up to you," I say, kissing his hair. "If it's bothering you that much, I'm sure Callum wouldn't mind if you and I discussed it first before he came home. But I don't know what it is or what you two agreed, so I'm afraid you'll have to make that decision yourself, babe. However, I *can* assure you that it's going to take something pretty fucking drastic to ever make me upset with you both."

Thankfully, that gets a weak chuckle out of him. Good. Because I mean it. I couldn't ever imagine being really angry with either of them. Sure, sometimes I roll my eyes because the kitchen hasn't been cleaned or someone left the loo seat up, but you just put up with things like that from the people you love.

Besides, now we're spreading our wings and looking for Daddies, I'm really trying hard to accept that there's a time limit on how long we're going to be living together. All this cosiness will be over sooner or later. So I'm determined to make the most out of the time we have left.

"So, um..." he begins. "I was worrying about meeting Daddy. About letting him...you know? Um, touch me. Because you know I can get very funny about that. So Callum, um, *hesuggestedwepractice.*"

I feel my eyebrows shoot up, and my pulse quickens. Did I just hear what I thought I heard? *Practice?*

"You and Callum...had sex?" I ask carefully.

But Luke shakes his head quickly. "No. I mean, well…not *sex* sex. Not like what Daddy is, um, offering us. Not all that."

My heart is still slamming in my chest. But it's a kind of excited feeling. I'm surprised. I'm still not quite sure what he's saying. However, my body is responding to it.

"But something happened between you?" I prompt.

Luke nods. "You know how we sometimes have fun together?" he asks. That doesn't do much to stop my heart from racing. I know exactly what he means.

"When we wank off together?"

"Yeah," Luke says in relief. "That's fun, isn't it? I, um, like when we do that."

My throat tightens. We *never* talk about this. It's like a naughty pact we have. It always seems okay in the moment because we're drunk. But we never speak of it again in the mornings after.

"I like it, too," I say faintly.

Luke stills beside me. "That's good," he says quietly. Bloody hell, I feel like we're caught in a spell that neither of us wants to break by speaking too loudly or making any sudden movements.

"Did you and Callum do that without me?" I say. "That's okay. If that's the case, I don't mind."

Luke wriggles beside me. "Sort of. Except…well, Callum was pretending to be Daddy, you see? So we kind of, well, we, um…" He screws up his face and takes a deep breath. *"Wewankedeachotheroff."*

I blink.

"Oh, wow," I say before I can think.

"Are you upset?" Luke whispers. "We weren't leaving you out on purpose, I promise. But you were with Daddy Wolf, and Callum helped me practice. I've never actually had someone else t-t-touch me down there, and I was worried about freaking out when it was my turn with Daddy Wolf. I even called him Daddy during it—Callum, I mean. So it wasn't really real but it was still kind of nice and—"

"That's hot," I say.

He leans back and looks up at me. "Really?" he squeaks.

I shrug. "Yeah," I say honestly. "Maybe I'm a tiny bit jealous, but I think it's great if that helped you. But was it also fun?"

He nods. "I…well, I knew Callum wasn't really my Daddy. It was good practice just because it was someone else. But it was kind of nice because it's Callum and I love him already, you know?"

"Yeah, I totally get that," I say. Then I chew my lip and hesitate, but fuck it. In for a penny, in for a pound. "Maybe we can all do it again someday. After we've all seen Daddy Wolf."

Luke stares at me for a moment. "I…I think I'd like that, Sammi. If that's okay? I know we all want Daddies, but what the three of us have…"

"It's different, but it's still good," I supply for him. "It's still love."

He gives another big sigh of relief, and cuddles against me again. "Exactly. I so hoped you'd understand, but I was scared you'd t-t-tell us off for messing everything up or be hurt that we left you out."

I mean, yeah, I do kind of wish I'd been there for that. But I can hardly complain. I was off having two of the best days of my whole life.

And if they'd be up for trying it again…

Yeah, that could be amazing.

For a while we just snuggle together on my bed. I rub his side, and he clings to my jumper. But after some time, it's like a charge has built up between us. I try and ignore it, because

I'm sure it has to just be in my imagination. However, then Luke takes a deep breath and looks at me with his pretty hazel eyes.

"Do you maybe want to kiss?" he whispers. "Just kiss. But that could be, um, nice."

I nod, leaning down towards him. "I think that's a lovely idea, babe."

We kiss all the time. But immediately, this becomes something more. I'm surprised when he's the one to push his tongue forward and lick my lips, asking to be let in. I oblige. I wrap my arm around him as we slide down the bed, and I cradle his face in my other hand.

This isn't just a friendly little peck on the lips like usual. This is snogging. We're making out.

And I love it.

It doesn't lead to anything more, but that's okay. There's a deep sensuality to it as we lose ourselves in one another.

I know this is going to keep me awake later. My whole world is being turned upside down one piece at a time. I have a strong feeling that no matter what direction the future is going to take, it's going to hold some serious heartbreak as well.

Daddy was never going to be mine to keep.

My best friends and I aren't really compatible for what we crave in a relationship.

Either way I look at it, I don't see a happy ending.

But for now, I just lose myself in this kiss, savouring the moment. I thought I was the only one who yearned for something more between the three of us. Before this all has to come to an end and we move on with the next chapters of our lives, I wouldn't mind knowing what it's like to be truly intimate with my best friends.

Someday, a moment like that could be a memory I

treasure just like my time with Daddy Wolf. I think the pain of knowing it was only temporary would maybe outweigh never experiencing it at all.

I guess only time will tell.

19

LUKE

I'M SITTING IN A LIMO. A REAL-LIFE LIMO.

I'm almost too afraid to touch anything, even though the nice driver explained to me that I can use the entertainment system and help myself to any of the food and drink available. It's all so fancy. How can it possibly just be for me?

My throat is dry with nerves as we make our way out of London, so I start by having a bottle of water. I'm worried about drinking too much in case I need the loo, but after we visit the first service station, the driver assures me that won't be an issue. The car is electric so we need to stop fairly regularly to charge and, in any case, if I need to go desperately or stretch my legs, he says I can just use the intercom to ask.

After we leave the city, we pretty much head straight down the M4, going west. Sam reminded me to keep an eye on my phone location, so I'd know where I was in the country. By now I'd hope that I was pretty safe meeting Daddy Wolf, but it gives me a small sense of control either way, knowing where I am.

There's a small refrigerator keeping the food cool, so

eventually I mellow out enough to consider eating, and am delighted when I discover that there's vegan sushi waiting for me amongst other things. I love Asian food the most, and I sort of remember that Daddy Wolf did ask us what we preferred. It's silly, but having something I like to eat puts my nerves further at ease.

Thanks to the way our shifts and Sam's classes worked out, the three of us have barely seen each other since Callum came home. Which is probably for the best, because out of all of us, he's absolutely the most likely to break Daddy Wolf's No Spilling the Beans rule. But it meant I only got a brief moment to confess to him that I had to let Sam know what happened between us.

He seemed totally fine with it. In fact, he said it was great that we'd already had that chat and that everything was good with all of us.

But I'm a nightmare. I need to dissect everything ten times over so my anxiety doesn't spiral out of control. He definitely *seemed* okay with it, but is he really? Was he just being kind? I'm not sure.

My consolation that I keep coming back to is that Sam has assured me several times in no uncertain terms that everything is fine between *us*, and he didn't just mean the fact that Callum and I got off together without him. He meant *that kiss*.

It's funny that a simple kiss can feel just as intimate and life changing as swapping hand jobs. There's no denying that things are changing irrevocably between the three of us. I just have to hope that it's for the best. Fingers crossed that when I get home, we'll have time to have a really good chat altogether to make sure everything's okay. Good, even. At least, that's my hope.

Thankfully, right now I have a pretty big distraction.

My pickup time was earlier than Sam's or Callum's, and

as we travel farther and farther down the motorway, I understand why. We appear to be heading all the way to Wales. I ultimately end up eating all the sushi because I'm so hungry, and hope that's okay. But I don't think I was expected to leave any for Daddy Wolf, so I try and calm my nerves.

I don't want to be a wreck when I finally meet this man.

It's difficult because my parents were so hyper critical of every little thing I did, and they were *always* changing the goal posts. If I messed up, my father would often lash out and not only hit me but also my mother, which led to *her* hounding me day and night as well to try and protect herself. I haven't spoken to either of them since I walked out after finishing sixth form, and I don't miss them at all.

With Sam and Callum, it's so different. They've never lost their tempers with me or even criticised me. They always try and help in such a nice way. So I think I'm getting better. I just wish I had money to afford a therapist so I could fix some of these issues for real. But in the meantime, I have to pray I can keep a lid on my crazy enough to fool Daddy Wolf.

I'd absolutely *hate* for him to think I was some sort of freak.

I basically kept debating whether or not to back out of this right until the last minute when Sam practically pushed me out of the door. What finally convinced me was when he handed me my piggy, Squish, and told me that I wouldn't be alone. He said that Squish would look after me, and that because he was there, it was kind of like Sam and Callum would be there with me, too. Both of my best friends stressed the importance of having Squish by my side, as per Daddy's request, so I gave in and allowed them to convince me that I wouldn't be on my own, even if that's make-believe with a stuffed animal.

I was the one who pushed for this plan to lose our

virginities. I was the one who was most determined to stop having this thing hanging over our heads like the Sword of Damocles. It's more than time that we all stopped getting in our own ways with regards to our dating lives.

Besides, Sam and Callum weren't able to spill any details, but they both assured me over and over again that Daddy Wolf is super nice and would be deeply in tune with my needs. I'm convinced there's something they're keeping from me, but hopefully it's just the specific details of their visits. They both promised that their intimate time with Daddy was amazing.

And now it's my turn. Am I really ready? Can I actually go through with it? Sam and Callum both agreed that they were treated like absolute princes.

If that's what's going to happen, that doesn't sound so bad to me.

I hug my piggy for most of the journey. I find a kids' film to put on the entertainment system that distracts me pretty well. But a lot of the time I'm just staring out of the window, looking at the countryside go by.

I've never been to Wales before, but from what I see, it's gorgeous. Lots of rolling hills and forests. I know I'm not going to Daddy Wolf's house—he explained that in his messages we got via Sam—but I'm starting to wonder why he couldn't find a nice hotel a bit closer to London. This seems like an awfully long way to travel just for a couple of days.

Then suddenly, I understand why we've come so far.

We round the corner of the road, and up ahead I see a castle.

Yup. A castle.

It's comparatively small. Half of it is only one storey and the rest is two. But there are at least *six* turrets that I can already see, with crenelations running around the top, and an archway over the front door that might actually have once held a portcullis.

"Is this where we're going?" I ask out loud. It was rhetorical, so I jump when the driver's voice comes through the intercom.

"Yes, sir. This is where you'll be meeting Mr Wolf and staying."

"Bloody hell," I mumble to myself.

Was this where Sam and Luke came as well? Or did they go to different places, since they left later in the day? Either way, if this is Daddy's standard, I admire them both for keeping their mouths shut. They weren't kidding when they promised that I'd be treated like a prince.

I've got my own *castle,* for crying out loud.

A nasty thought tries to push its way up to the surface to tell me that I'm not worth this. That it's too much. But Sam and Callum reminded me over and over again that I deserve to be spoiled for once because I'm special. I believe I'm special to *them,* at least.

As we pull up on the gravel driveway, I remind myself that this is a sort of game for Daddy Wolf. He's probably getting a real kick from de-flowering three virgins, one after another. All this flamboyance is more likely for him to try and show off and impress me, revelling in his own wealth. If I think about it like that, I can relax a bit and enjoy it more. It's all just a game.

I cling to Squish as I exit the car. The driver, Gerard, got the door for me and also fetched my luggage from the boot.

"Here is your key, sir," he says, handing it to me. "If you'll let yourself in, Mr Wolf requests that you make yourself comfortable and he'll join you shortly."

"Right," I say faintly, looking up at the castle once more. It's surrounded by trees and fields, and I can't help but feel like I'm in some kind of medieval fantasy. "Oh, thank you!" I remember to squeak before the driver gets back in the limo. He tips his cap at me, but then indicates that I should head inside. I guess I need to do that before he can take his leave. He probably has orders, too.

So I grab my little suitcase and make my way up the steps, my heart in my throat.

I assumed Daddy would be here to greet me, but apparently I'm going to have time to explore for myself before he arrives. That kinds of helps my nerves, knowing that I'll be able to settle myself before meeting him. It almost makes me feel like I've got a kind of upper hand, if that makes sense? Like this is *my* house and I'm inviting him over.

I laugh at myself. Now that really is a fantasy.

I hear the crunch of the gravel as the limo leaves, and I breathe a sigh of relief to finally be alone. Gerard was a nice guy, but I kind of felt like I was being watched.

The inside of the castle has been renovated and doesn't feel as cold as I feared it might. In fact, it's pretty cosy. The predominant colour scheme seems to be a rich red and cream that can be seen in plenty of velvet and silk finishes, accented with black metal and wood. I walk through an entrance way with a wrought iron chandelier hanging above me into a living space with huge windows that offer spectacular views of the surrounding area.

There's separate kitchen and dining rooms, as well as what I think is a sitting room or parlour? I don't really know what the difference is, but it's got an impressive fireplace, loads of comfy-looking armchairs and sofas, a coffee table in the middle, and bookcases with plenty of books and board games. I want to drop my suitcase off, though, so I go hunting for a bedroom.

There are several on the first floor, as well as a couple of bathrooms, which makes me think that this place is usually hired out by groups. Yet we have it all to ourselves. How incredible. I know which one is going to be our room when I find a bed with a hoodie laid on it and a note beside it with bootie slippers by the foot of the bed.

'Everything here is for you, Squish,' the note reads. 'Please make yourself comfortable.'

I touch the material of the hoodie, and it's ridiculously soft. Well…if it will make Daddy happy, then I should probably put it on.

I grin to myself as I take off my coat and do just that. The slippers are also the right size, which is pretty lucky. But then I take a peek in the wardrobe and find two sets of clothes. The smaller selection has just one of everything and looks pretty fancy. But the other has several of everything in various sizes, including alternate slipper booties—I assume in case these ones didn't fit. There are jeans, T-shirts, Henleys, shirts—even various options for underwear.

I realise that set is for me.

"Wow," I say out loud. Come to think of it, I *did* notice that both Sam and Callum came home with extra bags. I didn't ask because I assumed I wasn't allowed to.

Now I know. Daddy bought us clothes. I giggle, thinking of him dressing up his toys just the way he likes. Yes, this is definitely a game.

It's funny because when Sam came home, I was worried that this experience would feel fake and hollow. But now I'm here myself, treating it like role playing somehow makes it easier. I can be Daddy's boy. Not exactly a completely different person…more like…a version of Luke that I can perform. If it's not really me, then it means he can't really judge *me*. It's strange how that gives me comfort.

I'm still not quite done exploring yet, though. So I leave my case but take Squish with me, and go to nose around the last couple of rooms.

It's a good job I do.

The very last room I stumble upon has something quite remarkable inside. Looking around, it feels like some kind of playroom or nursery. There are toys neatly tidied in open top crates, model planes and hot air balloons hanging from the ceiling, big picture books on a shelf, a little nook with lots of colourful cushions, and a rainbow painted onto the back of the door.

It's not any of that that really grabs my attention, though.

Because a playpen has been set up. However, instead of a child inside it…there are three kittens.

I almost want to cry my heart aches so much as I cautiously make my way over to them. I'm no expert, but I'd say they're pretty young from how small and wobbly they are. There's a ginger, a calico, and one completely black one. They meow at each other as I carefully open the gate to the pen, then as I sit down, they notice me.

The black one is skittish and runs to hide up a small cat tree that's been erected in the corner of the pen. The ginger one gives me a look, then rolls over to start licking his paws. But the calico cautiously starts creeping towards me.

My heart in my throat, I reach out my hand like I do with the cats I make friends with on the street. He sniffs my fingers, then gives me a tiny meow, like he's asking who I am.

I mimic the sound, as if replying. *I'm a friend,* I try and tell him.

It must work because he rubs his head against my hand, then creeps a little closer.

Very carefully, I scoop him up and cradle him to my chest. He feels *so* fragile in my grasp. But he doesn't wriggle or complain. He just looks up at me with his huge green eyes.

I don't know why these kittens are here. I just think I'm in love, and that's all there is to it.

2 0

JACOB

I'M WAITING SO LONG AT THE FRONT DOOR THAT I START TO get worried. Gerard informed me that he dropped off boy number three, Luke, over half an hour ago. Have I got another naughty brat on my hands? I didn't think so from the information I received from the little piggies prior to our meeting.

I become slightly concerned. What if something's happened? He was told he had to answer the door to me with the passphrase, but what if he's hurt himself?

He could just be asleep, I suppose. Or walking around the grounds. He might have forgotten that he was meant to wait for the doorbell or thought he had more time before my arrival.

Either way, I'm impatient, and get my own key out to let myself inside.

By this point in the arrangement, I'm feeling slightly masochistic. I've managed to crack my heart with both Sam and Callum, so I figured it was best to fly at the last boy head-on and embrace the damage as it comes.

I can deal with the fallout when this is all over.

Saying goodbye to Callum was even harder than Sam, because Callum obviously got bratty. He didn't want to leave, and part of me wanted to believe that was because he'd fallen as hard for me as I had for him. But I'm sure that he just wanted to stay in our gorgeous log cabin longer, and he was *definitely* after more fucking, even though he wasn't recovered enough for that.

I managed to satisfy him by making him suck my cock again and getting him to wank off for me at my feet as he swallowed my cum. One last stunning memory to hold dear. But then I had to get firm and put him in the car to take him home.

And out of my life forever.

I sigh as I enter the final property, looking around. I'm not sure what exactly to expect from this last boy, except that he seemed somewhat fragile in the information I got in the messages I exchanged with Sam. In fact, more than once I got very protective vibes from Sam and Callum when it came to Luke.

I have a feeling I'm going to have to tread carefully.

Hopefully, that will make this more of an intellectual challenge rather than getting my feelings too involved. I've had a lot of precocious sugar babies in my time, but I've had a few more delicate boys as well. I enjoy playing therapist and figuring out what scene is going to help them best. It can be sexual, but in my experience, they've been more cathartic —sort of like what happened with Callum but with less fucking.

So as I move through the castle I've hired for the next couple of days, I keep that in mind. It's possible that this last little piggy won't completely break my heart.

"Hello, Luke?" I call out a couple of times. It isn't until I'm upstairs that I get a response.

I'm not even surprised this time. I was basically heading

straight for the nursery because I knew that's where he'd likely be.

"In here," a soft, dreamy voice calls out from behind the mostly closed door. "What's the passphrase?"

I'm pleased he remembered. I'm not sure he's the type to want to be punished. I knock on the door, eager to finally meet my final boy.

"Little piggy, be a good boy and let Daddy in."

"Come in," he calls instead of opening the door himself. I guess why, and it's confirmed when I make my way into the nursery space myself.

A young man with light brown hair is sat in the playpen with the three kitten brothers I arranged to be picked up from the rescue centre. There's a calico on his shoulder, a ginger in his lap, and a black one timidly sniffing his fingers. As I enter, the black one panics and makes a run for cover in the box part of the cat tree I had specially delivered.

I've never had a pet personally, but cats have always interested me. I must say the tiny little things are pretty adorable.

But not as adorable as my boy.

He's in the oversized hoodie and bootie slippers I had left out for him. His skin is pale with a few freckles and a slight flush on his cheeks. Everything about him looks soft and delicate. My immediate instinct is to wrap him up in my arms.

"Are you Daddy?" he asks, his voice light, almost like tinkling bells.

"I am," I confirm as I enter the playpen, careful to shut the gate behind me. The last thing I want is for one of the cats to escape and get lost. I have to find homes for each of them after mine and Luke's time together. I promised the rescue shelter. I'm not going to let one wander off into the forest or something.

"Did you get kittens especially for me?" he asks in awe.

I sit beside him. "I did," I say. "I thought you and Squish might enjoy their company whilst you're here." I see his little stuffed pig is also sat beside him, unlike with Callum when he forgot where he left him immediately.

Yes, I think I'm dealing with a third different boy altogether again. How interesting.

"I *love* cats, Daddy," he says, shaking his head and cuddling the ginger to his chest. "But I've never had one of my own. Thank you."

"It's my pleasure, baby boy," I say. That's not his name, but it will do for now.

I reach over to touch his cheek, but to my surprise, he jerks away, scaring both the cats. He looks around sadly as they run away, then back at me.

"I-I-I-I'm s-s-sorry," he stammers, then looks horrified. He claps his hands over his mouth as tears spring in his eyes.

My heart aches.

"No, I'm sorry," I say quickly and firmly. "I shouldn't have assumed it was okay to touch you. We can take that slowly going forwards."

He takes a few deep breaths, then rubs his eyes. "You just s-s-surprised me. I'm sorry. And I'm sorry about..."

He gestures to his mouth and bites his lip, clearly ashamed of his stammer.

Well, fuck that shit.

"You have nothing to apologise for, I assure you, baby boy. I'd really like to comfort you. How would you feel about a hug?"

He swallows and licks his lips. But then he nods.

Good. He needs looking after, but I can't do that if he doesn't let me.

"Wonderful," I say. I open my arms for him to come to me, which he does. It's tentative, but he leans against my chest. "Well done," I say genuinely as I wrap one arm around him. With the other, I reach over and pluck Squish the piggy from the spot where the calico kitten is sniffing him with interest. I hand him to Luke, who hugs him as I hug my boy.

For a while, we stay like that, quiet aside from the kittens' occasional meows. But then I feel Luke start to relax against me. "Thank you for the limo," he says after a time. "And the sushi. It was yummy."

"Of course, baby boy," I say, kissing his head.

But then I frown. I'm even more sure that 'baby boy' isn't really the right name for him. He's not a baby. He's delicate. Besides, I use that as a general moniker for a lot of my playdates. Just like Sam and Callum, Luke is special. He deserves a more unique name.

"What kind of boy are you?" I ask him. "What should I call you?"

"Not baby boy?" he asks.

I consider him a moment. "Not unless you absolutely want to," I say with conviction. "I don't think that's the best we can do."

He nods and licks his lips. "No, I agree. I don't think it's quite right."

Excellent. "Me neither. So do you have an idea what kind of boy you are—or what kind you'd *like* to be?"

He looks up at me with those pretty hazel eyes. "Um...I don't know, Daddy," he says softly.

"Well, I know you're a good boy," I say as I rub his back. He smiles gratefully at me, like acknowledging that is very important to him. I take note. I think praise is going to go a *long* way with this sweet one.

However, all three of these boys have been so good for me in their different ways. I've had a big boy and a naughty boy, but Luke is...well, he's like a porcelain doll. Fragile and beautiful... I wonder if he really knows that, though?

"Are you a pretty boy?" I ask.

His eyes flutter closed, and it's almost like he basks in the name. "I-I don't know," he whispers. "Am I, Daddy?"

I nuzzle our noses together, relieved when he lets me. Now that we're already hugging, he seems fine with all my other touches. "I think you're very pretty," I say gently. "Would you like that to be your name, pretty boy?"

He pants a little, his lips wet and oh-so kissable. His eyes are still closed as he thinks it over.

"Yes please, Daddy," he says eventually. "I think I'd l-like that."

"Wonderful," I tell him, kissing the corner of his beautiful mouth. "Well done, pretty boy. I'm so proud of you for making a big decision."

He wriggles against me at the praise, and my heart seems to thud extra loudly in my chest.

Bloody hell, these boys are dangerous to my health. Any hopes that I'd be able to keep my distance with this final boy is fading fast.

I look around at the nursery that we're sitting in. When I saw that the castle included it, that sealed the deal for me. I just got a feeling from some of the things mentioned about Luke that it might be a good idea.

"Can I ask you a couple more questions, pretty boy?" I say. "I want to get to know you a bit more, so I make sure I'm taking care of you properly."

He squirms against my chest, like he's trying to get even closer. I notice that the calico has crept back to him, and Luke holds his hand out to encourage the tiny creature to be braver.

"Of course, Daddy," Luke says. "You can ask me anything."

I smile and kiss his hair again. "Thank you," I say. "There was nothing mentioned in the messages, but I was wondering. Are you a little?"

It's not a kink I've particularly indulged in before, and I'm not sure how interested I am in it. But for Luke… Well, he's different. I already know I'd expand my horizons if he wanted me to.

He pulls at his piggy's jumper. There's a loose thread he's worrying at. "I don't think so," he says with a frown after a time, biting his pretty pink lip. He looks like he's struggling to find the right words, so I just wait patiently. It's not long before I'm rewarded. "I mean…I don't want to be a child," he explains. Then he screws up his eyes. "But maybe…maybe I want a safe space to enjoy childish things? Like I never got to growing up? That probably just makes me immature, doesn't it?"

I wrap my hand around his, partly to stop him pulling on the thread, partly to make him look at me. Both things work.

"On the contrary," I say. "Being brave enough to ask for what you need is very mature. I'm proud of you, pretty boy." His blush is all the reward I need. I smile at him and rub my thumb against the back of his hand. "There is nothing shameful in finding joy in pure, innocent things. I understand that completely, and I'll do my best to give you that safe space in the time we have together. For now, will you allow me to fetch some scissors so we can fix Squish's jumper? I'd hate for it to unravel."

Luke blinks at me then at the piggy, like he hadn't even realised he was fussing with the thread. He offers me a shaky smile, but it's earnest, and I feel like we've made a huge leap of progress. "Yes, please. Thank you, Daddy."

My heart soars.

I can only find a pair of safety scissors in a drawer, but they're still good enough to tidy up the thread. Then I resume my position cuddled up next to my boy, surrounded by timid little kittens.

Wow. If my old board of directors could see me now…

Well, they can't. And I don't even have a board anymore. I'm my own man, and this is why I fucking love being a Daddy.

The spankings and scenes are fun. But Luke is a special kind of boy. He's vulnerable and needs far more from me than an ordinary man can give.

Thank god he came to me. The thought of him under a less experienced hand turns my blood cold. I'm going to have to work extremely hard to do everything just right for him over our two days together.

And then pray to the universe that when the time comes, I'll be able to let him go with grace, and trust that whoever crosses his path in the future will do just as conscientious of a job as I will of looking after him.

I somehow doubt it, but that's life, isn't it?

21

———

CALLUM

"Finally, the essay of doom is over," Sam announces dramatically from my bedroom doorway, even lifting his hand to his head and pretending to swoon.

I pause my sewing machine and swivel around to face him fully. "Yay, congratulations! Does this warrant a celebration?"

He snorts. "I think you think any day ending with a 'Y' warrants a celebration."

I pretend to check my phone. "Luckily for you, today *does* end with a 'Y'! Terrible pink wine?"

Sam sighs. "Why not?"

I make sure my project is tidy enough for me to walk away from, then go join him in the kitchen. Luke left us a few hours ago but has only just messaged to say that he's arrived and everything's fine. It's crazy, but I'm more worried for him than I was for myself.

I'm also a teeny tiny bit jealous.

He still has his whole visit with Daddy before him. Mine is now a thing of the past.

Although my arse is still just about reminding me of what

happened whilst we were in that log cabin. Holy fucking shit, that was the most phenomenal first time I could have ever wished for. The fact that I've been sore for days somehow makes it even more perfect.

Like I was left with an undeniable reminder. Proof that it really happened, and it was just as incredible as I hoped it would be.

"Hello? Earth to Callum?"

I blink and realise that Sam is slowly waving a glass of rosé in front of my face.

"Shit, sorry," I say with a laugh. "Thank you. Cheers." We clink glasses and sip the cold, sweet-but-tangy drink. Sam arches an eyebrow at me. "What?" I ask.

"Come on, spill it," he says, leaning against the countertop. "Are you thinking about Luke? Or Daddy?"

I shrug and take another gulp of wine first. "Both?" I admit hesitantly.

There's a pause as we look at each other. We haven't really had a chance to talk since I got back, but now Sam's essay is finished…

"We should wait until Luke returns to discuss details, shouldn't we?" I say by way of an opener.

"Specific details, yes," Sam says resolutely. "But…well. We've been fucked by the same man. We're not virgins anymore. I think there are probably some general, overall things we can discuss."

We both laugh, but there's something kind of electric in the air between us now. Sam bites his lip, and I raise an eyebrow.

"Was it just fucking for you?" I ask.

For a moment, Sam simply holds my gaze. Then he slowly shakes his head. "No," he says, looking down into his wine with a sigh. "No, it was much, *much* more than that. I felt…I felt extremely cherished and taken care of by Daddy."

I breathe a sigh of relief. "Yes, me too. Exactly. It was like he reached into my head and knew exactly what I wanted. What I *needed*."

Sam beams at me. "I love that. Yes." He nods for a second and chews his lip before looking back at me. "Is it weird that I'm not jealous of you?"

I'm so glad he's said it. "Right?" I cry excitedly. "I was worried I would be, but hearing that from you…it's like it just makes my heart fuller. I'm so happy you got to experience that as well."

We share a look that feels like it has a lot of love in it. I know our situation is probably odd. I'm not sure I'd ever be able to explain it to anyone else. But that doesn't matter in this moment when it just feels *right*.

Our kitchen is so small that I'm able to reach my foot over and nudge Sam's shin. "Speaking of not being jealous, Luke said he told you about our little make-out session." I waggle my eyebrows at him, and he laughs, but there's a warm look in his eyes that I don't miss.

"Yeah. I mean, maybe I'm a *tiny* bit jealous. It sounded pretty hot."

"It was!" I cry, shimmying my shoulders in glee. "I know it was just pretend—role-playing really is therapeutic, you know—but it was also kind of amazing in its own right."

Sam hums and drinks a little more wine. "I said to Luke that maybe we can all do something like that when he's back. Together."

I blink. "Wow…I wasn't expecting you to suggest that," I admit.

He shrugs and looks away. *Shit*. I didn't mean to make him feel embarrassed.

"I just mean…not in a bad way, honestly," I try and qualify. "I suppose…well, we've all been looking for Daddies this whole time. But maybe there's something between the three of us as well. It's just surprising to me."

Thankfully, some of the tension leaves his body. "Yeah, that's what I thought. And…our lives are probably going to change soon if we want to start finding our own Daddies. It might be nice to try something between us before we go our separate ways."

I lick my lips, tasting the sugary wine. "I hope we'll always be close," I say. It's funny. I want things to change, but I also don't. There's something undeniably scary about the unknown.

"Oh, totally," Sam agrees firmly with a frown. "I'm sure we will. There's no one like us three little piggies."

I scoff. "Hell, we're all losing our V-cards to the same Daddy. There's close and then there's *that*."

Sam nods and the conversation lulls a little, presumably as we both get lost in our own thoughts for a minute. "We are kind of weird, aren't we?" Sam eventually laments.

I screw up my face. "And what's the alternative? Normal? Who wants to be boring and normal? Whatever that even means. I suspect that deep down most people are all freaks, in one way or another."

Sam gives me a small smile. "That's probably true."

"I know it is," I say and down another mouthful of terrible wine. "The world's full of weirdos. What matters is *happiness*. Too many people are afraid to go after what makes them happy just because of what others might think."

Sam hums thoughtfully. "You and Luke make me happy," he says quietly.

Something soft and tender unfurls in my chest. I cross the kitchen to lean against the counter beside him, bumping our shoulders together. "You and Luke make me happy as well," I say.

And, like, this isn't revolutionary news. We've been best friends for five years now. In fact, by this point, we're more like family. But there *is* something slightly different in the air, and I'm curious what it's going to mean once Luke returns.

Once we've all seen Daddy Wolf and he'll fade from our lives for good.

I chew my lip. I wish I could be sure that staying in this bubble with my besties would be enough for me. But then I recall the exquisite way in which Daddy pushed me to the edge, how he explored the humiliation kink I thought might have been lurking inside me all along and found a way to make me soar.

Luke and Sam could never, *ever* give me that. They love me too much. They're too kind and gentle. Daddy is kind as well, but he knows how to wield his power in different way. Like a surgeon with a scalpel.

"Daddy made me happy, too," I say quietly.

Sam wraps his arm around me and squeezes. "Yeah," he says heavily. "He was...amazing."

"He was everything," I say, shaking my head.

There's a pause, but eventually Sam speaks again.

"I think maybe I fell a bit in love with him."

A lump rises in my throat. I've been trying not to think like that. But I've *never* felt like I did with Daddy. I desperately didn't want to leave. And now it's like a part of me is missing, left behind in that picturesque log cabin.

Is that what love feels like?

"I think maybe I did a bit, too."

Sam places his wine down then turns to give me a hug. I return the embrace gratefully. "I wish we could split him in two and both have what we want," I say with a wet chuckle. "Or in three if Luke feels the same."

"Except that's not what Daddy wants," Sam points out. "We all agreed on one-time things…"

"Yeah, I know," I grumble. "I'm just being a brat."

"It must be a day ending with a 'Y'," Sam quips.

I laugh and tickle him in the ribs, making him squirm. "Bugger off," I tell him.

Sam laughs as well, but like me, I can feel the sadness. "Oh…what a strange situation we've got ourselves into."

"We never do anything normally, I guess," I say in agreement. "The three weird little piggies."

"Hopefully, one day, this will be a crazy story we reminisce about," Sam suggests.

"Yeah, hopefully."

Right now, though, it's confusing. I feel like my heart is being pulled in so many different directions. Some of it is good and exciting, but some of it is definitely going to hurt.

The deal with Daddy Wolf was clear. We all agreed to it, and it's for the best. Besides—we're getting what we wanted. An amazing and safe way to lose our virginities so that we can move on in life.

Keeping Daddy Wolf was never an option.

But unless something catastrophic happens, I'll always have my besties.

I'll just have to hope that when everything is said and done, that will be enough.

2 2

JACOB

THERE'S A VERY DIFFERENT VIBE BETWEEN ME AND LUKE compared to with Sam and Callum. But unfortunately, I'm not any less drawn to him than I was the other boys. It's just more fragile. We're not going to be rushing into anything, I can tell.

He's absolutely enraptured by the kittens, but it's not long before the little creatures fall dead asleep. So we leave them be, and take a puzzle Luke found in the nursery downstairs to start on in the living room.

I'm fascinated watching him work. He's very methodical at sifting through all the pieces to find the edges, turning every single one over as he goes. It's only a five-hundred-piece one, which at this rate I feel confident we'll be able to finish before our time is through.

Once we have the outline complete, I leave him to go start dinner. Unfortunately, unlike the other two properties, this layout isn't open plan. I find myself wishing I had something simpler to prepare, as I don't want to let him out of my sight for too long. I probably waste as much time popping my head around the kitchen door as I do making the damned meal.

In the end, though, Luke wanders in to join me of his own accord. "That smells good," he comments shyly.

I grin and head to the fridge. "It's a Thai green curry, but not too spicy. I hope that's okay?"

"That sounds delicious."

I beam at him from around the open fridge door. "I'm glad. Now, a little birdie told me that you like rosé wine. Would you like a glass?"

He raises his eyebrows. "I, um…I thought we wouldn't, because…uh…"

I'm incredibly glad that I saw Sam and Callum before meeting Luke. I've gleaned a lot about this special boy through them, and so far, my instincts have been spot on.

"We won't be doing a scene tonight, pretty boy," I inform him. I'd thought as much before I'd arrived, but now I know for sure. "We're going to take our time. So if you'd like to relax with some wine, that's absolutely fine. If you'd prefer, I have non-alcoholic rosé as well as a selection of flavoured sparkling waters and fruit juices. This is your holiday. What would make you happy?"

His shoulders drop from where they'd bunched up around his ears, and he smiles. "A glass of wine would be nice. I'm, um, a bit nervous still."

I pull out the bottle I had my eye on and shut the door. "Thank you for being honest with me, pretty boy. I won't tell you not to be nervous. I'm just going to do my best to make you feel at ease."

I pour two glasses, although I don't plan on doing anything more than giving mine a sip. We might not be doing a scene, but I'm still in control and need to make sure my boy is happy. However, I'm sure he'll get anxious if he thinks he's the only one drinking, so I'll give him the impression that we're sharing the bottle whilst I stick mostly to water.

"Cheers," I say as we touch the glasses together with a little ring through the air.

"Cheers," he agrees, taking a sip.

His eyes flutter shut and his throat bobs. As he licks his lips, desire floods through me. I know that he'll absolutely be worth waiting for, but I wish we had much longer than forty-eight hours to spend together.

I've wished that with all these boys. God damnit.

"That's so much better than our terrible corner shop rosé," he says with a laugh. "Thank you."

"You're very welcome," I murmur.

He hangs around whilst I finish cooking. I wouldn't have interrupted the fun he was having with the jigsaw, but I can't deny that I like having him by my side very much. He seems to delight in running off to the fridge to get the last few ingredients I ask for and drains the rice as soon as I request it.

He's eager to please. I find that very sexy in a boy. But that's a privilege I have to earn. Otherwise, I'll be abusing my power.

It doesn't take much longer to finish cooking, and we relocate to the dining room. I enjoy pulling Luke's chair out for him to sit at the table. The small act of chivalry seems to undo him. He blushes and bites his lip as he lowers himself down, looking up adoringly at me as I lay his napkin over his lap.

I'm glad I'm not drinking. I need my wits about me if I'm going to take it slowly with this boy.

I hand-fed the others for our first meals, but I get the sense that Luke wouldn't enjoy that. I have to be careful what control he wants me to take away from him. So, for now, he feeds himself.

"So, Luke," I say once we're both comfortable at the table. "Tell me about yourself."

He raises his eyebrows at me and seems genuinely confused by the question. "Me? Oh, um…I'm so boring."

"I can absolutely guarantee you that you're not, pretty boy."

Another delicious blush. I wish I could bottle them.

"Um, well…" he says, toying with the stem of his wine glass. "The most interesting thing about me is probably Sam and Callum, but you've met them already." He laughs, but I don't say anything, waiting for him to open up. I just smile in encouragement, my gaze fixed on him. "And, well, I don't really have any other friends. Not close ones. Sam and Callum are my family, I guess. They're kind of my everything."

He shakes his head and takes a mouthful of wine. I don't want him to have too much, but for now, I top him up. The alcohol does seem to be helping to unwind him.

"And other than that, I work in a pub. It pays the bills, you know?"

I nod. I do know how important it is to be able to pay the bills. It was just me and my mother when I was growing up, and sometimes we'd cry ourselves to sleep with hunger.

Now she lives in a five-bedroom house in the Cotswolds, and my useless absent father can rot in hell.

Luke doesn't mention his parents. I've worked out from the other boys that he's not in contact with them for a good reason, so I don't ask. I can completely sympathise with the hard-wired desire to be a self-made man.

"Work isn't everything," I assure him. "Besides, you're so young. You've got plenty of time to work out what direction you'd like to take your life."

He opens his mouth but then closes it again. Then he

pushes some of his food around his plate. I sense he wants to say something but is having trouble finding the words.

I wait patiently.

"There is something…" he says eventually.

I can't help but get the feeling that he might never have voiced whatever he's about to say before. I try not to lean forward or look too eager in case I spook him. Instead, I nod at him to go on. He licks his lips, then takes a deep breath.

"When I was desperate to leave home—but before we'd finished our A-Levels—I looked into some London LGBT charities in case I needed their help. There are people who help out queer kids in trouble. Find them places to sleep. Things like that. And there are community centres for adults to get therapy, do yoga, just get a cup of tea. Stuff like that. A lot of them rely on volunteers, and I couldn't afford to do that right now. But…I'd absolutely love to work somewhere like that. Somewhere that makes a real difference and helps people get back on their feet, or just offers a safe space to meet other LGBT people. If that, um, makes sense."

I blink. I wasn't expecting such passion from him, but it's beautiful.

"It makes perfect sense," I say honestly. "That sounds like a really wonderful idea. You seem very caring, pretty boy. I'm sure you'd have the capacity to positively impact more lives than you'd ever think possible if you got the chance."

He exhales, and a smile tweaks at his lips. "Um, thank you. Sorry, I'm talking too much about myself."

"That's the whole point of this evening," I remind him with raised eyebrows. "I want to get to know you. We're talking things slowly, remember?"

He smiles shyly but nods. "Yes, Daddy."

I can't help but feel that this one is going to need bossing around quite a bit for his own good. Sam and Callum both had a good sense of self-worth that Luke appears to be severely lacking. That won't do. If I think he's wonderful, then he needs to listen to his Daddy.

Even if the job is only temporarily mine.

"Why don't we relocate to the living room and get comfy?" I ask after he's had enough to eat. He automatically goes to pick up his plate, but I reach a hand out and stop him. "Daddy will take care of that later, pretty boy. You're on holiday. Your job is to relax."

He bites his lip and looks like he wants to protest, but then he eases and nods before I have to remind him who's in charge. Good, that's good.

"Okay, Daddy."

I pass him his drink and then take his hand to lead him out of the dining room. First, we drop by the kittens. They have a litter tray and food, so I'm confident they're okay mostly by themselves. Cats are appealing like that. But I know Luke would like to check on them, and he gets the sweetest happy smile on his face just from watching them sleep.

Satisfied that our four-legged friends are okay, I take him back downstairs and settle us on the sofa. "What do you usually do with your spare time?" I ask, hoping to keep the conversation going.

But I've let myself get distracted, and I make a stupid fucking mistake. I can't even blame the wine, because I hardly took a sip.

The touch is casual, at least by my standards. I just slip my hand over his knee, my fingers caressing his inner thigh through his jeans.

It's like I've given him an electric shock.

His entire body jerks, including the hand holding his wine glass. The pink liquid leaps into the air, suspended for a fraction of a second, before it splashes all over him, his clothes, and the cream-coloured couch.

His mouth drops open in horror as he looks down at the damage he's caused. I don't give a shit about wine stains. I'm horrified by the damage I've apparently done to *him.*

"Pretty boy, don't worry," I say, furious that I forgot myself. I'm already up, dashing to get a roll of kitchen towel. "Forgive me. That was completely unacceptable."

I'm already back to the sofa, crouching in front of him, wadding up some paper towel to mop him up. He has droplets of wine in his lashes as he blinks at me, clearly mortified.

"I'm s-s-s-so sorry," he whispers, his eyes getting wet with tears. "The couch—"

"I don't give a fuck about the couch," I say calmly. I take the wine glass from his hand before he breaks it in his grip, placing it on the table. Luckily, we were working on the jigsaw puzzle elsewhere, so that's safe. "I'll buy them a new one. This is my fault."

He shakes his head. I don't like being disagreed with, but I bite my tongue before snapping at him. He's devastated. Me being angry with myself shouldn't translate into getting snippy with him.

"I spilled the wine," he says, his voice quivering as tears tumble down his cheeks. "What the fuck is wrong with me?" He clenches his jaw and screws his eyes shut. "I'm such a fucking freak. This is why I'm still a virgin. It's all my problem. I'm so broken. I should just go. I'm sorry. I've wasted your time." He goes to stand up. "I—"

"Sit. Back. Down," I say firmly with my eyebrows raised, daring him to disobey me.

His eyes go impossibly wider, but he sits back on the couch.

Something unclenches in my chest that I didn't even realise had gone tight. Well, I don't like being disobeyed, I suppose. But I was right. He needs a firm hand like air. He can't be responsible for looking after himself, because it's obvious he will be far too hard on himself.

This is *my* fault. I have to make it right.

I exhale and relax. "Good boy," I say emphatically. "I'm so sorry I touched you intimately without permission. I told you I'd be careful, and then I made a mistake. *I'm* the one who has to apologise, not you. So I'd really like to comfort you now, but only if you'll let me."

He stares at me, looking confused. "I just ruined the couch because I'm such a mess that I can't even bear to be touched by a man I'm attracted to. Why aren't you kicking me out?"

"Pretty boy, are you questioning me?" I ask with a little smile, not letting my exasperation get the better of me. I appreciate he's not used to having a Daddy, but I'm not used to being defied (in a non-fun way, at least).

"No, Daddy," he says quickly, appeasing me greatly. But then he shakes his head. "I mean, not on purpose. I'm so confused. You don't have to be with me. I understand if you want me to leave. You wanted some fun sex, and I'm spoiling everything."

Now that pisses me off. I don't like being told what I want, especially when the other person is completely wrong. But I'm not angry with him. I'm angry with whoever has treated him so badly that he's afraid to be touched and so quick to demonise himself.

I take his chin firmly between my thumb and index finger, forcing him to look at me.

"What I *want*," I tell him, "is a good boy who'll let his Daddy take care of him. Good boys don't tell their Daddies what to do or think, do they?"

He shakes his head, looking mesmerised by me. I let out a breath and offer him a smile.

"You're a good boy, aren't you?" He nods even more

frantically. I remove my fingers. "I'm sorry. I asked for your permission to touch you, then did it anyway before you could answer. May I touch your face, pretty boy? May I hold you whilst we talk? I'd like to understand what just happened."

He swallows and stares at me a moment. Then he nods. "Yes, Daddy," he whispers. "That's o-okay. You, um, have my p-p-permission."

Something akin to relief washes through me.

Yes, I get what I want, usually because I take it. But in this instance, it feels much better to be given it, like a gift.

That couch is ruined, so I take his hands and guide him to stand. Then I lead us to an armchair, where I sit down. "I'd like to have you in my lap, please." It's not exactly an order, but it's what I want. However, I know we need to tread lightly when it comes to physical contact, so if he can't manage that for me right now, I'll find a compromise.

He looks down at the hoodie I bought him miserably. "I'm wet," he whispers. "And I ruined your lovely gift for me."

I bring his fingers to my mouth to kiss. "I'm sure we can get the stain out of the clothes, sweetheart. And I used the kitchen roll to get the worst of it off. I want to cuddle you. I'm not bothered about the wine. My only concern is whether you want to be touched like that."

He takes a shaky breath, but thankfully he then nods. "I'd like to be held. Thank you."

"Wonderful," I praise him. "Good boy. Come cuddle with Daddy. We'll make it all better."

"Okay."

Carefully, he climbs into my lap and lets his legs dangle over the arm of the chair. It reminds me of how I first pleasured Callum by the fire pit, but the two scenarios couldn't be more different.

"I need to ask you some difficult questions, pretty boy," I

murmur against his hair as I rub his arm. "You won't make me angry. But I'm afraid I don't understand the full picture, and I don't want to hurt you or scare you again."

"This is my worst nightmare," he whispers. "I knew I'd fuck this up. With you, I mean. I told Callum I would."

"You haven't fucked anything up, I promise," I assure him. "But I need to know what happened on the couch."

He takes a few ragged breaths. "I...I'm n-n-n-not used to being touched in a good way," he manages to force out.

My blood boils almost immediately, but I bite the inside of my cheek to remain calm. Luke doesn't need my rage right now. He needs me to be safe and calm for him.

"Did someone hurt you?" I ask.

He nods but doesn't speak for a few moments. "My dad," he says eventually. "He beat me. All the time. Sam and Callum...they rescued me. It took a while, but I like them touching me now. I've never let anyone else try, certainly not in a sexy way. Until today..." His face crumples. "I so wanted to be okay. I practised with Callum and everything!"

I'm not sure what that means, but my interest is piqued, and I hope we can revisit that particular comment later. This whole time, I've assumed that these boys are best friends in a platonic way. But now I want to know what 'practised' means.

That's a conversation for another time, though.

I'm not entirely shocked to learn that he suffered abuse at home. My overriding instinct is to track that fucker down and beat him with a cricket bat. But he can rot in hell with other monstrous fathers like my own. Who cares about them?

I care about my boy.

"I'm so desperately sorry, pretty boy," I say, hugging him tighter. "I'm honoured that you would let me try to touch you. I'll do everything I can not to surprise you again. But I need you to listen to me, because I'm Daddy and I know best, okay?"

He blinks spiky lashes at me. "Okay?"

"Everything is fine," I promise. "You haven't ruined anything. This is a journey that we're taking together, and you've already made such huge leaps. You're not alone, though." I chose this seat because I realised that his piggy was sitting nearby, so I'm able to reach down to get him and hand it to Luke. "See? Squish is right here with you. If ever you're not okay, that's your safeword. You call out for him, and I'll know to stop everything and check in with you. All right?"

He fondles the pig's ears thoughtfully, then nods. "Yes, Daddy."

"Good boy," I say and kiss his hair. "Is everything we're doing now okay with you?"

He pauses to give that proper thought, which makes me happy. I don't want him rushing into anything to appease me.

To my delight, he twists in my lap so that he's facing me more. In fact, our mouths are mere inches apart now.

"This is lovely, Daddy. I feel much better, thank you."

It's strange how relieved that makes me. Usually, I trust my judgement with boys implicitly. But Luke is teaching me a couple of things.

I guess I've never met a boy who didn't want to scene or get fucked as soon as possible.

I like this change of pace.

It seems my work isn't over, however. Not by a long shot.

"But…I really don't get it," he says, clearly still struggling. "Why would you want to waste your time on me when there are so many boys out there without these issues? Who know what they want?"

I laugh darkly. I can't help it. "Oh, yes," I agree. "They know what they want. They're precocious and confident. They want a sugar Daddy to spoil them and fuck them because they know how fabulous they are. They know they're worth it."

The tears shine in his eyes. I dislike that immensely, but I know I have to make my point.

"Exactly," he whispers.

I cup the side of his face, making him look at me as I raise my eyebrows. "They're boring," I say, not allowing him to turn away. "I'm tired of them. I want a boy who needs *me*. Not just my bank account or my firm hand. I want a broken little bird who needs Daddy to heal, to teach him how to be brave enough to fly again." I can't help but smile warmly. "That's why I had to have all *three* of you boys. Each of you are the opposite of boring. You see yourself as less than, pretty boy. But I see you as perfect."

He holds my gaze, and something tells me I'm finally getting through to him on some level.

"It makes me happy that you saw Sam and Callum first," he says quietly. "If you liked them, it makes me think you could actually like me."

"Of course, pretty boy," I say. "I lo—*like* all three of you so much. Meeting you has been one of the best things I've ever done."

I mean it. I do like these three little piggies.

Like them.

Because falling in love with anyone that fast is an absolutely absurd notion, let alone with all three boys together.

He sighs and snuggles against my chest with his piggy. "Thank you, Daddy," he whispers.

I'm not sure what for specifically, but I don't think that really matters. In that moment, I try and stop my own mind from whirring and just enjoy the gift he's giving me of lying so close to me.

I accept the fact there and then that we might not be able

to progress as far as he wanted sexually in the time we have together. But that will be okay. Because from what I'm seeing, we're already light years ahead of where he was before.

This isn't a race to check a certain box or put a notch on anyone's bedpost. It's clear to me that the next two days are going to be about healing, and that's all that matters.

LUKE

For the first time in my life, I'm able to stop myself from completely spiralling when disaster strikes.

Don't get me wrong, I'm still mortified about what happened on the couch. But I'm also starting to trust Daddy when he says things are okay.

Aside from that, we had a lovely evening. Dinner was delicious, and once I calmed down, we were able to talk for a while longer cuddled up in the living room. Daddy seems genuinely interested in all sorts of things about me.

I've never felt more special, more *seen*. Except with Sam and Callum, of course. But I'm ashamed to admit that because we see each other every day, it's not as remarkable anymore.

Maybe after the break of being with Daddy, it will get more special again. I love them dearly, after all.

But right now, I bask in the attention from my very first Daddy. That is, until I start to fall asleep right there on his lap.

Oops.

"Come on, sweet boy," Daddy murmurs as he nudges me gently. "Time for bed."

I don't care if it's childish. I cuddle Squish to me as I stand and rub my eyes. It's been a long day, and I'm emotionally and physically wrecked. "Can we check the kittens first, though?" I ask.

Daddy smiles at me. "Of course, pretty boy. They've probably woken up now, so we need to make sure they're happy and have everything they need."

Daddy's right. When we enter the playroom and turn on the light, all three of the babies are awake and playing. In fact, they're beating each other up, which makes me laugh. Daddy told me they're brothers, so that makes sense.

I go and sit with them for a few minutes, letting them come up and sniff me. The black one is getting braver, but the calico just runs right up and sits on my head, much to my delight.

"Will you keep them after we've had our holiday here?" I ask.

Daddy shakes his head. "I fear I work too much. I'm going to find loving homes for every one of them, though."

I don't like the idea of them being separated, but maybe someone will want to adopt all three.

I wish it could be me, but I know with absolute certainty that our landlord would get apoplectic if he found pets in our crappy apartment. We'd be evicted for sure.

The most important thing is that the little ones are loved and safe. I'm lucky that I'll get to spend this time with them now.

Much like Daddy.

Sam and Callum promised he'd be nice, and he is. Even if that means being stern. I understand when he does it, it's because he's trying to take care of me. The firm hand he has is actually calming to me. When he's in charge, I don't need to worry about anything.

Even the touching is getting better fast. He holds my hand as we turn off the light and leave the kittens be for the night. Then he places his other hand on my lower back as he steers me to the en suite attached to the bedroom where I found the slippers and hoodie. I was right—it is where we're going to sleep.

Having his hands on me is surprisingly soothing. I like how he guides and moves me. *This* is why I need a Daddy. When someone I trust takes charge, everything becomes so much better. When I have to make decisions, there's always so much stress that I'm going to get something wrong and be punished. This way, I don't have to worry.

The wine stain doesn't seem so bad now it's dried, and I really hope we can get it out like Daddy said. I'd love to keep this jumper as a memento. For now, he gives me time and space in the bathroom to brush my teeth and get changed into my pyjamas.

When I return, he's in a pair of boxers and a T-shirt. Still mostly covered up, but it's the most I've seen of his body so far, and it makes my heart skip a beat.

He's such a *man.* He's not some built gym bunny, but he is muscular, and his legs are nice and hairy and...

Oh no, I'm staring.

He laughs, though, and gestures me to come towards him. "Are you ready for bed?" he asks.

I lean into him, so he knows I feel okay to hug—even if it *is* different now he has fewer clothes on. But I don't feel intimidated (much). He promised that we wouldn't push things too fast, and I believe him.

Sure enough, he gets me into the bed—which is *enormous,* oh my god—then goes to brush his teeth as well. When he returns, he turns off the lights, gets under the covers...

Then doesn't come near me.

"Good night, pretty boy," he says in the darkness from his side of the mattress, which, considering how big it is, might as well be back in London.

"Oh, um. Night night," I say.

I lie there for a while, hardly daring to move. My anxiety is bubbling back up in me again, until I realise I have to make a choice. Ask for what I want or get no sleep all night?

"Um, Daddy?" I say eventually.

I'm afraid he's already fallen asleep, but his voice is clear and alert when he replies, "Yes, sweetheart?"

I sigh in relief, then ask my question before I can chicken out. "Could we maybe snuggle?"

There's hardly any light, but I just about make out his smile in the gloom. It's a big one. "Of course, pretty boy. Come here. I'm really proud of you for asking for what you need."

My heart feels like it wants to burst as I wriggle over to him and huddle against his chest. He wraps me up tightly in his arms and kisses my hair.

"Good boy," he tells me.

I sigh with happiness.

After that, it takes me no time at all to fall asleep.

THROUGHOUT THE NEXT DAY, I continue to relax and get used to being around Daddy. When I wake up, I realise he's allowed me to sleep in but has left me a cup of tea in a thermos, so it doesn't get cold. I know it's only tea, but it's also one of the most romantic things anyone has ever done for me.

I shower and dress in some of the new clothes he's bought for me. I never buy myself stuff unless it's absolutely necessary, so I take my time trying various items on in front of the mirror, marvelling at how well everything fits.

I had eighteen Christmases and birthdays with my no-good parents. They never once made me feel this cherished.

Once I finally settle on my favourite ensemble, I leave the bedroom and head straight to the nursery to visit the kittens and make sure they have breakfast.

To my surprise, Daddy is already sat there at the desk, reading a newspaper and drinking a cup of tea of his own. I thought he'd be downstairs in the dining room on the laptop I assume he's brought with him, doing important grown-up stuff.

"Good morning, pretty boy," he says, sounding genuinely delighted, immediately folding his paper to give me all his attention. "I knew you'd head straight here."

My heart does a strange flippy thing in my chest. One, he already knows me well enough to guess where I'd go when I woke. And two, he made sure he was wherever *I'd* be?

Wow.

"Hi, Daddy," I say shyly.

He beckons me to him and opens his arms in an invitation. I don't know if he just wants a hug, but I seize my courage and go ahead and sit in his lap instead. He practically throws his arms around me and buries his face against my neck. Knowing that he likes when I'm brave and let him touch me makes it easier to do.

"Did you sleep well, beautiful?" he asks.

I nod, then look down at our little mini pride. They're sleepy and yawning, but they do seem to be stirring at our talking. "Are they all right?"

"They're wonderful," he assures me. "But I thought you'd like to put their food down, so I held off. They've been asleep —like you—so don't worry that they've been hungry."

I bite my lip but can't stop my grin. He really *does* know me well.

After we sort the cats, he makes us a proper English breakfast but all vegan, even though he eats meat, then we head out into the countryside to walk it off. The rest of the day is mostly taken up with my preoccupation to finish the bloody puzzle because I really don't want to leave it unfinished when I go home tomorrow.

Yikes. I can't believe I'll be leaving *tomorrow.*

That makes me look up from what I'm doing and pause. I'm kind of surprised that Daddy would want to work on the puzzle with me. It's a picture of puppies and kittens causing trouble in a greenhouse, so not exactly mature. But he seems just as engrossed as I am.

"Are you sure you wouldn't rather be doing something else?" I blurt out at one point.

He looks up and raises an eyebrow. "Do *you* want to do anything else, pretty boy? Because all I want to do is help you relax. If this is how you want to spend the afternoon, then I'm delighted to join you." He grins and drops the piece he's trying to place before walking around the table to me. "I just want to be where you are, gorgeous boy."

He wraps his arms around me and nuzzles my neck. I feel like I'm enveloped in flames, but in the best way.

And then I don't think.

I just turn my head and sort of *bump* my mouth into his.

It's clumsy, but Daddy takes charge instantly, knowing what I want. Of course he does. The kiss is searing and all-consuming. He holds my back and cards his fingers through my hair, claiming me with his body and his lips and tongue.

It's incredible.

When he releases me, I cling to his shirt, panting. "Whoa," I rasp.

He grins and kisses the tip of my nose. "'Whoa' indeed, pretty boy. Feel free to do that any time."

Well…maybe I will.

We had simple sandwiches for lunch, but for dinner we're having a big veggie stir fry with crispy tofu. Daddy said I could keep working on my puzzle. However ,I want to help. I love following his orders and feeling useful. He makes the sauce from scratch—not from a jar or *anything*. I'm super impressed.

I notice he doesn't offer me wine at all. Not even the non-alcoholic stuff I've seen in the fridge. We still drink out of Champagne flutes, but it's some sort of refreshing sparkling apple and raspberry concoction.

No drinking. Does that mean he thinks we're ready to play this evening?

I have butterflies in my tummy as we eat at the dining room table. He's put some classical music on as well as lit some candles in an actual candelabra on the table. It's so intimate and romantic.

Luckily, he's also good at keeping me talking. Otherwise, I would probably have spent the entire meal in nervous silence. But Daddy is great at asking me questions about my life, past and present, without bringing up too many painful memories connected to my family. When I'm with him, I feel like maybe I *am* sort of interesting, after all?

And he finds all kinds of ways to make me feel important as well. Like when he produces vegan ice cream for dessert that actually tastes amazing. I've had some pretty bad ones in my time, so I tend not to bother now in case it's a waste of money. But this one is chocolate and caramel with marshmallows and jelly beans.

If I wasn't fighting with my nerves, I'd have probably had a second bowl.

As it is, I've drunk several glasses of the sparkling fruit

juice in an attempt to keep my teeth free from bits in case more kissing is on the cards. But then that means I need to pee, so I excuse myself to do that, then am able to check my reflection in the mirror anyway.

Is this it? Am I ready? I'm going home tomorrow, so if anything's going to happen, I figure it has to be tonight.

I send a silent prayer up to whoever might be listening that it's not a complete disaster, then head back downstairs.

LUKE

"I HAVE AN IDEA," DADDY SAYS TO ME WHEN I COME BACK downstairs. He takes my hand and leads me from the dining room. I regard him with wide eyes as we head back up the stairs, the way I just came.

Expect this time, we're going towards the bedroom.

I gulp.

Am I ready for that yet?

He chuckles, but it's not mean. "Don't worry," he assures me as we step through the doorway. "I won't make you run before you can crawl. However, I thought there might be something in here that could help us play."

I like the idea of playing. Daddy would be in charge, and he'd make me feel good. At least that's what I hope. I remind myself that I'd promised to try anything this weekend. I'm tired of being afraid.

"Okay, Daddy," I say quietly. "I'll do what you say."

"Good boy," he says, and my heart melts like warm chocolate.

He's been good about not touching me unexpectedly. I still feel so ashamed about the wine on the couch, but he was very clear that it wasn't a problem and he'd fix it. So as he places his hand on the small of my back, I take a breath and manage not to freak out. It's so hard for me, though.

He moves us to a drawer, opening it to reveal several sets of pyjamas.

He rests his finger on one silky-looking set in dark blue. "I want you to put these on," he says to me, looking me in the eye. "They're your size. You can change in the en suite."

He juts his head towards the bathroom behind us, then hands me the pyjamas.

I bite my lip. "Okay, Daddy."

I'm not sure what his plan is, but I quite like the idea of changing into some new comfy PJs. I offer him a smile, then go into the bathroom and close the door behind me. It's funny to me that this is just the en suite. It's bigger than the bathroom all three of us share at home.

Quick as I can, I strip out of my new clothes and leave them folded neatly in a pile on the loo seat. I look at myself naked in the mirror for a second, wondering what it is he sees. I'm smaller than both Sam and Callum, with a soft tummy and not much body hair. I used to worry I was too boyish, but when I discovered I could in fact *be a boy* with kink, it bothered me less.

I realise I've got lost in thought. I don't want to keep Daddy waiting, though, and I don't need to be worrying about this now anyway. He's not asked me to go back to him naked.

I hurriedly pull the jammies on, marvelling again at how well the clothes he's bought for me fit. Wow, the silk feels *incredible* against my skin. It makes me all tingly and shivery. I love it.

Conscious of how much time I've wasted already, I take a deep breath, collect up my clothes and ease the door back open, making sure to turn off the light. It's pretty dark in the bedroom as well, but I can just about see that Daddy is reclining on the bed, propped up against the pillows. I'd half expected him to be naked or in his T-shirt and briefs again, but he's still in his shirt and trousers.

My knee-jerk reaction is relief, but then that makes me cross with myself.

Don't I *want* to lose my virginity, for heaven's sake?

Daddy smiles at the sight of me, though, dragging me away from my thoughts. Pleasing him feels *so* good. "Pretty boy," he murmurs, patting the bed beside him. "Come snuggle with Daddy."

I look down at my clothes before deciding to discard them on the dressing table in front of the mirror. I look back at Daddy, who nods at me. Good. I made the right choice to put them down.

Slowly, I approach the bed. I have a feeling that this is going to be different from last night. It also won't be like cuddling with Sam and Callum. For a crazy second, I really, *really* wish they were here with me. But that's ridiculous. Some things I just have to do by myself.

I sit on the edge of the bed, but he pats the pillow beside the one he's leaning against, so I lie down. "Good boy," he murmurs, making me flush with pride.

See, this is easy. I can do what Daddy says. He'll take care of me.

I curl up on my side to look at him, and he rolls over too. He's propped up on his elbow, however, so he's above me, illuminated by the small amount of light coming from the hallway. "May I touch you through your pyjamas, pretty boy?" he asks.

I blink, fighting back the moment of panic. I want to ask him where he wants to touch me. But then I realise how good it is to just let Daddy decide, so I simply nod, making myself trust him.

He reaches across the distance between us and rests a hand on my hip. He circles his thumb, and I shiver at the contact. It's nice through the silk, but my heart is on the verge of racing. It's almost like I *want* to panic.

"I'm right here, pretty boy," Daddy says in a warm murmur. "You're doing so well. It must be really hard to work out what's a good touch when you've had so many bad touches. Would it maybe help if you closed your eyes? I'll tell you if I want to move my hand."

I swallow and consider what he's suggesting. "I'll try it," I say with a nod.

"Good boy," he says.

I don't think I'll ever get tired of being called a good boy. I get a little rush every single time. The high helps me close my eyes with a smile.

I worried blocking out my sight would have made me anxious, but something weird happens. I'm able to just focus on how nice the weight of Daddy's hand feels against my hip. I like the firm pressure of his thumb rubbing through the pyjamas. It's sensual but also kind of ticklish.

"That's nice, Daddy," I whisper.

I feel the bed shift slightly. "I'm going to kiss you now, pretty boy, as I caress your side and down your thigh, okay?"

My breath catches in my throat, but it's from excitement, not fear. "Okay, Daddy," I tell him.

His mouth claims mine with a passion I haven't experienced from him before. Hell, from *anyone* before. He pushes his tongue through my lips, licking his way into my mouth. He tastes warm and sweet from the ice cream. I kiss him back with more confidence than I've ever felt with anyone else, all whilst keeping my eyes shut like he told me to do.

I lose myself for a few moments until I become aware of his hand travelling up and down my side. The panic is almost like a ghost now. Because I can't *see* someone's touching me, my brain isn't automatically making the bad connections. I don't feel scared.

It's incredible.

In the darkness there's just Daddy's touch, his scent, and his gruff moans of pleasure.

I'm doing that. This ridiculously hot man is being turned on by little old *me*. It's a pretty intoxicating feeling.

I'm not sure I'm even aware when I roll my hips, seeking more friction between our bodies. But when the silk brushes against my sensitive, thickening cock, I can't help but gasp right into his mouth.

That feels fucking amazing.

Daddy laughs at me, but it's not an unkind sound. "Does that feel good, pretty boy?" he asks teasingly.

I nod, brushing my nose against his cheek. "Oh my god, so good."

"I thought it might," he mumbles against my lips. "How would you feel about Daddy trying to touch your cock through the pyjamas? Do you think that could feel nice?"

My breath hitches and my heart thumps in my chest. It's like my head is still trying to panic, but my body really, *really* likes the idea of him doing that.

"Uh, yeah," I manage to utter. "That could feel nice. We can try."

"Good boy," he says, still caressing my side. "Remind me. What are your colours?"

"Green, yellow, and red," I say automatically.

"Good boy," he repeats, sending a shiver down my spine. I love being good so much. "And your safeword?"

"Squish."

"Good boy. What colour are you now?"

"Green," I tell him breathlessly.

Then he slides his hand from my hip, over my tummy,

then strokes my cock.

"Fuck!" I cry out, my eyes flying open in shock. Holy hell, that feels *amazing*. Why haven't I tried this before? The silk adds something so incredible against my sensitive skin.

I'm panting and trying to push my cock back into his hand, but Daddy stills my shoulders and makes me look into his eyes. "What's your colour, pretty boy?"

"Green," I whisper, aware I sound desperate, but I don't care. Right now, I'll do anything for him to touch me like that again. "So green, I promise, Daddy."

He chuckles warmly. "That's my good boy. Would you like some help keeping your eyes closed? I have a sleep mask you can wear if you want."

I'm still trying to catch my breath, but I make myself calm down and consider what he's saying. Closing my eyes did feel really amazing as it made me focus on only the good touch and not anticipate a bad touch. It took so much stress away from me. I worry what will happen if I change my mind, but Daddy hasn't restrained my hands in case I feel the need to take it off, and I also have my colours and safeword. I can stop any time if something feels wrong.

"I'd like to try that, please, Daddy."

He smiles at me and kisses the corner of my mouth sweetly. "That's very brave of you, pretty boy. Thank you for trusting me."

Like the pyjamas, the eye mask is silky. It feels plush like a little pillow as Daddy settles it on my face. Even the elastic around my head is covered with the soft material.

Daddy holds my hand and puts his other one on my hip again. "I'm right here, pretty boy. You look extremely gorgeous right now. How does that feel?"

I like the pressure of the mask on my eyelids, and also the way his breath is ghosting over my lips and skin. "Green," I tell him.

"Amazing. Let me know if anything changes. Otherwise, you just lie back and relax."

I gasp as he kisses my neck and caresses my cock again. I'm pretty hard, but as he glides his fingers up and down my shaft, my erection thickens even more, and I start leaking. I almost worry about making a mess of the nice pyjamas, but it's not my job to worry. If Daddy's not concerned, then I don't need to be either.

I just need to chill out and enjoy myself.

Except, I don't feel like being that passive. It surprises me, but I pretty quickly realise that I *want* to reach out and run my hands over Daddy's chest and shoulders. With the blindfold on, I focus extra hard on the softness of his shirt, the hardness of his muscles, and the wiry texture of his short beard on his chin.

My body feels amazing all over, not just my erection in his hand. Daddy's hand is firm in mine. The silk against my skin as it touches the bed and parts of his body light me up like fireworks. There's absolutely none of that fear I had before. All the bad feelings have melted away. I feel like I'm flying through the night sky like an angel.

"Daddy," I whimper between kisses. "Daddy…please…"

"What do you need, pretty boy?" he asks.

"More."

I don't really know what I mean, but Daddy does, naturally. It's effortless as he moves his hand and slips it under the waistband of the pyjamas.

And then he's actually touching my cock.

Holy fuck, it's *so good.* Even better than when Callum did it, and I thought that was pretty epic. His hand is big and strong, and it's just such a thrill to realise that it's not me touching myself. With the help of the eye mask, I'm hyper aware of every stroke along my shaft, of the way he slides his thumb over my slit, of the way he squeezes and twists with his palm. Fuck me sideways, I really hoped that being with a Daddy would mean more experience, and I can feel that now.

Daddy Wolf knows what the hell he's doing.

I'm babbling nonsense, whining and gasping for air as my climax builds. But I don't know if that's what I'm supposed to do. "Daddy, I'm going to…I'm close…*urgh.*"

"It's okay, pretty boy," he says as he holds me tightly to his chest, his hand flying over my cock. "Let go. It's okay. I've got you."

It takes me only seconds after that. I've never felt an orgasm like it. It's as if I shatter into a million pieces, and yet Daddy is right there, holding me together.

I shiver and shake and choke my way through it, clinging to his shoulders for dear life.

Then suddenly, it's like I can breathe again, and I'm gulping down air. I don't even realise I'm fumbling trying to take the mask off until Daddy does it for me. I blink like a newborn. The room seems so much brighter than it did before. I look around to remind myself where I am, but then I launch at Daddy, kissing him like the world's about to end.

He reciprocates with equal fervour, clutching at my hair and digging his fingers into my back. It feels so raw and feral even though we're both still almost completely clothed.

But I need more.

It doesn't matter that I'm still shaking from my orgasm. I'm as high as a kite and I've got no intention of coming back down to Earth anytime soon.

"Please, Daddy, *please*," I moan as my fingers scramble over his shirt buttons. But then he grabs my hands and stills me, looking into my eyes.

"Pretty boy, what do you want?"

My mouth opens and closes a couple of times, the words suddenly stuck in my throat. However, if I'm brave enough to want it, then I have to be brave enough to say it out loud.

"I want you inside me," I manage to whisper.

My words are quiet, but it feels monumental to me, especially as I don't flinch or look away from Daddy's gaze. I hold it, feeling brazen. My heart is pounding in my chest, and I'm trembling, covered in sweat, but for once in my life I know what I want, and I refuse to be too afraid to reach out and take it.

Daddy drops my hands to cup either side of my face and kisses me passionately. "Good boy," he tells me several times. "I'm so proud of you. Daddy's going to take such good care of you. Just tell me if anything doesn't feel good, okay?"

I nod, but then he's undoing the buttons on my pyjama top and—*oh wow*—I guess we're getting naked now.

But rather than be afraid, my hands fly up to help him, not just with my shirt, but with his. Then we kick off our bottoms, and then...

Holy *fuck*. He's laying his entire body over mine, pinning me down. It's so delicious. So much skin on skin. And his thick, hard cock is digging into my hip as he grinds down.

His kisses are hot and possessive, and I kind of just want to stay like this. But then he moves away from me, reaching for the drawer...

Oh, shit. He's got a bottle of lube.

Before I can start to overthink, he's back kissing me. I hear the bottle opening and feel him moving around me. "This is going to feel cold, baby boy," he says. I note that he called me 'baby' instead of 'pretty', and maybe that's because he's warning me of a bad touch and wants to be extra protective.

"Okay," I say to let him know I understand.

"It will warm up, though," he promises. "And when I push my fingers inside you, it's going to burn and feel strange. But I'll give you plenty of time to get used to it."

"Okay, Daddy," I tell him. "I'm ready."

He's right. It is bloody cold, and I jerk in surprise. But because I knew it was coming, I can grit my teeth and start to relax. That allows me to appreciate that for the first time in my life, someone else is touching my most intimate area.

And it's *amazing*.

He's kissing me again as he strokes his slippery fingers against my puckered hole. Like he's coaxing a frightened animal out from its burrow. I suppose, in a way, he is. Then he takes his middle digit and starts to push.

I've fingered myself before, but it's different when it's someone else doing it, and Daddy's hands are definitely bigger than mine. Still, it actually feels fine.

It's when he tries two digits that I let out a little hiss. But he's true to his word and goes slowly, and before long he's added a third. All the while he keeps kissing me and whispering sweet nothings about how good and gorgeous I am. He uses his other hand to fondle my dick, gradually getting me hard again. My whole world is him, and it's beyond amazing.

It gives me the confidence to drop my hand down his stomach, feeling the rippled planes of his torso and the ticklish hair that grows coarser and thicker below his belly button. "Can I, Daddy?" I whisper.

"Of course, pretty boy. I'm all yours."

His shaft is like velvet over steel and throbbingly hot in my hand. He moans as I tentatively caress it, getting used to the feel of it against my palm. I wonder what it would be like to suck it. I've never given a blow job before. The thought of it has always intimidated me, but I feel like—no, I *know*—that Daddy would be patient and careful with me whilst I explored.

I don't think there's going to be time for that tonight, though. We're on a mission.

Daddy slows his movements before easing his fingers out

from within me. "I think you're ready for me now, sweetheart," he says, nuzzling his nose against my cheek. "It will be more comfortable if you're on all fours, but how does that make you feel?"

I shake my head. "No, Daddy," I say quickly. "I want to see you. Can I be on my back?"

"Of course, pretty boy," he tells me before giving me a heart-melting kiss. "I want to see you, too. Wait one second."

He wipes his fingers on a tissue from the box by the bed before gently rolling me over so I'm on my back like I wanted. Then he gets one of the pillows that isn't under my head, gets me to lift my hips, then slips it under, elevating my pelvis. Once he's certain I'm comfortable, he gets the tube of lubricant again, drizzling another load between my crack before slathering a good amount along his shaft.

"You're going to want to keep your knees up, pretty boy," he tells me, using his palms to push them back. "You can either hold them or wrap your legs around my waist— whatever feels best for you."

I nod, understanding. For now, I hold them as close to my chest as I can, watching in fascination as he positions himself between my legs, angling his cock at my stretched-out hole.

Holy fucking *shit*. This is really happening.

As if reading my thoughts, he pauses as he rests the tip against my entrance, then reaches out with his dry hand to caress the side of my face. "Everything still all right, beautiful?"

I nod eagerly. I'd be lying if I said I wasn't slightly nervous as I'm about to go through something brand new. But what is there really to be afraid of? I know Daddy will take good care of me. He's experienced and knows what's best. He won't judge me. He said we'll go slow.

"I'm ready," I tell him.

He leans down to capture my mouth, and in that moment,

I feel truly loved. This might not be for more than one night, but it's not a game or make-believe.

It's real.

"Deep breath in," he murmurs to me. "Then breathe out and relax."

I do as he says, and as I exhale, he pushes forwards, breaching my tight ring of muscle.

Even with all the stretching, it's a squeeze. I try my best to relax and let him in, but it takes a lot of effort. He warned me it would burn, and it does, but he keeps kissing me and stroking my cock, distracting me as he demands more and more of my hole.

Somewhere along the way, the burning starts to feel kind of pleasant. And the *fullness.* I've never experienced anything like it in my life. It's so invasive, but in a way that makes me feel claimed and protected and whole.

When it seems like he's as far inside me as he's going to fit, I shift around a bit to see how I feel. It's *weird,* I can't deny, but I kind of love it. I definitely love how our bodies feel amazing pressed together, slick with perspiration. We're both panting between kisses, and the way Daddy is staring at me, it's like I'm the most precious thing in the world to him.

I try what he said and wrap my legs around his waist, enjoying how that makes it feel as though he's deeper inside me. And then—wordlessly—he moves.

It's just one thrust, but the end of his cock pushes against the back of my insides, and it's like a million kilowatts light up the room.

"*Oh my god!*" I shriek as I cling to him.

I don't know what the hell that was, but I need him to do it again.

He chuckles and nips at my earlobe. "Did you like that, then, pretty boy?"

I nod my head against his and gasp for air. Belatedly, I

realise that must have been my prostate. There's a massive difference between knowing there's a bundle of nerves up your arse, and having a big cock hit it, apparently.

"Holy fuck, I love it. More, Daddy, *please*."

"Your wish is my command, gorgeous boy."

He kisses me then starts to move his hips in a regular rhythm, and I can't describe how amazing it is. My thoughts have gone to jelly for anything other than the way my Daddy is fucking me.

I can't believe I almost ran away from this. This is one of the best things that's ever happened in my entire *life*. I want this every day! Holy *shit!*

"Good boy," Daddy gasps as he digs his fingers into my back. "Good boy. So good for Daddy."

"Please, please, please." I'm gibbering.

I'm not really sure what I'm asking for. Please don't stop. Please keep going. Please don't let go.

Please love me.

I know it's nonsense, but it feels so real to me in the moment. But then all thoughts cease completely when Daddy reaches between us and takes my cock in hand for the second time that evening.

There's no warning. It's like my orgasm explodes like a bomb. I shatter apart again as I scream, coming all over myself as I hold on to Daddy's shoulders for dear life. He keeps moving his hand and thrusting inside me, like he's trying to wring every last drop of pleasure from my body.

And then he arches his back, and I can feel his cock throbbing inside me as he releases. I'm dizzy and shaky, my mouth is dry, and my arse is already sore. But I also feel perfect in a way that wouldn't have seemed possible to me before today.

I feel complete. Safe. Exhilarated.

And it's all because of Daddy.

2 5

SAM

The flat is immaculate.

I've hoovered the floor, dusted every surface, scrubbed the toilet, and even wiped down the inside of the bloody windows. Right now, I'm elbow deep in the washing up. I'm not just cleaning what we've used recently. I've got out all the eggcups, baking trays, and even the gravy boat that hasn't been used since Christmas.

It's slightly possible that I need a distraction.

"I just want it to be nice for when Luke returns," I've said at least three times to Callum, who's chosen to hide himself away in his room rather than deal with my fit of madness.

I don't blame him.

It's difficult to pinpoint exactly what it is that's making me this crazy. My thoughts feel like soup. But I figured when I came home from my time with Daddy that would be the most intense period for me, when I'd be missing him the most.

But everything has changed so much since then, and my longing for him isn't dissipating. If anything, it's getting stronger.

The conversation I had with Callum two days ago is playing over and over in my mind. I still feel like we both did then in the kitchen. I'm not jealous of him spending time with Daddy, not at all. In fact, I'm over the moon that he had just a deep and meaningful time with him as I did.

But it's clear that both of us have caught feels, and if *we* have, I'm not sure Luke ever stood a chance. I guess we'll find out soon enough. He's been keeping us apprised of his journey home, and his ETA is imminent.

I was a fool. I was so worried about the physical implications we would all face losing our virginity—like would it hurt or whatever—and whether or not Daddy Wolf would treat us kindly or whether we'd be left feeling cheap and used.

The idea that we'd be left heartbroken never crossed my mind.

I've tried to convince myself that if the dynamic between us three besties is changing, then that could perhaps fill the void. I'm a little nervous that we're crossing a line that we can't uncross, but I'm starting to feel like life is too short, and why the hell shouldn't we try?

But…that only solves part of the problem, for me anyway. Yes, the idea of being intimate with my best friends even more than we already have gives me a thrill. But as much as I adore them, I *know* they'll end up turning to me for Daddying, and that's not what I want at all. In fact, I'm certain *that* would be what would damage our relationship beyond measure, and that's inconceivable to me.

So I'd rather we didn't do anything at all than risk that.

Perhaps I'm just in the weeds. In a couple of weeks, this won't seem so bad. I'm just consumed with thoughts of Daddy, as I know Luke is with him right now.

Or…he was. See? Now it's in the past for all of us. Once

I'm not constantly being reminded of Daddy's existence, I'm sure these aching pangs will fade.

I hear Luke's key in the door and splash half the washing-up water all over myself. I blink droplets from my eyes for a second, then hurriedly grab a tea towel to mop myself down.

"Hey?" Luke calls out tentatively.

Callum beats me to it. Before I can get my arse out of the kitchen, there are several banging, sliding, and crashing noises, followed by Luke's pitiable squeak. I rush out to find him enveloped by Callum's embrace as he rocks them back and forth, slowly rotating on the spot like a drunken ballerina in a music box.

"You're home!" Callum cries. "We missed you so much!"

I can't help but laugh fondly. You'd think Luke was back from deployment in Afghanistan, not returning from a luxury mini-break. But I don't burst Callum's bubble. I just go join in the hug. I have to admit it *does* feel good to have us all back under the same roof again. None of us has work this evening, either, so we can actually have a quality catch up.

"How was it?" I ask when we finally break apart. Luke looks tired, but happy, so that gives me hope.

He shakes his head. "Just…incredible. I'm still processing it all. It was everything I could have dreamed of. But—it wasn't perfect—that's not what I mean. It was kind of messy, actually. But that's what made it so amazing, you know? Imperfectly perfect."

Both Callum and I sigh. "Yeah," I agree. He's hit the nail on the head there.

Callum grabs his hand and drags him over to the bed, so I follow. "Can we *finally* all talk about everything now, then?" he asks, jumping on the mattress and pulling Luke with him. "No more secrets?"

"I guess so," I say with a shrug as I crawl over and join them. We end up all sat with our backs against the pillows, like we're watching TV, although this conversation is bound to be way more fascinating than anything we could put on the screen.

Callum claps his hands in glee. "How adorable were the alpacas?"

Both Luke and I stare at him. "What alpacas?" Luke asks.

"Don't you mean peacocks?" I ask.

Now it's their turn to stare at me. "Peacocks?" Callum practically shrieks.

"Daddy organised some kittens especially to keep me company," Luke says sadly. "I *hated* leaving them behind, but he promised me that he'd make sure they all got amazing, loving homes."

I shake my head. "It seems we all had quite different experiences, didn't we?"

"We had one thing in common, I bet," Luke says quietly, looking at me and Callum. "Daddy was just as wonderful as you promised he would be."

I hum and nod. "Yeah, that much is true."

"I miss him," says Callum in an unusually sombre tone for him.

My heart twists in my chest. I was starting to believe that I'd embellished my time with Daddy to the point where he's become this impossibly unreal larger-than-life figure. But seeing the way my best friends get misty-eyed in that moment, I think perhaps he really was that incredible.

As we talk, we discover that we each went to totally different but equally amazing sounding locations in three different parts of the country. He tailored each of our visits to us specifically, including food, entertainment, clothing that he gifted us to take home, and although we don't go into it too much, I'm sure the sex was dramatically different for us all as well.

Maybe after some terrible pink wine, we'll be brave enough to share more of those details.

For now, one thing is abundantly clear, and that's that Luke is right. Daddy managed to steal all three of our hearts in the short time we spent together.

Perhaps it's because we all know that it was just a one-time thing for all of us that none of us are getting jealous of the others. That was the condition of the deal we made with Daddy. It's not like he's going to choose one of us to see again. I'm sure that would alter how we felt quite dramatically.

As it is…we're all equal. We all got the same amount of time with him, and during that time he treated us each like we were the most important boy in the world.

I come back to my thoughts from when I was washing up. This will heal soon enough. We made a pact that we'd lose our V-cards by New Year's, but by the time the holidays roll around, I bet our memories of Daddy will be fond and the pain will have faded away.

Until then, we just have to look after each other, like we always do. Perhaps our futures will hold different Daddies of our own to take us into the next stages of our lives. But for now, it's the three little piggies.

And the love we have for each other will have to be enough.

26

JACOB

This is ridiculous.

I take another sip of red wine and scowl as I keep flipping through the profiles on my phone without even really looking at them. All these boys are perfectly fine. Delicious, actually. If I wanted to find a willing hole for my cock tonight, there are several eager candidates I could have at my home in an hour with just a click of my fingers.

But that's not what I want.

I can't have what I want.

Because I absolutely would go for some tight arse right now, but my stupid *heart* is getting in the way of a perfectly fine fuck.

I don't want an anonymous hook-up. I want my three boys back in my arms. Back in my bed. I want to see their faces light up from my praise. I want to hear their moans of ecstasy. I want to do everything to make their wildest dreams come true. I want to see Luke working on another jigsaw puzzle—a bigger one, though, because he'll have the time to complete it. I want to help Sam study. I want to see what garment Callum is bringing to life with his magic hands.

I'm unaccustomed to not getting what I want.

I bite my thumbnail, a habit I haven't indulged in for years. I resent feeling this helpless to my own bloody feelings and desires. I'm not used to being unable to fix a problem. I'm certainly not used to not being able to forget my troubles with a decent fuck or a bottle of something from my top shelf.

I dislike this feeling immensely.

Well, I might not have a boy, but I have my liquor collection at least. Perhaps I should move on to something stronger than wine so I can try and obliterate these feelings. I said goodbye to Luke yesterday, and since then I've done nothing but try and numb my pain.

I curse Harris's name. She was totally right, of course. I was looking for a boy to fill a much bigger chasm in my life than could be found in just a few days. What I need is a real relationship. I thought taking on the challenge from the little piggies would be a good bridge between that and getting away from the endless parade of sugar babies.

I didn't expect to fall for all three of them.

Urgh, this is self-indulgent nonsense. I'm not *in love*. It's just a kind of infatuation. I'm only imagining all three boys here in my penthouse, so it doesn't feel as empty.

Well...*almost* empty, now.

Especially not when Harris steps through my front door, as if I'd summoned her with my seething. She takes one look at me in yesterday's shirt, clutching my wine glass as I hunker down farther in the armchair I'm gradually becoming one with, and raises her eyebrows.

"It's that bad, is it?" she drawls.

"It's bloody worse," I cry, pointing to the pile of sleeping kittens in the basket across from my feet.

Because of course I didn't have the shelter come and pick

them up from the castle like I'd planned. Of *course* I've brought them home, telling myself that it's just until I can get them adopted, whilst I spent the whole day kitten-proofing the entire penthouse to keep them safe.

But, quite frankly, if I can't have my boys, why can't I have the kittens that remind me of them? Just for a little while until my stupid heart stops breaking. The black one is timid, like Luke. The ginger is steady and content, like Sam, and the calico is a little bit wild, like Callum.

I miss my fucking boys. Good lord, who have I become?

"Then do something about it," Harris says, heading to the sideboard and helping herself to a glass so she can pour herself some of my very expensive wine. I don't even have the strength to muster up a protest.

Not about the wine, anyway.

"Do what?" I snap, aware I'm being a git but also aware that she's as tough as nails and won't care. "We had an agreement. They weren't looking for a long-term thing, and I am. With one boy—*one*. These three are a package deal."

She sips her wine and looks down at the kittens as the ginger one yawns widely. "There are three of them," she comments, gesturing to the basket.

I frown. "Yes. They're brothers. Some arsehole left them in a bloody box by the side of the road. I'll, um, find them a home. Soon."

"And you arranged three peacocks," she muses. "And three alpacas."

"They all went back to the sanctuaries I hired them from," I say with a scoff. "Don't worry, they're not lurking in the bathroom waiting to watch you pee."

She sighs and rolls her eyes. "*Three* of each for just one boy."

I stare at her for a moment. "Yes. I can do basic maths."

"You say that, and yet here you are, all alone. One." She smirks at me and leans back in her chair.

I open and close my mouth, not entirely sure what she's getting at. "That was the deal."

"That was the deal *before* you met them and turned into this pathetic sack of feelings I see before me." She waves her hands up and down, indicating my general vicinity. "You've been utterly useless since they messaged."

"Are you saying I shouldn't have agreed to this?" I ask, getting defensive. I know I'm extremely pathetic right now, but the idea of never meeting my piggies makes my heart clench in my chest in a horribly painful way.

I'd rather be wallowing in torment right now than never having met them at all. That's a no-brainer.

But Harris sighs irritably. "I'm *saying* that you're lying to yourself, and it's annoying me. I've never seen you so dense about anything. You *like* these boys. What's stopping you from at least asking if they'd be willing to see you again?"

"That wasn't the deal," I repeat petulantly, because I can't allow myself even a little glimmer of hope that I could see them again.

I never told them that I was looking for a forever boy. It was irrelevant. Our arrangement didn't lend itself to that, and they explicitly said that wasn't what they wanted from me.

"Deals change all the time," Harris says, something dangerous dancing in her eyes. "You've made a career out of changing people's minds. As loathe as I am to admit it, you can be a charming, romantic, and thoroughly delightful motherfucker when you care about something—or someone. How do you know they haven't completely fallen in love with you and aren't waiting anxiously by the phone for your call like some eighties rom-com?"

For a few moments, I just stare at her. The idea of

reaching out to the boys and making myself vulnerable by asking for more is…unsettling. But I didn't get where I am in life by taking the easy way out. Not ever.

I swirl my wine in the glass, looking at the liquid as it swishes around. "I can't pick just one of them."

"Then don't," she cries, looking at me like I'm mad. "When have you ever been afraid to ask for what you want?" She indicates my home with all its exquisite art and furnishings imported from around the globe. "You said it yourself—they're a package deal. You're a billionaire. Would it really be so extravagant to get yourself a harem?"

Something pings in my brain akin to a lightbulb flicking on or a penny dropping.

Could I see *all three* of them again? Together? At the same time?

Luke never did elaborate on what he meant by him and Callum 'practising'. But Callum mentioned that they kissed each other all the time and often shared beds. Sam stressed how they loved each other *more* than just friends. I don't know how far it extends, but I'm certain that there's *some* degree of intimacy between them.

Would they want to share a scene together with me?

My blood is suddenly pumping in my veins. It would be crazy to think that they'd agree to something like that long-term. It's so unconventional. But just for a night? A chance to see what it would be like to love them all as one…

That has some potential.

"Are you done moping?" Harris asks.

I rub my chin. "Maybe," I concede. "I think I have a message to draft."

She swallows the last of her wine and places the glass down on a table coaster. "Then my work here is done. Don't forget to feed those cats."

I scoff as she heads towards the door. "As if I would."

I'm Daddy. I look after *everyone*. Be that three kittens...or three little piggies.

27

———

LUKE

"And that's why it's really important that we store the beer coasters alphabetically, Luke," my manager tells me like he's talking to a toddler. "Not by shape. Do you see?"

"Hmm hmm," I respond, reminding myself that I really need this job at the moment and don't have the strength to hunt for a new one.

We're in a particularly slow lull between lunchtime and evening customers at the pub right now, so my manager has taken it upon himself to inflict some extra 'training' on me. Which basically involves him moaning at me for every tiny thing I don't do to his exact specifications.

Kill me now.

No, that's not the right attitude to have. This is just temporary. I need to be grateful that I have a regular job so that I can afford the rent with my besties. I'm saving a little each month as well—it's not much, but it's something. Maybe soon I'll be able to get a part-time office job like Sam has, and then I could start volunteering at the youth LGBT charity I was telling Daddy about.

I wish I could ask his advice. So badly.

I'm actually proud of myself for how brave I was leaving the castle the day before last. I really kept my shit together. On the outside, anyway.

On the inside, I was an absolute mess. I wanted to spend a whole month there in that perfect cosy bubble with my Daddy and our kittens. We could maybe work on another puzzle (seeing as we finished the greenhouse one), but we could also go for long walks and read books and…

Life isn't a holiday, though. I'm sure Daddy would have got bored of all that very quickly. So it was probably for the best that our time was kept short. That way, I can remember it for what it was.

Perfectly imperfect.

Even if I did cry my way down half of the M4.

The nice driver, Gerard, didn't say a word about it. But he did produce a box of tissues after our first service station stop. I took them gratefully. By the time we made it back to London, I was reasonably composed again.

But it's been obvious between the three of us at home that something's not quite right.

It's not like I thought we'd break into a pillow fight the moment we stepped through the door then have an epic make-out session. But things are different now that I've wanked off with Callum and properly kissed Sam.

And then there's the fact that we're not virgins anymore.

I have to blink and force myself to tune in to what my manager is droning on about, because the temptation to relive every delicious detail of my amazing night with Daddy is *strong*. If it had to be only one time, I couldn't have asked for anything better. It was beautiful. I felt treasured and exquisite.

But it was over far too fast. And now my chest aches at the loss of that wonderful man.

Time heals all wounds, I know. Sam keeps saying to me

and Callum that everything's going to be okay, but I know they feel it, too.

We haven't opened up about the specifics of each of our sexual encounters yet, but I'm keen to. Knowing that there are still things yet to learn about Daddy is what's keeping me going right now.

Once that's done, I know the pain is going to be tough to bear. But I'm trying to live in the present.

Well, not *completely* in the present. I'm definitely wishing the time away until I can get out of this blasted pub, but that won't be for hours yet.

However, something totally unexpected does happen that breaks up my day very nicely.

Sam and Callum come rushing through the front door, looking around excitedly until they spy where I am.

"Oh, look, customers," I say cheerfully to my manager as I pretty much launch myself away from him. My besties have never been to visit me here before, so it's not like he's going to warn me off wasting time serving them. In fact, he mumbles something about tax returns that need his attention, and mercifully slinks off out back to his office.

I glance around, but the other couple of customers seem content with the drinks they're nursing, and it's too early for the kitchen to be open, so no one's going to be bugging me for food. Therefore, once the coast is definitely clear, I whirl around to my best friends and almost snap myself in half leaning over the bar to give them a hug.

"What are you doing here?" I ask. "Not that you need a reason. I'm delighted to see you. Oh! What can I get you to drink?"

"Champagne?" Callum suggests as they sit on barstools, grinning like a loon.

Sam waves a hand in front of his face, as if telling him to

be quiet. "We've got some news. Have you got a minute to talk?"

I glance over my shoulder. In theory, my manager could come back any second. But I'm allowed to be friendly with customers.

"I can if I serve you," I say. "Do you want some water?" I'm aware neither of them is made of money.

But Sam shares a look with Callum, who's practically bouncing off his seat, then he rolls his eyes and laughs. "Okay. Not Champagne, but maybe you have some terrible pink wine, Luke?"

"We have some quite nice pink wine, actually," I inform him. "Two glasses?"

"Nope," Sam says firmly. "A bottle and three glasses. You can have a sip."

The one good thing about working here is they actually don't mind us having a little tipple with customers so long as we don't get smashed. I've never done it before, but apparently, today's the day.

"What's going on?" I ask as I ring up the order on the till and charge Sam's card. We're not a particularly pricey pub, but a bottle of wine here is still three times as expensive as our corner shop, so I pull out a fiver from my pocket and insist that Sam takes it. Callum does the same. There we go. I prefer it when the three of us are equal.

Callum nudges Sam with his shoulder. "Show him," he whispers. Is it my imagination, or does emotion catch in his voice? It's not *bad* emotion, though, so I don't think we've been robbed or anything.

But now I'm really baffled as to what the hell is going on.

I watch as Sam gets his phone out of his pocket, unlocks it, then navigates to a certain screen. He hands it over for me to look at, and my breath suddenly hitches as I realise it's the Collr messenger. This is how we've been talking to Daddy.

How we *were* talking to Daddy.

No! I let out a little squeak as I realise there's a new message sent just under an hour ago.

My little piggies, it reads.

I know we had an agreement in place, and if that's how you wish to leave our time together, I respect that. However, I have a proposition for you. If you are interested, please keep reading.

The visits we had were very special to me. Each of you gave me something unique and wonderful. I know you are close, so I hope my suggestion isn't too out of turn for you. Again, if you're not interested, I respect that.

I pause. Wow. He sounds…*nervous.* Since when is Daddy nervous?

"Have you read to the end?" Callum asks impatiently. I shake my head, and he huffs. "Then what are you waiting for? Go!"

I laugh but do as I'm told.

What I propose is one final night together. The four of us. I would Daddy all three of you in a group scene. We can set as many or few ground rules as you want. But I know we could create something really beautiful. Think of it as a send-off before we all go on with our lives.

I await your response,

Daddy Wolf

I'm pretty sure my jaw is hanging open. I can't believe this is actually happening.

"Okay, *now* he's got to the end," Callum mutters into his wine glass with a smirk.

"What do you think?" Sam asks.

I stare at him a second, then cast my gaze down once more to reread the message.

Daddy wants to see us all together.

My heart is racing. Naturally, my brain wants to go into overdrive and conjure up all the reasons why this is a truly *horrible* idea. But for once, I don't want to listen to it at all.

I just want to listen to my heart.

"I think it sounds amazing," I say as I hand Sam back his phone. "I think it could be exciting…really special…the perfect way to end our time together with some ceremony."

Callum is nodding eagerly. Sam looks between us both, always the sensible one. "Do we think we'll be able to really walk away after that? For good?"

I chew my lip then gulp down half my wine glass, hoping the liquid courage will keep my anxiety from rearing its head like it's so close to doing. I'm listening to my *heart* now.

I'm not an idiot. I pretty much figured we'd all fallen hard and fast for Daddy and were kind of grieving together. I appreciate this could be throwing petrol on an open flame. But…

Oh, if there's one thing I've learned recently, it's that life is too bloody short.

"We're going to have to walk away in any case. This way, we all get to see Daddy one more time. And…" I take a deep breath and look them both in the eyes. "I think it could be something really special to share with you both. I know things are shifting between us. We might have to say goodbye to Daddy Wolf, but maybe he can show us a way the three of us can make each other happy. At least until we find different Daddies of our own."

Sam raises his eyebrows, then nods as he looks between me and Callum. "You make a compelling argument," he says seriously.

"Wow, I just wanted a gang bang, but you brought *feelings* into it," Callum quips with a snort.

Sam hits him over the back of the head, but I'm laughing. The whole thing is pretty ridiculous. I know we're trying to protect our hearts, but I think we also need to have fun with it as well.

Being with Daddy was *so* fun.

But…so was being with Callum as well. And my kiss with Sam was gorgeous.

"Have we got anything to lose?" I ask diplomatically.

They shrug. "No more than we have already," Sam says.

"So…" Callum waggles his eyebrows. "Shall we message him back? Now?"

I bite my lip as I grin. "I say yes."

"Yes," Callum agrees.

Sam hums and shakes his head. "That's three yeses, then."

He unlocks his phone again, but I shoot my hand out. "Wait!"

They both raise their eyebrows at me this time.

"Have you still got that photo of us holding our piggies?" I ask.

Sam smiles, I guess as he cottons on to what I'm suggesting. "I certainly do."

I nod. "Send that with the message," I suggest. "Tell Daddies that his little piggies can't wait to see him."

And that's exactly what we do.

28

———

JACOB

WHEN THE INTERCOM BUZZES, MY HEART LEAPS INTO MY throat like I'm a damned teenager waiting for my first-ever boyfriend to pick me up. It's ridiculous, but I long ago resigned myself to the fact that this whole situation is pretty ridiculous.

I might as well embrace the madness.

"Hello?"

Sam's voice pierces straight through my heart, but not nearly as much as seeing the live video screen of the lobby downstairs.

There my boys are. All three of them, together. They look as though they're huddled for warmth as Sam talks into the speaker.

"What's the passphrase?" I murmur on my end.

Sam leans in closer, like he's worried he'll be overheard.

As if I've let anyone in this building hurt them. They're under my protection now.

"Daddy Wolf, we're very good boys. Please let us in."

My heart flips and my cock jumps in my trousers. Well,

this is it. I've invited them into my home. For better or worse, there's no going back now.

"You are very good boys," I say, pressing the release button to grant them access. "I'm waiting for you on the top floor."

I brace my hand against the wall by the lift doors, putting the other on my hip. I take a few deep breaths, trying to mentally prepare myself for what's about to happen. But the truth is even with my extensive experience, I'm not sure I'll ever be ready.

It's not like I haven't had more than one boy in my bed before. It's *these* boys in particular that make this so exciting.

The lift dings, announcing their arrival, so I stand back with my hands behind my back and wait for the doors to open. I sent Gerard to fetch them from their flat over the river and instructed them each to pack an overnight bag. But what I'm not expecting when the doors open is for them each to be clutching their piggies that they obviously got out on the way up.

My breath hitches.

Sam is in the middle and is practically radiating protective vibes towards the other two. He even has his free hand on Luke's back. They're all looking at me with wide eyes, and I know I need to say something, but I'm just so mesmerised by the sight of all three of them side by side.

I may have been filthy rich for many years, but in this moment, I feel like I've just won the lottery.

Before the lift doors can start to close again, I step forwards, blocking their path. I reach out and caress the sides of Luke's and Callum's faces, not quite believing that they're here with me again.

"My boys," I murmur.

I pull them all against me for a heartfelt embrace, delighted when they automatically hug each other as well. It's completely natural for me to find Luke's mouth for a kiss, then Sam's, then Callum's.

"My beautiful boys."

It's going to take me a little while to wrap my head around how best to share them. For example, with just two, I could have given them a hand each to hold. The best I can do now is take Luke's hand and guide him out of the lift. I'd rather leave two together than leave one out. To my delight, Sam automatically reaches out for Callum's hand so they can walk into the entrance hall together.

I've never brought any boys home before. It always felt like crossing a line. But tonight is special.

I'm trying not to think of it as a goodbye. More like an epic finale to an incredible moment in my life that I'll never forget. It might not be possible for me to be their forever Daddy, but I'll *always* be their first Daddy, and they'll always be my three little piggies.

The only person aside from staff who is ever really in my home is Harris. I don't like that I feel nervous as I let them enter ahead of me, but at least I try not to let it show on my face.

"Whoa, Daddy!" Callum cries, looking around with his jaw unabashedly hanging open. "This is all yours?"

"It's lovely," Sam says warmly.

It's funny, but I was pretty proud of this place until quite recently. Now, I fear it looks cold and impersonal, like a hotel room or a spread in a magazine.

Well, aside from one aspect that's recently changed.

"*Ohmygod!*" Luke actually screams. For a second, I fear that he's going to burst into tears. He's close. When he turns to look at me, his eyes are shimmering. But instead, he throws his arms around me and makes a sort of keening noise. "You *kept* them."

The kittens have made a run for it, no doubt terrified by

his enthusiasm. But as Sam and Callum swivel around to get a better look, the calico comes creeping out again. He's been the boldest of the three from the start.

"Kittens?" Callum squeaks.

I shrug. What I *mean* to say is something about how it's just temporary and I'll have to find them their forever homes soon. But instead, what comes out of my mouth is, "I'm glad I did, pretty boy."

I give the three boys some time to take their shoes off and get comfortable, by which I mean determinedly make three kittens come out to say hello to them. Luckily, the cats are naturally curious, and make their own way towards the boys for a sniff.

It's by far the cutest thing that's ever happened between these four walls, and I love it.

But before long, the atmosphere starts to shift. One by one, three pairs of eyes turn my way expectantly. Good. I want my boys relaxed, but I'm also *very* eager to begin our evening together.

They've sat themselves on the floor, so that works with me on the sofa as I'm elevated above them. I've got my legs spread open and am leaning one elbow on the armrest. All I have to do is beckon with one finger, and they all come crawling to kneel at my feet.

The power I feel is *intoxicating,* but the responsibility is also looming. My mistakes with Luke hang heavy in my mind. These aren't playthings. They are my precious babies, and I must treat them with the delicacy of handling fine china.

Emotionally, I mean.

Physically, I know some of them can handle a lot more.

"Who's in charge?" I ask them.

"Daddy," they reply in a chorus that sends electricity zinging throughout my body and straight to my balls.

"Who knows best?"

"Daddy," they agree again.

"That's right. Daddy knows each of you very well. And he knows that you have different needs. Not every little piggy likes the same thing. So if I ask one of you to do something that another doesn't understand, that's okay. You don't have to worry. Everybody has their colours and their safewords that they know how to use."

They nod as they stare at me in awe.

I reach down and touch each of their sweet faces one after the other. "I can't split myself in three, but I will do my best to give you equal attention during this scene. I adore each of you the same. That's a promise."

That gets more of a reaction than I'd anticipated. Luke bites his lip. Callum nods eagerly. Sam glances between his two best friends and rubs their backs briefly.

Yes. These boys are in it together.

I was going to ask what they were comfortable with, but I decide in that moment to go with my gut. They've got their colours in case something makes them uneasy, but I really hope it won't come to that.

"Stand up and hold hands."

They do as they're told quickly. Luke takes a second to look over his shoulder at the kittens and whisper, "Bye."

I move around them, placing a hand each on Luke's and Callum's back before kissing the top of Sam's head. I love how he's always in the middle of them both.

"All right, this way, little piggies."

I gently guide them to my bedroom. I always thought it was a bit ridiculous that I had a super king-sized bed all to myself, but now I'm confident that it will just about fit the four of us.

I've already prepared for their arrival with clean sheets and the lighting set up just how I want it. Low and romantic, but still more than enough illumination for us all to see. I think it's very important that everyone remains fully present in the moment.

I haven't prepared any toys or equipment. I'm pretty certain having the four of us together will be enough kink in itself.

Time to test that theory.

I leave them standing as I go and sit in the corner of the room in the armchair I had delivered especially for this purpose. I'm not taking three boys to bed and missing out on the opportunity for a voyeur's perch. They watch me as I lean back and rest one ankle on the opposite knee.

"Kiss," is all I say.

They're still holding hands, and they all look between themselves. This is the first real test. If this doesn't work, I'll abandon everything.

But it's my darling, delicate Luke who tilts his head and exhales as he looks at Sam. Then he lets go of Sam's hand to cup his face, and kisses him with such passion I can feel the true love simmering below it. He's still got hold of Callum's hand, and then turns to kiss him with the same fervour.

I'm not sure what happens, but then Sam joins them, and it's a messy three-way embrace that makes my heart pound in my chest and my dick jump in my underwear.

There's no doubt in my mind that these boys are ready.

"Stop, my darlings," I say quietly, unmoving.

A thrill shoots up my spine as they obey immediately. Good. They know that Daddy knows best. I won't steer them wrong.

I give them my next command. "Undress each other, please."

Luke's breath hitches, and he turns to look at Sam. But Callum grins and lunges for Luke's T-shirt, pulling it over his head. "See, it's easy," he says to them.

Luke looks from him to Sam, then tentatively reaches up to begin tackling the buttons on Sam's shirt. I thought I'd have to reprimand at least one of them for attempting to remove something from themselves, but they're remarkably good at remembering my simple instruction.

I resist the urge to groan or adjust myself where I'm sitting. I don't want to disturb them. It's like I'm watching my own personal erotic nature documentary. I love how they giggle and smile at each another as one by one the clothes all come off.

Except for their underwear.

When they've each only got the one item of clothing left on, they pause and regard one another. There's a beat where I wonder if I've going to have to intervene, but then Callum's the one to move. Sam may be the caretaker, but it's becoming clear that Callum is the most sexually adventurous of them by far.

He sinks to his knees, running his hands down Luke's sides before holding his hips. "Can I?"

Luke's breathing heavily. He looks at Sam and then me, but I'm just a spectator here. I need to see how they handle this by themselves before we start sticking things recklessly in holes.

Sam surprises me. He also drops to his knees, and Callum moves his hand wordlessly so they can both take hold of the top of Luke's briefs. Luke pants as he looks down at them, touching the sides of their faces. Then he nods.

Carefully, they strip him naked. He sways a little on the spot as he steps out of his underwear, but aside from that, he doesn't move. He certainly doesn't flinch or try and cover himself.

"Your turn, Sam," Callum says excitedly. Yes, he's definitely taking charge, not Sam. That's interesting.

I think we can use that for a little kink later, but I'll let them finish this task first.

Sam nods and gets to his feet. Then it's as if Luke comes back to life. He gives out a little laugh as he drops to his knees beside Callum, and they divest Sam of his last item of clothing quicker.

Callum practically springs to his feet and jams his fists proudly on his hips, grinning as the other two take his briefs off him. Rather than wait for them to stand again, he drops back to the floor, grabbing their hands and shaking them excitedly.

They're all pretty hard already. It's like having to watch a delicious meal be slowly served, knowing that I can't have a bite until the very end.

But I can certainly inhale the tantalising scent.

"Come here to Daddy, little piggies," I growl. "Walk on your knees. I want to see your gorgeous cocks on display."

They don't have to move far, but their erections sway fantastically as they come to me. I'm tempted to have them lie on their backs on the bed and just switch between them, sucking them off. But that's not the power dynamic I'm looking for tonight.

I *almost* think 'maybe next time', but I just shut that down. It's best not to go there.

There's only tonight.

Callum is in the middle for a change, but that's good. It's time to introduce a new dynamic.

"We love our naughty boy, don't we?" I ask the others as I stroke my fingers under his chin. "Even when he's being a bossy little slut."

Sam's head snaps towards me, his eyes wide with horror. But Luke regards Callum thoughtfully, tilting his head. Callum pants, fixated on me, a blush creeping onto his cheeks and across his chest.

I tut loudly. "I saw you looking at those tasty cocks," I say with a laugh. "You can't wait to suck them, can you?"

"I'm sorry, Daddy," Callum whimpers. "I'm so bad."

"You are, but it's a good job that Daddy wants to see some filthy cock-sucking." I switch my gaze to Luke and caress the side of his face. "Will you be good for Daddy, pretty boy?"

"Yes, yes," he says with a nod.

"Of course you will," I say proudly. "All you have to do is stand up. You can touch our naughty boy with your hands and make as much noise as you like. But you must stay standing, okay?"

"Yes, Daddy." He hurriedly gets to his feet, his arms by his sides, then takes a couple of steps backwards. "Is this okay?"

"Perfect," I tell him warmly. "I'm going to ask our naughty boy to touch you now. Is that okay, or would you like a blindfold?"

Luke looks around at all of us. "No. I want to see."

My heart swells with pride. "Good boy. You let me know if that changes."

"I will," he promises.

I turn my attention back to Sam. "Now big boy, come and sit on Daddy's lap. We're going to watch this bad, dirty boy swallow all that delicious cock down his throat until he chokes."

Callum bites his lip and looks back at Luke. But he doesn't move yet. Good boy.

Sam is hesitant, however. "Daddy?" he says uncertainly from where he's still kneeling on the floor.

I arch an eyebrow at him. "Do I have to ask you twice, sweetheart? I know you're a good boy."

He glances at Callum, but when Callum grins and nods at him, that seems to give him some permission he needed. I know I told him back in the living room to trust me, but his protectiveness and loyalty are warring within him. I can't really blame him. It's actually very endearing. But at the end of the day, there's only one person in charge of this scene, and that's me.

"I'm sorry, Daddy," he says as he gets up and settles across my lap. He hugs my neck and looks questioningly at me.

"This is what makes our naughty boy happy," I murmur, brushing my fingers along his stubbly chin. "I promise it will be okay. Daddy knows what he's doing."

Sam bites his lip and looks down at Callum.

I take the opportunity to keep the scene going, and scoff down at him as well. "What are you waiting for, cum bucket? Crawl over there and do your job. It's all you're good for."

"It's okay, Sam," Luke says breathlessly. "I want it. I think Callum will be really good at it."

I wonder if that's going to break into Callum's subspace, but he pretty much spins on his knees and scrambles over to his friend. He runs his hands up Luke's legs then takes the base of his cock in hand, wrapping his lips over the shaft and putting on a show.

"Good boys," I tell them. "So pretty for Daddy."

I glance at Sam again, who finally nods at me. "Okay, Daddy," he says quietly. "I think I understand."

"Good boy." I slip my hand around his cock, making him jump and moan. "Let's watch the performance together. Isn't it hot?"

We turn our heads. Luke is trembling, doing his best to stay on his feet as Callum uses all his tricks to make him come undone. Luke's got one hand on Callum's head and the other on his shoulder, using that to prop himself up. I stroke Sam's length, loving the way he shivers against me.

I don't want anyone to come yet, though. "Enough, greedy boy. Stop." He pops off Luke's cock, making our pretty boy cry out and screw his eyes shut.

Good. If he was close, I intervened just in time.

I turn to the boy in my lap. "Are you ready to play, big boy?"

He nods eagerly. Excellent.

"Naughty boy," I bark. "Lie on your back on the bed like a good little slut."

It's almost comical how fast he scrambles up there, leaving Luke standing. I encourage Sam to get to his feet, freeing me from the armchair, and I lead him by the hand over to where Luke is.

"Can I hug you, pretty boy?"

He pants and nods. "Of course, Daddy. That's a *good* touch."

I pull him to my side, kissing his damp hair. "Thank you. Now, big boy, there's a dirty boy over there desperate to get his cock sucked. Do you want to give it a try? If you do it well, Daddy will give you a nice spanking."

Sam's eyebrows raise, and he quickly looks at Luke and Callum. But Luke immediately reaches out and grabs his hand.

"Is that a good touch?" he asks.

Sam considers him a second. "I guess it is," he says with a nervous laugh.

Luke squeezes his hand. "Then you should go have a nice time."

I'm amazed that this is the same boy who threw wine all over himself because he was so scared only a few days ago. He's flushed and breathless, but more importantly he's having *fun* playing with his friends. It's a beautiful thing to behold.

I keep him pressed to my side as we both watch Sam crawl towards Callum's red, leaking cock. Callum's got his hands under his head, looking down with a grin at the sight of his friend approaching. He nods, and tentatively, Sam reaches out to wrap his hand around the base of the shaft and cautiously slip his lips over the tip.

Callum writhes and moans. "Yes, I love it, Sam. Suck me hard."

I swallow down a snort, but it's difficult as my heart is so full of fondness for this naughty little brat. His confidence in what he wants is also helping Sam be bolder, which I also love.

I kiss Luke's temple and rub his side as we watch Sam get into a rhythm. As soon as I feel like he's getting the hang of it, I move to sit on the bed in a good position with Luke snuggled up against me. I raise my eyebrows at him, and he nods.

"Good boys," I say, but that's all the warning I give before I bring my hand down against Sam's arse. A loud clap rings through the air, but that's nothing compared to the filthy moan that Sam lets out. He stills with Callum's cock down his throat, digging his fingers into Callum's hips, making him cry out as well.

Fucking hell, that's a delicious sight.

I rub Sam's bum tenderly. "Keep going, big boy. You look absolutely perfect."

"Amazing," Luke agrees in awe.

I don't know everything. But I'm sure this is much further than any of them have gone together before. I'm not sensing kickback from any of them, however. In fact, Luke is rubbing his chest and licking his lips as he watches Sam suck off Callum and me spank Sam.

"Play with your nipples, pretty boy," I whisper in his ear after I've given Sam a few more hard slaps. "It's good that you like this."

"I love it, Daddy," he whispers back with a gasp as he gives his hardening buds a tweak.

I grin. "Would you like to get involved and play? I think it's big boy's turn to get a blow job."

Luke looks at me thoughtfully. "Could I be blindfolded for that?" he asks quietly. "Then I can feel everything better."

My heart skips a beat. "Yes, good boy," I say, overcome with pride. "Well done for asking for what you need. Of course, Daddy will sort that for you."

I move from him and run my hand over Sam's hair, encouraging him to come up for air. "That's enough, big boy," I tell him. "You were gorgeous. I want you to play with Luke now, please."

His lips are red and swollen. So delectable. "Yes, Daddy," he says, then he and Callum share such a lovely smile and kiss to end their moment together, it makes my heart ache.

Within seconds, I get Luke on his knees with a new sleep mask on because I let him take the other one home with him. I pull Sam aside before he approaches him.

"He's relying on you to take care of him," I murmur against his ear. "You need to take your juicy cock and fuck his mouth. But ask him before you start, okay?"

"Yes, Daddy," Sam says.

"I don't know if he's ever done this before," Callum says from behind us. His voice is soft, like he doesn't really want Luke to hear. My heart aches. I love how these boys look out for each other.

Okay, so this is a big deal. But…it also doesn't have to have a ton of ceremony if Luke doesn't need it.

"Pretty boy, what's your colour?" I ask.

"Green," he says.

"And what do you do if you're not happy and you can't speak?"

"I raise my hand."

I sigh happily. "Good boy."

I kiss Sam and nod for him to begin. Luke is beautifully

submissive as he lets his best friend feed him his cock, his hands resting on his thighs, whimpering as Sam thrusts his decent-sized dick down his throat.

I look over my shoulder where Callum is still reclining on the bed like that cat that caught the canary. I'm beyond proud of him for speaking up for his friend. But the scene isn't over yet.

I click my fingers at him. "Who said you could rest? Get down here and kneel by my feet."

It's almost comical how Callum twists and practically falls off the bed in his haste to get to me. He throws himself at my feet facing me, but I pull his hair and turn him so he can watch his friends.

Don't get me wrong. My cock wants to rip its way out of my trousers right now. But I can wait. Each of my boys needs their moment to shine.

But the time is coming. Soon. I know exactly how I want the rest of this scene to play out.

2 9

JACOB

WHEN I DECIDE THE BOYS HAVE HAD ENOUGH, I DON'T SAY anything. I simply stand and release Callum's hair, then move over to wrap my arms around Sam's chest. "Good boy. You can stop now. I think our pretty boy enjoyed that a lot. I hope you did, too."

"Oh, yes, Daddy," Sam says breathlessly. He looks at me as he withdraws from Luke's mouth, leaving Luke gasping for air. His lips are shiny and swollen, and spit dribbles down his chin.

I kiss Sam's cheek then crouch down to wipe Luke's face with my thumb before carefully removing the mask. "How was that, pretty boy?" I ask, giving his jaw a gentle massage.

"Holy fuck," he squeaks as he blinks. "Uh, yeah. Good, Daddy. I loved it. Oh my god."

I chuckle and hug him to me. I wonder if after tonight, these boys are going to be a *lot* more open to sucking each other off.

The pang of jealousy is sharp and hard, but it's also fast. I can nurture that tomorrow. Tonight, I still have work to do.

I place the sleeping mask on a dresser, then help Luke to

get up on wobbly legs. "Everyone stand by the end of the bed, please. Then lean over on your elbows with your palms facing up."

Callum leaps up from where he was kneeling at the end of the bed, spinning on the spot, then shoving his arse in the air. Sam and Luke take a little more time, but soon I'm faced with the most delicious array of bottoms. It looks like they're worshipping, which is funny, because that's exactly what I intend on doing.

I don't rush as I make my way to stand behind them. Sam is naturally in the middle again with Callum on the left and Luke on the right. I caress and fondle their cheeks, enjoying their pretty hums and moans. Callum tries to grind his cock against the mattress, earning himself a hard swat to his arse.

"Bad boy," I growl. "Did I say you could pleasure yourself?"

"No?" he says with a giggle, deliberately making it sound like a question. "But Daddy, I *need* to. It feels so good!"

"Do you want another smack?" I ask him, my eyebrow raised even though he can't see me.

There's a pause. "Maybe?" he replies, the sass clear in his voice.

I grin and spank the other cheek twice in quick succession, loving how he moans.

Again, the thought crosses my mind that both Sam and Callum liking spankings in different ways could make for more interesting play. Sam as pleasure and Callum as punishment. But...I won't be planning another scene, so the point is moot. I shake myself and force my thoughts to remain in the moment.

I do that by walking around the bed to my nightstand to fetch my personal lube. For each of our getaways I bought the boys new bottles. But now...well, it feels fitting to pop open this well used one for them.

"Raise up your dominant hand, please."

I must admit, I know a lot about my little piggies by now, but which hand they write with isn't something I picked up on. Sam and Callum lift their right palm slightly higher, whilst Luke raises his left. I squeeze a good dollop of lubricant onto those fingers for them each.

"You have until I take my clothes off to stretch yourselves. Then you'll be at my mercy of what I want to give you. I suggest you start now."

Luke squeaks whilst Callum laughs, but all three of them reach out and hurriedly shove at least one finger up their own arses.

My god, what a sight.

I have no intention of rushing. I don't want to hurt them. So for a little while, I just watch them, soaking up their moans and laughter.

"Daddy?" Sam pipes up.

"Yes, big boy?" I reply as I finally begin to take one of my cufflinks out.

He pauses a moment. "Can we kiss?" he asks eventually.

My heart melts. "Of course, sweetheart," I tell him.

I sort of wish I'd got them all facing each other so they'd all be able to do that again. But they don't seem unhappy as Sam leans over and first captures Luke's mouth, then turns to Callum to do the same.

By the time I've finally got my shirt off, they've all got two or three digits inside them. Excellent. I give them a little longer as I finish undressing, then I reach for where I discarded the lube and make sure I've got a good amount on my cock.

"Hands down," I instruct them.

Luke and Sam respond immediately, but Callum requires another spank to get him to comply. For that, he gets me shoving *my* two fingers inside him without warning. He yelps and wiggles in delight.

"Who do you belong to?" I ask.

"Daddy," all three say.

"Who's going to take care of you tonight?"

"Daddy." I love how that response is more emphatic.

"That's right," I say as I remove my fingers from Callum's arse. "So now I'm going to take you one by one. All you have to do is stay still and enjoy yourselves. You can make as much noise as you like. You can hold hands. You can kiss. Do you understand?"

"Yes, Daddy," they moan wantonly. There's no doubt in my mind that they're very eager for what's about to happen, and so is my poor neglected cock.

I'm sure this little play session will require a couple of top ups, so I still leave the bottle of lube close by. But for now, I angle myself and start pushing my way into Callum. He's a bit tight, but I know he'll enjoy the roughness, so I forge ahead. He cries out and gnashes his teeth, and Sam fumbles to grab his hand.

My sweet boys.

It doesn't take long before I can begin fucking in earnest. I glance over to see Sam and Luke watching us, their breathing heavy and their skin damp with perspiration. I can just imagine how their pulses are racing as they wait for their turn, the adrenaline spiking in their system.

I feel like a king, and for a short while, I'm truly able to forget that this is all just temporary.

All three boys accept me beautifully. I take more time entering Sam and Luke, but once I'm in, I ram them hard, bringing myself to the brink before moving on to the next. I'm not normally a fan of edging myself, but the need to take each of these boys equally drives me forwards.

By the time I ease out of Luke, they're all a total mess,

grinding against the bed even though I didn't say they could, biting their lips, whimpering, and generally unravelling. For a brief second, I consider stretching this out even more, but that wouldn't be right. We said one scene, and it's time for this one to come to its natural conclusion.

I wipe my brow with the back of my hand and step backwards. "Turn and face me on your knees, little piggies," I say, surprisingly breathless. It's not just the physical exertion, I know. My heart is pounding in my chest from the emotion of it all as well.

This time, they're all much slower and shakier as they follow my instruction. They huddle together in a group, their shoulders touching as they look up at me with wide eyes. They all have spiky lashes, swollen lips, and hard, leaking cocks.

It's a mental image I will treasure for as long as live.

I give my length a few leisurely strokes as I catch my breath, looking down on my boys. My harem, as Harris called them. "Touch yourselves," I rasp as I start to pick up my own pace. "My gorgeous boys. Show Daddy how good and pretty you are. You can come whenever you like. Make sure you enjoy it."

There's a lot of whimpering and moaning that accompanies the delicious sounds of skin slapping against skin. The air stinks of musk and the artificial tang of lube. I take it deep into my lungs, secure in the knowledge that this is all mine. I own it. I created it. I control it.

Callum is the first to spill all over his hand, gnashing his teeth and crying out. I'm so fucking close, but I force myself to hold on. I have to see this through.

Mercifully, it's not long before Luke comes, his eyes squeezed shut. Then it's just Sam left.

"Good boy," I murmur, reaching clumsily out with my

free hand to touch his face. He gasps as he looks into my eyes. "Good boy. I've got you. You can let go."

But then something happens that threatens to break my heart, probably into three pieces as that seems to be the only number I care about these days.

Sam is the boy who takes care of everyone else. Who just needs a little extra TLC to let go and allow himself to be cared for, just for once. I don't know how much Luke and Callum are aware of this, but regardless, they rest the sides of their heads against Sam's shoulders, hugging against his side, showing him that they are there for him, too.

A sob escapes his chest as a tear tumbles down his cheek. Then finally his orgasm hits, making him spill all over his hand.

My own fist is flying over my cock as he gasps his way through his climax. I let go, dropping my head back with a bellow, but managing to keep my eyes on my boys as I start to spurt.

They hardly flinch at all at I paint them with my cum, claiming them with powerful ropes of cream that hit their bodies and faces. I feel like a caveman banging my chest.

I don't care who the fuck comes after me. These boys were mine first, and they'll *always* be mine in one way or another. I'm inside them, all over them. I'm their Daddy.

Forever.

30

SAM

I know Daddy told us all to pack overnight bags, but there was still a part of me that expected him to ask us to leave as soon as we all came down from our orgasms.

The first thing I notice when I blink the stars from my eyes is how absolutely magnificent he is towering above us with his cock in his hand as he milks the last of his cum from his balls. I wonder if I should feel dirty or ashamed that he's jizzed all over me and my best friends, then I decide I couldn't care less what I'm 'supposed' to feel.

I just know that I'm content to my bones and definitely in love.

I'm in love with my best friends. That's not such a shock, however the nature of that love has certainly changed. If it hadn't before we all sucked each other off, it absolutely has now.

But I also know I love Daddy. Seeing him tend to all three of us differently showed me just how emotionally intelligent he is. He's deeply in tune with all our needs, effortlessly switching between us to lean into what we desire most.

He proves that further by dropping to his knees and

hugging Callum first. "Good boy. Such a good boy. Are you all right?"

I won't lie. Seeing Callum's kink come into play was uncomfortable for me, but I eventually sort of got my head around it. He's never mentioned anything like that to us before, but I guess it ties in with being a brat in some way.

All I care about is that he clings to Daddy and nods. "I'm fine, Daddy," he says with conviction. "That wasn't as intense as last time, but it was still fun." He lifts his head and smiles at me and Luke. "I loved sharing it with my besties."

Now that I do understand. Knowing that Daddy spanked me in front of them was fucking exhilarating. I feel like I shared a part of me that's so secret and special. It's freeing and humbling and a bunch of other things I haven't unravelled yet. I hope that's how Callum feels, and Luke as well after asking to be blindfolded. We never did confess the most intimate details of our time alone with Daddy, but I get the sense that we all got a glimpse of the others' experiences tonight.

"My boys, my boys," Daddy mumbles as he hugs all three of us to him, rubbing our backs and kissing wherever his lips can find. "So perfect for your Daddy. So beautiful."

We stay on the floor a little longer until I unfortunately shiver and break the moment. That's when I think Daddy might send us on our way.

Of course he doesn't. Once we've all got some composure back, he leads us to his massive bathroom and sits us on the floor before dashing off. Within moments, he's back with three cartons of apple juice that he pierces the straws of for us before handing them to us. Then he gets the awesome walk-in shower running hot.

I'm pretty body-confident, but I've never just casually hung around other guys naked. However, I have to say in that moment it's hardly an issue that crosses my mind. I feel so at home in my own skin and completely at ease with these men I love. I know Daddy will be gone soon, but I feel like he's given us a gift to share between us three. Something we can take away and cherish forever.

Once we've drunk our juice, Daddy guides us into the shower. We can't quite all fit, but he rotates us and washes us down one by one before giving himself the fastest rinse. I love that we all smell of the same hair and body gel. It's like a pine forest, and I breath it deeply into my lungs.

He takes his time to dry us off, and then dresses us in our pyjamas from our bags. And I literally mean *dress*. He holds out the bottoms for us to step into and pulls the tops over our heads or—in Luke's case with his fancy new silk pair—does up all the buttons.

Once he has his own briefs and T-shirt on, he herds us like a sheepdog into the bed, pulling up the covers. "I'll be back in a second," he tells us. "I have to check on the kittens before we turn in for the night."

Luke gives a little whimper that echoes my own feelings. "Thank you, Daddy," I say. I'm not as attached to the tiny creatures as Luke is yet, but I love that Daddy hasn't forgotten them.

I promise myself that I'm going to try and stay awake until he returns. I'm vaguely aware of him turning off various lights and appliances, but when I hear him murmuring nonsense to our kitten friends, I can't help but let my eyelids drop with a big smile on my face.

SAYING GOODBYE IS AWFUL.

Just awful.

And not because it's tearful and messy. But because it's not.

I can tell Luke and Callum are putting on brave faces like I am, acting cheerful during breakfast like everything's fine and it's just an ordinary day. Daddy is nice, of course, but it's like a glass wall has come down between us and him.

It all feels fake, and I hate it, because absolutely nothing has felt fake until this point. But there's nothing I can do about it. I guess he's done with us now. It's the end of the deal.

We collect up our bags and stuffed piggies and say goodbye to the kittens. Luke almost loses it then. He bites his lip, and I can see him swallowing down tears as he pets each of them twice, telling them that he loves them and that he hopes they find wonderful homes. I have to admit I've got a lump in my throat as well as I cradle the black one to my chest. These little fellows are quite the heartbreakers.

It's easier to focus on them than it is Daddy, though. Our experiment has come to an end. We got a fantastic extra night together that none of us bargained on. We should be grateful.

This arrangement was never designed to last.

But I feel numb as I hug him by the private lift. No one else uses it, so it's just been sat there waiting for us since the night before, its doors opening immediately as soon as Daddy presses the button.

He hugs us all equally. I wonder if he's counting the seconds in his head to try and make it as precise and fair as possible. Then he steps back and puts his hands in his pockets.

"Take care of yourselves," he says with a nod. It's not cold, but…it feels careful. Neutral.

And that's the last we see him.

It's a bit of a blur as we travel down in the lift and exit into the lobby of his super posh building. We don't say anything as we hurry out of there. I think we all feel like we don't belong, and want to make an escape before anyone questions why we're there.

But once we get onto the pavement, we all look at each other. Well, Luke and Callum look at me, waiting for a decision. For once, I don't mind making it at all. I know what will make me feel a tiny bit better, and that's living in a bubble for a few hours more. It's a Sunday, so none of us has work or anything for the rest of the day. Tomorrow, we'll have to face reality. But for now, I just want to enjoy the company of my best friends.

Maybe we can help each other heal.

"How about we go to the park?" I suggest, seeing as it's a gorgeous day. "We can lie around in the sun and get fish and chips from one of those cheap vans for lunch."

"The one that does the vegan burger," Callum suggests, always thinking of the group.

"That place does vegan ice cream, too," Luke adds happily.

There we go. It's hardly the Battle of Trafalgar, but it's enough of a plan for me.

We don't talk much. I'm not sure what there is to be said right now. But as we lay on the grass there are a lot of heads in laps, hand holding, feet reaching out and touching.

We might be heartbroken, but we're also new versions of ourselves. We've evolved. This closeness is completely natural, and it feels like a balm on my troubled soul.

We'll get through this. Together. The three piggies.

Little do I know just *how much* we're going to have to get through.

It's evening by the time we return to our pokey flat. Considering we haven't done much all day, we're all bone-tired. So at first, when my key doesn't work, I assume I've made a mistake. But then I try it again.

And again.

"Uhh?" I say, raising my eyebrows in question at the others. "Do one of you maybe want to give it a try?"

Luke gets his keys out of his jeans pocket, but to my increasing horror, he doesn't have any luck either. By the time Callum also fails, I'm not even surprised. With a shaking hand, I get out my phone, and with a sinking heart find our landlord's number to call. We only ever text, and I'm already dreading him picking up, but this isn't a situation we can hang around for.

"Yeah?" he barks as the call connects. The background noise makes me think he's down the pub watching a football match. I wince as there's a collective groan from around him, presumably as someone fails to kick the ball where it's supposed to go.

"Um, hi. It's Sam from Number Twelve Dartmoor Court. There seems to be a problem with our door."

There's a pause before he scoffs. "Oh. Yeah. You three. You didn't make rent, so I changed the locks. I've seen you all coming and going with your suitcases anyway. You don't want to live there? Fine. I'll get someone in who pays better. *Oi! Ref! You blind?*"

I jerk my phone away from my ear in shock as he yells, but then I put it right back. "You can't do that!" I cry. "You can't just kick us out! That's illegal! What about all our stuff? And…what do you mean about the rent? We pay by direct debit. It should be fine!"

Luke and Callum are staring at me like they're both about to burst into tears. I don't blame them. That's exactly what I want to do. But I hold on to my nerve as I wait for our arsehole of a landlord to reply.

He laughs. "Then go get a fucking lawyer. You poofs were terrible tenants anyway. Never should have agreed to house a bunch of queers. Good riddance."

I open my mouth to yell at him in disgust, but the line goes dead.

An icy coldness washes through me. He can't do this. It's completely illegal.

But that doesn't help us right now.

I lick my lips, desperately trying to scramble up a plan when I'm so dizzy I could faint. "We, uh, have a problem."

Callum's on his phone when suddenly he makes a horrible keening noise and scrunches up his face. "It's my fault!" he cries, tears spilling down his face. "Oh my fucking god, it's *my fault!* I didn't have enough in my account for the rent payment. Oh, shit, shit, *shit.*"

Luke and I throw our arms around him as he starts to shake uncontrollably. "It's okay," I tell him fiercely. "It's not your fault. He should never have done that."

"He's a homophobic wanker!" Luke agrees vehemently.

Whatever the case, it's kind of irrelevant. We have to work out what we're going to do right now.

Call Daddy.

No, absolutely *not.* He doesn't owe us anything out of the bedroom. We're not going to break the agreement. The pain of being rejected by him now would be unbearable, and I can't risk it, not just for myself but for my best friends either. From the way no one else suggests it, I know they feel the same way.

We have to look after ourselves.

Right, first things first. We need somewhere to spend the night. Callum is already broke and Luke and I have infuriatingly just sent a good chunk of change to that arsehole that we'll now never see again.

Money is extremely tight.

I try and breathe calmly to stop the panic from creeping in. A hotel is out of the question, but there must be other options.

"We could try and find a hostel or something for tonight, maybe?" I suggest.

Luke swallows and looks between us both. "Or the park?"

My stomach drops. "The park?"

Luke shifts on his feet. He's also got his phone out, and he waves it at us. "It's going to be warm tonight, and a low chance of rain. We could save some money and take all day to regroup tomorrow."

I feel so sick. We can't actually be homeless, can we? That's…well, that's a really terrifying thought. I scrub my face. The thought of saving money right now is really tempting. And tomorrow is Monday. Places will be open that we can call. Hostels to find beds. Maybe even a bloody lawyer.

But it would be dangerous in the park.

I look at Callum's stricken face and decide that saving money is our top priority.

"Good idea, Luke," I say, faking a confidence I don't feel. "We'll be fine. We can sort all this out in the morning, so there's no sense in wasting money tonight."

Callum exhales in relief and nods tearfully. "Yeah, it'll be fine for one night. Just a couple of hours, probably. Tomorrow we can sort this out."

I can put a hold on my degree and start working full-time. I can take on a second job, even. We'll find a way out of this.

If we stick together, everything will be okay.

I knew this morning we were embarking on the next chapter of our lives, but this wasn't what I had in mind.

Fucking hell.

3 1

JACOB

RIGHT. TOMORROW IS A NEW DAWN, A NEW DAY. I WILL GET back to work. I will begin looking for someone I can start a real long-term relationship with.

Once I get out of this silk bathrobe. And probably stop lying on the living room carpet as well.

I'm on my back staring at the ceiling. The kittens are using my body as a climbing frame. I haven't eaten anything all day, and my stomach is still sloshing around the couple of cups of black coffee I forced down at breakfast.

When I said goodbye to my boys.

This is for the best. If I'm ever to get another business off the ground, people need to take me seriously. I can have a younger boyfriend. I can't have three live-in boy toys. Tongues would wag. They'd say I was eccentric and not to be trusted.

I'm pretty sure I've never given a fuck as to what anyone thinks of me in my life, but giving myself a concrete reason for walking away from this helps.

I also keep telling myself that the boys wouldn't want to be my harem. They need to find real relationships. They're all young. They'll have plenty of time to find their perfect forever Daddies.

It will all work itself out.

Tomorrow morning, I will put a fresh suit on, change my bedsheets, and set about finding homes for these cats. Or just one home, actually. I want them to stay together. That's not too much to ask for, is it?

I'll have a proper breakfast then open my work emails for the first time in two weeks. Going through them will easily take up most of the day. I'll schedule time with Harris, and she can organise for me to meet with some of those promising start-ups she's been badgering me about. I'll pick a couple to invest in and start the business of making new money again.

Life will continue as it did before.

I bite the inside of my cheek to try and stop myself from dwelling on the fact that *I* will no longer be the same as I was before. That those boys changed me. I've *never* been needed like I was with them. I was able to nurture them and bring out the best in them like I never have with any other boy.

I know that's partly because I never tried. I can see now how easy all those sugar babies were in comparison. God, none of that was real in the slightest.

I've been wrestling all day with the idea of helping out my little piggies financially. I could at least help set them up in some way so money wouldn't be an issue for them like it clearly is. I don't want to make the relationship feel transactional, but I have a ridiculous amount of wealth. I wouldn't even notice if ten or twenty grand went missing, but it could literally change their lives.

However, when I start down that path, I can't help but go further and question why they couldn't move in with me and benefit from my support. They said they didn't want to be sugar babies, but would it really be like that? Surely, it would just be giving them the opportunity to follow their passions free from the financial burden that's been holding them back since school. I wouldn't have got where I am today without that first leg up from my first boss.

That would be a relationship, though, the one thing they said they didn't want right from the start. And I lied and went along with that. We had a deal.

I broke the rules already. The boys said they would come over together just once. One night with the four of us to scratch the itch. Anything long-term would be impractical.

Wouldn't it?

Nothing about this arrangement has turned out how I expected. I thought it would be a fun side-project to keep me occupied for a week or two, but not something I'd want to navigate every day. I thought that would be way too much of a commitment. I've never made an effort to maintain a relationship with just one boy. How could I possibly juggle three?

Except they don't feel like a burden on my time.

They feel like they give me purpose.

I absently pet the calico kitten that's settled down on my chest. "Ohhh, what the hell am I going to do?" I ask him.

He gives me a big yawn in response.

I shrug. Sleeping in it isn't the worst idea. Maybe tomorrow I'll be able to wake up and actually see my plan to get back to normal through.

My front door bursting open sends all three kittens hurtling under the sofa to their favourite hiding position. I sigh. "Hello, Harris," I say heavily.

"Jacob? Where are you?"

The panic in her voice is completely irregular. In fact, I quickly become convinced that aliens must have invaded London, so I sit up with a frown to see her.

"What's going on?"

She takes a breath, then marches over to me. The fact that she doesn't comment on my state of undress really gets me worried.

Seriously, have my stocks vanished or something?

"Your boys—"

"I don't have any boys," I interrupt her sadly.

"Shut up," she snaps, looking murderous. "We don't have time for your nonsense. We can have a big fight about how you're lying to yourself later. Right now, they need you."

A cold shiver runs down my spine. "They need me?"

She waves her hand in the air. "Obviously I've been keeping tabs on them, because I knew *this* would happen."

Ah, there we go. She shakes her hand at me, apparently finally noticing that I look like that guy from that film who just cared about his rug.

"Tabs?" I repeat. "You mean surveillance?"

She narrows her gaze at me. "Don't question my methods. I have eyes everywhere. That's not important. What's *important* is that their skeevy landlord has evicted them onto the streets without warning. He booked a locksmith last night and put the flat up to rent today. Given the timeframe, I'm not sure they would have even had time to get much of their stuff, if any."

A whistling noise has started in my brain. I stare at her as my vision darkens around the edges. The fury that's beginning to boil in my veins is like a kraken waiting to be unleashed.

"Some prick kicked them out of their home?" I say in a dangerously low whisper.

Harris doesn't flinch, though. In fact, her eyes blaze in triumph. She knows I'm paying attention now. "So it seems."

"And where are they now?"

She shakes her head. "None of them have used their debit

cards today. That's why I came to you. I'm at a dead end, but you—"

"I'm not," I finish her sentence for her.

I don't walk. I run to my laptop, firing it up as I get out my phone. Much like Harris, I have my own methods of doing things that might raise some eyebrows over at The Met. I don't care what the police think, though. Especially right now when it could really help. I never indulge in anything more than a little light industrial espionage. Everyone does it. I just never get caught.

I'm the Big Bad Jacob Wolf, and nothing stands in the way of what I want.

"Sam," I mutter to myself as my fingers fly over the keys. "Please don't have deleted the app. *Please...*"

I never exchanged numbers with any of the boys. All I have is Collr. But if it's still active on his phone...

"Ah-ha!" I cry, punching the air as relief makes me dizzy. "Gotcha." But then I frown as I zoom the map in on the location. It's a small park between Peckham and Lewisham by a cemetery. It's one o'clock in the morning. A thunderstorm rolled in about an hour ago. What the hell are they doing there...?

Holy fuck. I snap my head towards Harris. "They're sleeping rough?"

She looks between me and the screen, raising her eyebrows. "They don't seem to be moving, do they?"

I zoom in again and stare at the little dot. It certainly looks stationary to me.

I throw off the silk robe and jump to my feet, jabbing a finger at my EA. "Get the car."

She has the audacity to smirk at me. "It's already downstairs, you dickhead. Now hurry up and go rescue your boys. And *this* time, try not to lose them, hmm?"

3 2

LUKE

LUCKILY, SAM HAD AN UMBRELLA IN HIS BAG, BECAUSE HE'S organised like that.

Unfortunately, we need it.

Callum and I are huddled against his sides as he holds the brolly above our heads. We were against a tree a while ago, but when the thunder and lightning started, we had to venture out into the open bit of the park.

We've managed to keep the bags hugged against our chests, but there's not much room for our feet and legs. I can't feel my toes anymore. Overhead, thunder rumbles and forks of lightning pierce the sky in the distance.

When the heavens opened, Callum said that Sam and I should go try and find a hotel or a hostel. I said we should *all* try, and that Sam and I could pay for Callum. But Sam checked his phone and it forecasted the rain wasn't supposed to last even half an hour, so that we should just stick it out.

That was almost two hours ago.

Now, though, I figure we should just try and see it through. I can't face the thought of moving. I'm not convinced we'd be able to find anything close by, either. I've been searching on my phone as the battery dwindled, but there's nothing. A taxi would be a shocking waste of money, and the tube has now closed.

So there's no sense in torturing ourselves. At least I've decided to just try and get some sleep. Feeling sorry for ourselves won't do any good.

Callum apologised so many times that even I had to get firm with him in the end, which seemed to have shocked him out of his horrible guilt. But this isn't his fault. It's our despicable landlord's. We always knew he was a grubby, scheming crook, but this goes beyond the pale.

It would be lovely to think that karma is going to come back and bite him in the arse, but life isn't fair like that.

"Do you want me to hold the umbrella for a while, Sam?" I ask.

He gives me a small smile. "That's okay, babe. This is the best way to keep us all dry. You just try and get some sleep."

"Oh, fuck," Callum croaks. Sam and I both snap our heads to look at him as he points into the night.

Towards the cemetery.

"What fresh fuckery is this?" Callum rasps.

My stomach drops and fear rinses through me. There's a light bobbing through the darkness and the rain. A torch.

Someone's out there.

"Let's go," Sam says, the urgency in his voice compelling us to scramble to our feet, hurriedly trying to get our backpacks on.

We don't care about the rain now. There's no telling what kind of trouble is coming our way.

"Quick, over here," Sam whispers, jutting his head towards the wooded area where we were seated before. "We can hide in the trees."

"What about the lightning?" I ask.

Sam pauses for just a second. "I think it's worth the risk."

There isn't much of a moon, even if there weren't loads of clouds, so hopefully whoever that person is, they haven't seen us yet. Sam tries to keep the umbrella over all three of us as we start squelching over the grass.

Then we hear it.

The voice calls out. In fact, I think someone is screaming.

Callum stops walking, turning back to look the way we just came. "Did they just say…"

"Callum, no," I beg as Sam and I stop as well.

But he shakes his head mulishly. "Just…wait."

And then it comes again, a faint roar over the rain.

"SAM? BOYS? WHERE ARE YOU?"

I look at my best friends. No…it couldn't possibly be…

"BOYS?"

"DADDY!" Callum bellows, waving his arms like he's trying to flag down a plane. "DADDY, WE'RE HERE!"

"Callum, no!" Sam cries, mimicking me and trying to shush him.

He's probably right. It's probably just a massive case of wishful thinking, and letting someone know where we are is going to get us in serious trouble.

Except I turn and look back as well. I see someone running at a hell of a rate through the rain…

"BOYS?"

"Daddy?" I whisper.

"No, it can't…" Sam says, shaking his head.

"BOYS!" the figure yells yet again. We can't see anything with the torch pointed at us, jumping around like crazy in the dark. We should run, they're getting closer…

We don't get the chance.

Daddy barrels into us with the force of a steam train, throwing his arms around all of us, dragging us to the ground and sending the umbrella flying. I'm so stunned I can only stare at him as he grabs for us, kissing Sam, then Callum hard on the mouth. When it's my turn, it's all I can do to submit.

"Are you okay?" he cries as the rain pours down his face. He's still got the torch light on his phone, and it's casting dark shadows over all of us.

"How did you find us?" I ask incredulously.

He shakes his head. "That doesn't matter. I heard what happened with your flat. Are you hurt? You must be so cold."

"We're okay," Sam says, shivering. We're all shivering. "But yeah…this rain isn't ideal."

"Were you going to *sleep* out here?" Daddy demands. It's the first time I've ever heard him angry.

"It seemed like the best idea…" Sam mumbles sheepishly.

"No, no, *no*," Daddy rants. "You should have messaged me. I would never have let this happen."

"B-b-but the agreement?" I say in a small voice.

I hate confrontation, but I know we all felt the same way. We were ashamed. Mortified. Daddy never signed on to take care of our *lives*. How could we have burdened him with this?

However, he shakes his head now with fierce passion. "I don't give a *fuck* about that. You are going to come home with me, right now. You can stay as long as you need. I…I know you don't want a long-term relationship, but I'll have you for as long as I can keep you. You boys are *mine* and I *love* you."

I can't help it. I'm so tired and stressed, and I've been holding it together for hours. I burst into tears and throw my arms around Daddy's neck, clinging to him like he's a life raft. I feel as Sam and Callum bump into me, joining the embrace.

"It's okay," he says over the noise of the storm. "It's okay. I've got you. Everything's going to be all right. Daddy's got you. You're safe."

I know it's crazy, but I believe him.

And I don't just mean about where we're going to sleep tonight. He said that we're *his* and that he *loves* us. He said we can stay as long as we want.

I'm not sure what that means exactly, but I can't help but feel like the deal we made might not be over yet after all.

CALLUM

THE FIRST THING THAT LUKE DOES WHEN WE GET BACK TO THE penthouse is gather up the three kittens in his arms, then place them carefully on the bed. "I want us all together," he says in a small, wobbly voice.

We're all still pretty soaked from the rain, so whilst the kittens explore the bed, sniffing the sheets and making biscuits with their tiny paws, Daddy sets about undressing all of us. He's got a grim determination about him that's making my heart race.

Honestly—running out in the rain to rescue us? That's like some shit from a Jane Austen novel. And then not asking but *telling* us that we were coming home with him was the Daddiest Daddying I've ever heard of.

He was so angry that we didn't break the rules of the deal and contact him when we realised we were up shit's creek without a paddle. Now he's all possessive and growly, muttering about us being his bad boys and how much trouble we'll be in the morning.

It's the hottest thing I've ever seen in my life.

Just like last night, once the three of us are naked, he

steers us into the bathroom and gets the shower going. He's still dressed, though. Soaked to the skin. I don't know if he doesn't realise or doesn't care, but it hurts my heart.

"Daddy, stop," I say, placing my hands on his chest. I know he's the one usually giving the orders, but this is a strange night. He stills and looks at me as steam fills the room. "You're cold, too."

"I'm fine," he says in a clipped tone, but Sam shakes his head and touches Daddy's arm.

"We're sorry, Daddy," he says tearfully. "We were scared to contact you. We thought now the deal was done, you wouldn't want us."

It's like a knife twists in my chest.

I'm still frightened of that.

But Daddy's face crumples, and—*holyshit*—tears spring from his eyes. He fumbles with his arms, but the three of us are already there, hugging him.

"I want you so much," he whispers. "I tried to respect your wishes. But I need you boys. You scared the shit out of me. If anything had happened to you…"

"It didn't," Luke says firmly. "You saved us."

"You were amazing," Sam adds in awe.

"That was like something out of a *movie*," I insist. "Daddy Wolf to the rescue!"

He takes a shaky breath in and rubs his face as he regards us. "Come on. Let's get you warmed up."

It shows what a state of shock I'm still in that I don't say something lewd about different ways to warm up. In fact, I'm still mortified and guilt-stricken that I got us into this mess in the first place. I know Luke and Sam are convinced that our douchebag landlord broke the law, but we wouldn't be in this situation if I'd kept an eye on my money like I'm supposed to.

But then…Daddy wouldn't have come and rescued us.

The universe works in funny ways, I guess.

He tries to usher us into the shower, but my bratty side takes over.

"No, Daddy," I say again, shaking my head. "We need to look after you, too."

This is one of those moments that prove to me why my besties are my besties. Without a word, they follow my lead as I start to undo Daddy's shirt buttons. Sam tackles the cufflinks and tie. Luke is the one brave enough to go for the belt and trouser zip. I'm so proud of how far he's come in such a short time.

Daddy doesn't say anything. He just watches us with a soft expression that I adore. He moves his limbs as we guide him, but otherwise, he lets us call the shots until he's as naked as we are.

"There we go," I say, satisfied. "Much better. Now we can all warm up together."

"My boys," he mumbles, shaking his head as he pulls us in for another cuddle. "Such little angels."

The water from the shower is blissfully hot. We take turns crowding under the stream, washing with the same hair and body wash that we used last night.

Again, like last night, Dady also dries and dresses us in our pyjamas. I'm amazed that the kittens are still on the bed. They've all found spots at the foot of the mattress, so we try not to disturb them as we crawl under the duvet.

We sit up against the pillows. Daddy hugs Luke and Sam to his sides, and I spoon with Luke. I don't mind being on the outside, as that means Daddy can rub my back, and it feels lovely.

"Tomorrow, we'll go get your stuff from the flat," Daddy says. "Then we can decide how we want to proceed."

"Our landlord changed the locks, remember?" Sam says unhappily.

Yeah, that was an *epic* dick move.

Daddy tilts his head. "Good job I bought the building and your apartment within it, then."

The three of us sit up and stare at him. "You bought the *building?*" I cry.

Daddy checks the clock on the wall. "Well, technically, I'll have bought it in about five hours when the paperwork can go through. But rest assured I'll have a new locksmith ready and waiting for the second we're allowed to get back into your flat."

I mean…I'm not an idiot. I can see the penthouse suite that we're in. I knew Daddy was rich. But *that* rich? *That* powerful?

"So we could move back in?" Luke says quietly.

Daddy drops his gaze to look at him sadly. "Don't you want to stay here?"

Luke looks at me and Sam. "We can't, can we?"

Something reckless takes over me. "Why can't we? Daddy says we can stay as long as we want. What if that's forever?"

Now everyone looks at me like I'm mad. *Shit.* Maybe they don't feel the same way?

Bollocks to it. If tonight taught us anything, it's that life is short.

"Would you want us to stay, Daddy?"

He looks between us all then back at me. He swallows, and something *breaks* on his face.

"Desperately. You boys are precious to me. I…" He closes his eyes, nods, then opens them again. "I know it's complicated, but I want you in my life. I know you said that you weren't looking for long-term relationships and that you just wanted to lose your virginities, but—"

I wave my hands to stop him from talking. "That was the plan before, yeah. But then we all kind of fell in love with you. Then we came here last night and saw how it could work with all four of us. Am I the only one that wants to give that a chance? That wants Daddy to take care of all three of us? We could be best friends *and* boyfriends and love Daddy all the time. Come on!"

Sam and Luke look at each other nervously. Luke bites his lip, but he gives the smallest of nods. "That sounds like heaven," Sam whispers.

We all look at Daddy.

He closes his eyes, and two tears slip down his face. Then he hugs us to him so tightly we're in danger of getting bruised.

I don't care, though. In fact, it's the best feeling in the world. Like he's showing us how he's going to keep hold of us and never let us go.

"I would love nothing more than to be Daddy to all of you," he says eventually. "I have enough love for three, I have no doubt."

"I love you all," I mumble from the middle of our cuddle.

"I love you all, too," Sam and Luke say in unison.

"So is that settled?" I lift my head and ask, not afraid to be the brat. "We're staying? It's official?"

"It is, naughty boy," Daddy says warmly. Hearing him say my special name again makes it really sink in for me.

This is happening.

"And the kittens?" Luke asks.

Daddy scoffs and rolls his eyes. "I think it's finally time I admit that I was *never* going to let go of those blasted kittens. Much like certain little piggies I know."

My heart melts right there in my chest. "I don't want you to ever let us go," I say, hugging him and Luke, and taking Sam's hand in mine.

Daddy holds my gaze for a moment, then shakes his head. "Never again. I *promise*."

And I believe him.

EPILOGUE

Jacob – Seven Months Later

"Dinner's almost ready!"

I smile at the chaotic scene in my home. I've never known a Christmas Day like it.

My heart is overflowing.

Sam has spent all morning in the kitchen slaving over a spectacular meal for all of us. He's asked for a bit of help when needed, but mostly he said he wanted to do this as a present for us all. I respect that. And who am I to tell my big boy that he can't show his family love?

I've been playing a game with Callum and Luke that seems to involve collecting certain values of smiley-faced sushi on different cards to make the highest scoring platter. We've had the pink Champagne flowing since we woke up, so I'm honestly not sure what the hell is going on, but the boys seem to be having a whale of a time. So if they're happy, I'm happy.

Even if I hate losing because apparently I didn't have enough laughing edamame bean cards.

These past several months have been a bit of a blur, much like today. Chaotic, but very happy. Imperfectly perfect, as Luke likes to say.

It was easy to move the boys out of that hovel they'd been living in. I'd already decided to get them out of there, but upon seeing the place I was doubly—triply—glad. It was barely enough space for one of them, let alone three. Now they have plenty of room for all their passions here in the penthouse, and my bedroom immediately became *ours*. I love seeing all their clothes in the wardrobe and their toothbrushes in the bathroom. And there are so many photos *everywhere*.

It pained me to pay off their scumbag of a landlord, but at least I got the satisfaction of deducting all the renovating costs first. He was lucky I didn't have his homophobic arse thrown in jail, but the boys didn't want to punish him. They just wanted to move on and forget about him, which I respected.

That apartment is now a halfway home for one of the LGBT charities that Luke spends his time volunteering for. When a teen in need requires a bed for a night or a week, they now have that nicely refurbished flat as one of their options. In fact, I've done up several such flats over the past few months and insist on not taking a penny's rent from the charities. Why would I need to?

Since September, Sammi has been studying for his degree full-time. He stopped working as soon as he moved in—they all did. Except for Callum, because he just really loves teaching pole dancing. He's saving that money in a 'treat' fund, which I suspect he's just using to buy sex toys, but I *really* can't complain about that.

I won't have any of my boys wasting their days on jobs

that don't fulfil them. Their time is precious. I know Sam will make a wonderful primary school teacher, and now he's not tired out by having to work stupid hours as well just to make rent.

Callum is also studying the fashion course he could never dream of before. We've talked extensively about what he'd like to work towards, and the thinking currently is a small, exclusive boutique of fun handmade garments with a couple of queer staff members. He's not ready for that, yet, but it's so beautiful for me to see these boys all start to dream, and dream big.

I want anything to be possible for them.

Luke's one and only request of my funds was to pay for therapy. It only took him a couple of weeks to ask me, which stunned me initially. But our sweet, delicate boy is remarkably strong too, and he's working really hard to overcome all the bullshit his parents put him through.

I look at him with such fondness, tickling Callum's ribs as he accuses him of cheating on the sushi game. He's wearing the hoodie I got for him for the first day we met. The wine stain is ever so slightly still visible, but I think that's part of why it's Luke's favourite and he wears it all the time. I think he likes to see the journey we've all been on together, and I'm also sure that embracing the bad that comes with or before the good is part of his new and improved mental health regime.

I'm proud of him. I'm so proud of all of them.

The kittens have almost grown into cats now, and they had the time of their lives with all the Christmas wrapping paper this morning. It's crazy how much *movement* there is in my home now. I went very fast from just me to three boys and three cats, and now it feels like there's life in every single corner of this home.

And the sex.

Fucking hell.

It's not been as tricky as I thought it would be, navigating this unconventional arrangement. We often do group scenes, but there's also the spare bedroom that I've done up all cosy for if anyone wants space to themselves. It's a good job I'm still reasonably young, fit, and virile, though, because these boys demand a *lot* of my attention.

And I'm always thrilled to give it.

I smile to myself as I recall how just this morning, they decided that the best way to wake up Daddy was with his first Christmas present: all three of them under the sheets, worshipping my cock, balls, and hole. Merry fucking Christmas to *me*.

I love that in the space of a year I've gone from lonely bachelor to having a whole bloody family. My mother adores them. We all met a couple of months ago for a ten-mile hike, because she's a maniac. But cleverly, she worked out that would be a good length of time to grill all my boys one after another.

Apparently, she was very satisfied with the results.

She's insisting on hosting New Years's at hers for us with a bunch of her lady cruise friends. We all agreed that would be an absolutely brilliant way to ring in the new year—with a bunch of women who have seen everything, been everywhere, and really don't give a fuck about anything but having fun anymore.

I was nervous at first that she wouldn't understand the nature of our relationship, but the woman who raised me from nothing is just as awesome as ever. She said she didn't have to comprehend all the details. She could see how happy we all were together, and that was all that mattered.

Harris pretends like she tolerates them, and likes to call them 'Boy One, Boy Two,' et cetera, instead of their names. But they've taken to her teasing remarkably well. Even sensitive Luke. They can see as I do that she's proud as punch that we've all found such happiness together.

It sticks in my throat that for the most part these boys aren't close with their families or are just not in contact at all. It seems like the only parents who might be interested in meeting us are Callum's, but even then, they seem more content to just call him a couple of times a month.

Sam's family might possibly reply to an email. But I'm glad that we've all universally decided that Luke's so-called parents can jump in the sea.

No matter. I'm their family now. And they'll never want for love nor comfort again.

"Okay, ready!" Sam announces happily, indicating the four overflowing plates he's dished up on the breakfast bar. He's done a fine job of creating a fest for meat-eaters and vegans alike, and I know that our stomachs are going to be bursting before long.

Callum and Luke cheer, abandoning the game to collect their food. I see to it that there's a fresh bottle of Champagne in a chilled bucket on the table, then ensure everyone sits in the right place.

I've got one more present to give them.

"Crackers first," I say before they get a chance to dig in.

"Of course," Callum agrees, grabbing his.

Luke inspects his carefully. "These are very fancy, Daddy," he says.

I try and hide my grin behind my Champagne flute as I take a sip. "I had them specially made," is all I tell him.

We each take our crackers in hand and cross arms. When they bang, there's lots of shrieking that sends the cats running from where they were coming to investigate the tasty food smells. I laugh, but my eyes are sharp, making sure they all pick up the right boxes that popped out from the middle of the crackers.

Sam is the first to hold his between his fingers, and he looks sharply at me.

He can see it's a ring box. We each have one.

"Daddy?" Sam asks.

My boys' eyes go wide as they all pick them up. I place mine by my knife. I don't need to open it just yet. I already know what's inside.

"How about you all open them on the count of three?" I suggest. It's my favourite number now, after all.

They look at each other in anticipation. Then as one, they count, "One, two, *three.*"

Their faces as they look inside are my last present of the day. Luke's jaw drops open. Callum gasps. Sam bites his lip and blinks glassy eyes.

The bands are platinum with a ring of tiny diamonds running through the middle. Each should fit their boy's finger perfectly. I've spent a lot of time snooping these past few months, and Harris has obviously put her skills to the best use.

I pick up my box and open it to show my boys that I have a matching one as well. "These are a promise," I tell them. "A promise for us all that we will love each other no matter what. If you would like to have a ceremony to celebrate this, we can. We could go on holiday or have a few people gathered together here in London. Or we don't have to do anything at all other than slip them on our hands right now. All the legal nonsense is already covered and will be finalised with signatures from all of you. But it was important for me that you boys know how much I love you, and that I will do for the rest of my life. That is my promise."

I'm amazed I got through the whole speech. I've been practicing it for weeks, but as they all started crying one by one during it, it was very hard to keep my cool. But now I'm done, I allow myself a little sniffle, and my nerves rise as I wait for them to answer.

They share a look between them, then suddenly it's like a race who can get their ring on their hand first.

"Oh, Daddy!" Sam cries, jumping from his chair and throwing his arms around me. Luke and Callum follow immediately after. I laugh as I hug and kiss them all.

"So that's a 'yes', then?" I tease.

Callum spins around and grabs my box, carefully taking the band out. I automatically offer out my hand, and he slips it on the right finger for me.

"Now it's a 'yes'," he announces proudly.

"Forever," Luke agrees.

We all hold our hands out together, admiring the way the rings sparkle. This is it. My happily ever after.

The big bad wolf and his three little piggies.

THANK you so much for reading the story of Daddy Wolf and his three little piggies! If you want a super hot bonus Halloween scene, just click **here!**

If you want more contemporary fairy tale retellings with Daddies, keep reading to discover **Golden** (Goldilocks and the Three Bears) and **Wild Ride** (Little Red Riding Hood). For my other fairy tales, check out the **three-book box set** of Cinderella, Beauty and the Beast, and Rapunzel!

If you'd like to discover my contemporary American pen name, HJ Welch, please take a look at the **Pine Cove** complete cox set, available in eBook and audio!

IF YOU'D LIKE to be the first to know what fairy tale I'll be working on next, make sure to join my Facebook group, **Helen's Jewels**. We also have a lot of fun with games and giveaways, as well as ARC opportunities.

THANK YOU TO MY TEAM!

Cover Design: Cate Ashwood

Editing: Meg Cooper

Proof Reading: Tanja Ongkiehong

General awesomeness: Ed Davies, AK Faulkner, my hubby, and our cats.

Golden

Can three very hungry bears find their own sweet golden boy?

GOLDIE

Thanks to my no-good ex, I'm up to my eyeballs in debt…to an adult entertainment company. The owner offers me the chance of a lifetime: if I keep my lips zipped about why I'm there, I can work off the loan in front of the camera. I'm thrilled, but self-conscious: who wants to work with a skinny twink like me? Then the biggest, scariest star of all asks for me. In fact, Daddy *demands* me. And, like both his partners warn me: what Daddy wants, Daddy gets. Can I really handle three bears? As they close in on me, I realise…it's too late to run.

DADDY

Goldie is shy, innocent, brand-new…and totally irresistible. I'm going to make him ours. The three of us have enough love for a fourth. It's supposed to be only for a weekend, but our golden angel's secrets betray a broken soul that needs mending…and I'm the man to do it. Goldie's sleazy ex is too cold for him, and this weekend might be too hot. But the four of us together? That feels just right. And when I find out why Goldie's really there, we'll stop at nothing to save our golden boy.

Golden *is a super steamy, standalone MMMM gay romance novella featuring a picturesque cottage in the English countryside, lashings of praise for a shy boy, one very fat cat who knows best, enough porridge for four hungry tummies, and a guaranteed HEA with absolutely no cliffhanger.*

Click here to get the Golden eBook

ALSO AVAILABLE

Wild Ride

A sexy surprise is waiting in the woods...

RED

Chased into the forest in the middle of the night, my only hope of survival is the man I used to obsess over. Now I'm all grown up, I won't miss this opportunity to thank him. Our chemistry is immediate and off the charts, and I'm not looking for a Forever Daddy. My Very First Daddy is all I need. But when he surprises me with a present that awakens something new in me, I know I can't quit.

HUNTER

I've never been anyone's Daddy before, but Red needs me in a way that melts my grizzly heart. I'll do anything for him. But if my recent, brutal divorce has taught me anything, it's that I'm not much of a catch. Does a beautiful young thing like Red really want me? His brother might be my best friend, but his father hates us both and will do all he can to keep us apart. When trouble comes knocking on my door, though, I know I'll do anything to save this boy I've fallen for.

Wild Ride is a super steamy, standalone MM gay romance novella featuring a boy who discovers a love of lingerie, a sassy grandma, a loyal pooch the size of a wolf, something scary lurking in the woods, and a guaranteed HEA with absolutely no cliffhanger.

Click here to get the Wild Ride eBook

ALSO AVAILABLE

The Fairy Tale Collection: Contemporary MM Retellings

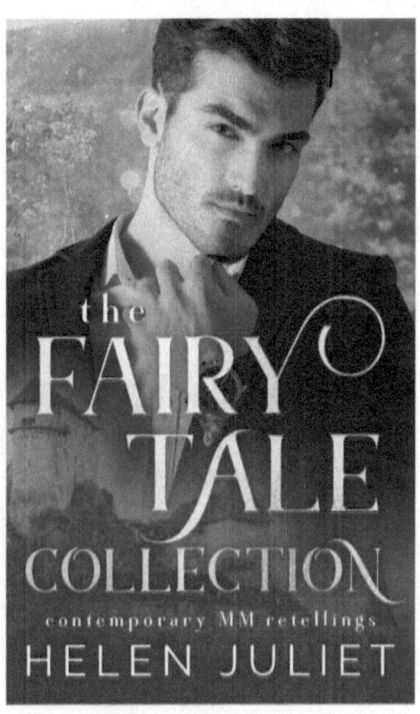

Experience Beauty and the Beast, Cinderella, and Rapunzel as you've never seen them before in this thousand page box set of contemporary adaptations! Available together for the first time, each book is a standalone with its own HEA, but watch out for familiar faces!

Thorn in His Side

Beautiful, innocent Joshua Bellamy finds himself in an arranged marriage to the older, brutish, and scarred Darius Legrand. But in Darius's secluded mansion, Joshua begins to see that Darius isn't so scary after all. In fact, despite being a little grumpy, he's actually very protective and caring. When danger comes knocking on their door, will Joshua and Darius's blossoming love be strong enough to save each other?

A Right Royal Affair

Nobody knows that Prince James of the United Kingdom is bisexual, and as he's sixth in line to the throne, it needs to stay that way. But when he meets the cheeky, outrageously gay Essex boy, Theo Glass, everything could change. Against his better judgement, James asks Theo to help him put on a royal charity ball to remember. Can they resist their mutual attraction for a whole week alone in a picturesque castle, or will true love bloom?

Hair Out of Place

Raphael d'Oro is a secret prince who has spent his entire life exiled in a London penthouse. But now he's in a race against time to get back to his tiny European nation to claim the throne that's rightfully his and save his people. Good thing he has his insanely hot older bodyguard to take care of him. But Griff Thompson would never want someone as inexperienced as Raphie, would he? Even *if* they keep finding themselves in places with only one bed…

Click here for the Fairy Tale Collection eBook

Click here for the Fairy Tale Collection audio

ALSO AVAILABLE

Pine Cove Box Set by HJ Welch

Welcome to Pine Cove, where true love lives happily ever after! **This 2000 page box set contains all six novels as well as all five companion short stories.**

-

Safe Harbor

Robin Coal needs a fake boyfriend for his high school reunion. He asks his housemate: a gorgeous, totally straight ex-Marine. What could go wrong? There's only one bed, and Dair might not be so straight after all... When Robin's past threatens their future, only Dair can save him.

-

Sweet Spot

It's Halloween and Robin has prepared a sexy little surprise for his boyfriend Dair when he gets home from work. Hold on to your horses, Marine!

-

Troubled Waters

Bodyguard Scout Duffy doesn't know what's worse: the fact that his scorching one-night-stand, Emery Klein, is his bratty new client, or the fact that he doesn't even remember Scout. But Emery's life is in danger thanks to his out and proud charity work, and once he finally recognizes Scout, their chemistry in undeniable.

-

Homeward Bound

Swift Coal just found out he's a father, and his daughter (and her cranky cat) are coming to stay. His best friend's younger brother, Micha Perkins, has nowhere to go and a wrongfully tattered reputation. He's relieved when Swift asks him to be a live-in babysitter. He just has to hide his lifelong crush. Easy, because Swift is straight—right?

-

Bright Horizon

With sixteen years between them, baker Ben Turner and lawyer Elias Solomon have no idea their crush is mutual. But when Ben inherits his long-lost family's estate and becomes an overnight millionaire, Elias swears to protect the innocent younger man from the vultures circling him. To unravel the mystery of the inheritance, they must go to England to confront Ben's estranged relatives…and their feelings for each other.

-

Crossed Paths

Raj Bhat is done living in the shadows. It's time for him to take charge of his own destiny and tell the man he's fallen for how he really feels.

-

Midnight Sky

It's the night before New Year's Eve. Taylan Demir is all alone, and he's just lost his dog. Except when his handsome customer, Hudson Perkins, comes to his rescue, Taylan doesn't just get his dog back. He's suddenly got a hot date, and maybe someone to kiss when the clock strikes midnight.

-

Memory Lane

Angel Shields saved Jay Coal's life in high school, and Jay has secretly loved his straight best friend ever since. Now Angel's back in town with amnesia after a suspicious work accident and it's Jay's turn to rescue him. He pretends to be Angel's fiancé to see him in the hospital, but with his scrambled-up memory, Angel's not sure it's fictional after all. He just knows he loves Jay more than ever.

-

Thin Ice

Kamran's ex broke his heart, tricked him into aiding a bank robbery, and now he wants him to do one last job. There's only one way to say no: seek the protective custody of the biggest, grumpiest FBI agent ever, Lee Marshall. And pretend to be his boyfriend for a week-long family reunion in their giant mansion. Wait, what?

-

Calm Shores

Gorgeous, sophisticated Dante walks into Oliver's bar and orders…a boyfriend?! Dante needs a man to keep his mother from setting him back up with his awful, cheating ex, and Oliver is up for the challenge.

-

Fresh Snow

Emery Klein is throwing the best Christmas party ever, but his fiancé, Scout Duffy, and all their friends have something more exciting in mind.

-

Each Pine Cove book can be read as a stand alone and has its own happy ever after. But if you read the whole series, you'll see a lot of familiar faces!

Click here to get the Pine Cove eBook bundle

Click here to get the Pine Cove audio bundle

ABOUT THE AUTHOR

Helen Juliet is a contemporary MM romance author living in London with her husband and two balls of fluff that occasionally pretend to be cats. She began writing at an early age, later honing her craft online in the world of fanfiction on sites like Wattpad. Fifteen years and over half a million words later, she sought out original MM novels to read. By the end of 2016 she had written her first book of her own, and in 2017 she achieved her lifelong dream of becoming a fulltime author.

Helen also writes contemporary American MM romance as HJ Welch.

You can contact Helen Juliet via social media:
Newsletter (with FREE original stories) – https://www.
subscribepage.com/helenjuliet
Website – www.helenjuliet.com
Facebook Group – Helen's Jewels
Facebook Page – @helenjulietauthor
Instagram – @helenjwrites
Twitter – @helenjwrites

www.ingramcontent.com/pod-product-compliance
Lightning Source LLC
Chambersburg PA
CBHW030810210726

48290CB00002B/509